THE FAWN

T0349290

Also by Magda Szabó in English translation

The Door (2005)
Iza's Ballad (2015)
Katalin Street (2017)
Abigail (2020)

Magda Szabó

THE FAWN

Translated from the Hungarian by
Len Rix

MACLEHOSE PRESS
QUERCUS · LONDON

First published in the Hungarian language as *Az őz*
by Szépirodalmi Könyvkiadó, 1959
First published in Great Britain in 2023 by MacLehose Press
This paperback edition published in 2024 by

MacLehose Press
An imprint of Quercus Publishing Ltd
Carmelite House
50 Victoria Embankment
London EC4Y 0DZ
An Hachette UK company

The authorised representative in the EEA is Hachette Ireland, 8 Castlecourt
Centre, Dublin 15, D15 XTP3, Ireland (email: info@hbgi.ie)

Copyright © 1959 Éditions Viviane Hamy and Magda Szabo estate
English translation copyright © 2022 by Len Rix

The moral right of Magda Szabó to be identified
as the author of this work has been asserted in accordance with
the Copyright, Designs and Patents Act, 1988.

Len Rix asserts his moral right to be identified as the translator of the work.

All rights reserved. No part of this publication may be reproduced
or transmitted in any form or by any means, electronic or mechanical,
including photocopy, recording, or any information storage and retrieval
system, without permission in writing from the publisher.

A CIP catalogue record for this book is available from the British Library.

ISBN (MMP) 978 1 52942 565 9
ISBN (Ebook) 978 1 52942 566 6

This book is a work of fiction. Names, characters, businesses,
organisations, places and events are either the product of the author's
imagination or are used fictitiously. Any resemblance to actual persons,
living or dead, events or locales is entirely coincidental.

Designed and typeset in Scala by Libanus Press, Marlborough
Printed and bound in Great Britain by Clays Ltd, Elcograf S.p.A.

MIX
Paper | Supporting
responsible forestry
FSC® C104740

Papers used by MacLehose Press are from well-managed forests
and other responsible sources.

TRANSLATOR'S FOREWORD

"I wanted to be with you sooner, but I had to wait for Gyurica and you know he's always late . . ." the novel begins, and it ends with the cry, "Wait for me, I'm coming." But who is the speaker of those opening words, who is she addressing, and where and in what circumstances will they be reunited? The reader must wait until the final chapter before the last of these questions is answered. The journey will take her less than a day, from mid-morning to nightfall, yet in those few short hours we will have travelled through a lifetime spanning three decades of major social and political upheaval.

The story begins with Eszter's growing-up in ultra-conservative inter-war Hungary: private schools and religious institutions are permitted and professional and wealthy people like the Graffs and her aristocratic relations the Martons thrive. In March 1944 the country is annexed by Hitler; in August that year Eszter stars in a university student production of Goethe's *Iphigenia at Tauris* chosen specifically to please the occupying forces; her final exam takes place just before Christmas, under the non-stop Allied bombardment that reduces Budapest to rubble, and by January 1945 the Soviets are in control. They install a puppet regime and impose the full apparatus of dogmatic Marxism, but because she works in a state cooperative theatre Eszter is allowed not only to become famous but is sufficiently well paid to buy her own house in a leafy suburb. Her real problems are personal. They arise from the degrading circumstances of her childhood, her unresolved feelings of anger and resentment and a desperate need to be accepted for the person she feels she really is. We learn much about the way she sees herself from the roles with which she most closely identifies: Goethe's Iphigenia, sacrificed by her father at Aulis, Shaw's rebellious commoner Joan, Shakespeare's tragic Ophelia, and Shakespeare's irresponsibly mischievous Puck.

She is certainly no moral exemplar. Playful and quick-witted she may be, but she is capable of saying and doing wicked, even horrifying, things. She is strangely aroused by the idea of destruction; she revels in the winds and the driving snow; extreme cold, a city aflame under the bombs, the obliteration of her childhood home – nothing can daunt her spirit; and yet, though entirely without personal vanity, she is painfully hyper-sensitive about her one physical defect, the deformed foot that symbolises her humiliating past. She has an instinctive sympathy for stray animals and small children, but her sense of having been neglected and exploited as a child has made her scornful of everything she considers soft, pampered or meekly conformist. That this should extend to her former classmate, the beautiful and virtuous Angéla, is predictable; that her hatred and envy should become all-consuming when she discovers that this despised paragon is the wife of the man she loves is a recipe for disaster – and disaster is what she duly delivers. Yet somehow she never quite forfeits our sympathy, and the manner of her ending, appalling as it is, touches on the sublime.

Len Rix, February 2022

DRAMATIS PERSONAE

Principal characters

Eszter Encsy, actress, narrator

Eszter's father, non-practising lawyer

Eszter's mother, piano teacher

The Martons, Eszter's aristocratic relatives on her mother's side

Auntie Irma, Eszter's widowed aunt on her mother's side

Kárász néni, Eszter's next-door neighbour

Kárász Béla, neighbour's son

Ambrus, Eszter's other next-door neighbour

Károly, younger brother of Ambrus

Gizi, affectionately "Gizike", Eszter's friend

Józsi and Juszti, Gizi's parents, who run the Three Hussars

Gyurica, Eszter's doctor

Juli, Eszter's maid

Angéla Graff, Eszter's fellow pupil

"Uncle" Domi and "Auntie" Ilu, Angéla's parents

Emil, Angéla's brother

Elza, housekeeper to the Graff family

Péter, Angéla's pet bird

Lőrinc, university lecturer and translator

Pipi, Eszter's fellow actor

Hella, Eszter's fellow actor

Árvai, Eszter's fellow actor

Ványa, Party-appointed theatre director

Ramocsay, sculptor

Note

néni (Auntie) and *bácsi* (Uncle) are used familiarly for
    non-relatives

"a" (as in "Graff", "Marton") is pronounced like the English
    "salt", "Baltic"

"c" (as in "Gyurica") is pronounced like "ts"

"cs" as in "Ramocsay" is pronounced like the English "ch"

"g" (as in "Gizi") is always hard, as in "good"

"j" (as in "Juli") is pronounced like the "y" in "you"

"s" (as in "Ambrus") is pronounced as "sh" in English

"sz" (as in "Eszter") is pronounced like the "s" in English"

Dates and places

Eszter is born *c.*1928 in the city of Szolnok in central Hungary

The Germans occupy Hungary in March 1944

Budapest is besieged by the Allies in the winter of 1944/45

In 1948 the Russians impose a puppet Communist regime

The action of the novel takes place in Budapest in 1954

1

I wanted to be here sooner, but I had to wait for Gyurica and you know he's always late; he said he'd be with me by nine but it was well after eleven when I saw him stepping through the door. Everyone thinks he's a Party education worker or a person delivering Party leaflets, though he always has his doctor's bag with him. He stopped in the middle of the courtyard, blinked several times, looked around for the number he had been called to, number 39; as soon as he spotted it the women left the gallery, shut their doors and went back into their kitchens; when he finally got inside he took a deep breath, mopped his brow and asked Gizi for a glass of water. As for my foot, it's nothing serious, I just need to avoid walking on it and keep applying the cold compresses; the swelling won't go for another twenty-four hours yet and no-one is going to ask me to jump down from a tree between now and then. As Puck says: "Up and down, up and down, / I shall lead them up and down."

He didn't mention you, not for reasons of tact, I think, but because he had nothing more to say – and what is there to say? He stared at Gizi, sitting at the table bolt upright with her hands on her knees, very much the mistress of the house. When he stood up she unfolded a fresh towel and handed it to him. The bed had been made but my bag and gloves were still there; he must have realised that I had spent the night there. Józsi's walking stick and plastic raincoat were on the hanger, and his shaving brush and stick of soap were in full view on the shelf over the washstand. I was wearing Gizi's dressing gown, the one with the huge flowers; she was already in her black dress, she'd been ironing her apron when he arrived. While he was examining my foot the cat, her enormous three-coloured tabby, came in from the corridor, padded over to him and rubbed its hair all over his trousers. When he left, Gizi scrubbed the bowl out as if it were infectious.

My first idea had been to spend the night on Margaret Island. I was alone all afternoon – Juli had gone off to church. I wrote her a note to say I was going to the Grand Hotel for the night, packed my bags and called a taxi. I stopped and paid the driver in Szabad Tér. I could hear music playing inside the hotel and I was just about to go in when they started folding up two of the awnings over the tables; it was sundown, they were cranking the long handles and the blue cloth was slowly folding up as the metal frames collapsed and closed shut. I caught a brief glimpse of the patch we had watched the upholsterer stitch on and I caught a sudden whiff of the storm that had torn it; I also saw the big glass window of the restaurant where we sat looking on in wonder as the rain rattled and crashed against the pane.

I turned round and went back into town. When I got to the flat I found Gizi sitting on the front steps with her dress pulled tightly down over her knees. She was waiting for me. It was her day off and she had come to ask if I would spend the night with her – we weren't in the habit of explaining things to one another. She lives in one of these horrible Budapest blocks where every flat on the same floor opens out onto a central gallery – hers is number 39, but there's also a 60, next to the steps going up to the attic; there's a cage on a hook outside nearly every door, children screaming down in the courtyard, cooking smells coming out of the windows and the toilet doors in the communal washroom never close properly.

As I went into the building I stumbled against the waste bin and half an hour later my ankle had swollen again. I had supper lying in bed; Gizi had cooked some *lángos – lángos* with sour cream. There are two beds in her room, but she had made up only hers for us to sleep in. Juszti's wedding photograph is on the wall above it, a very young-looking bride with her eyes lowered, holding a tiny spray of myrtle in her hand. I don't know where she had sent Józsi, I didn't want to ask.

Neither of us slept well – my foot was throbbing and Gizi kept getting up to change the compress. In the morning she went down to the grocery store and phoned for the doctor; the rest you know. After Gyurica had gone she called a taxi for me. She came with me to the square – it was only a hundred metres from the Swan. The flower sellers were sitting outside the gate; they called out to me but then left me alone. Once again

I had lost my hairpins so I bought a dozen at a stall. As I was about to leave the square by the main gate I spotted a flowering tree leaning over the wall and stopped. I hadn't noticed it there the day before, or hadn't looked at it properly. I now realised that it was a bignonia.

Do you know what a bignonia is?

Father would have been able to give you its botanical name. I used to know it myself, it'll come back to me soon. If you have ever been in Köves Street you would know what it looks like: a tall, twisted shrub, very aggressive, growing on a trellis, with flowers like hunting horns. The first time I went there to see Angéla she was standing on the fence, clinging on to the lattice-work with a red bignonia flower between her teeth.

Anyway I didn't go in, I carried on towards the chapel. I was hobbling a bit now, I was wearing Gizi's shoes, her feet are bigger than mine, but even so they were pinching and my big toe had started to throb. I took them off as soon as I got inside and tucked my feet under the kneeling board; the stone floor was nice and cool.

There was one other person in there, an old fellow, kneeling before the statue of St Antony. His lips were moving and his hands were clasped in prayer, the way Pipi did it in *Joan of Arc*, the perfect image of ardent devotion. When he had finished he tossed a coin into the purse, a twenty fillér piece; as soon as I got outside I burst into tears. Ványa was so fond of my "melodious sobbings", he should have heard these strangled gaspings and heavings. I have no idea what I was crying about,

I don't think it was about you, or because it had been so dark in the chapel – I don't know when I was last inside one. The red glow of the light in the sanctuary, the great floppy yellow roses on the altar to Mary – it was absolutely wonderful to be in there, unspeakably good. If I believed in God – if I believed in anything at all – it wouldn't have been the same. I would have instantly leaped up and started pleading with the Heavens, I would have whined and whimpered and lamented and begged and pleaded and promised to do anything in return, and wept uncontrollably; but I knew there was no help to be had, and I didn't want any anyway, so there was no point in asking: even if I could have brought myself to beg for it, it would still have been no good, I could never have undertaken to be a good girl and never to tell lies, I would simply have offloaded all my burdens onto Heaven, gone away with a shining face full of tears, and it would have cost me nothing; I would have been able to let myself go for a moment – and everything would have been even harder than before. So I really can't explain why it was so unbelievably good just to be in there.

When I decided to leave I could barely stand the pain of trying to force Gizi's shoe on the foot again; I couldn't do up the laces – but I needn't have worried, the swelling was so tight that it fell off. I got to the front gate but I didn't want to go past the bignonia again, so I came in through the side gate. I hope nobody calls round, nobody who knows me. I've taken the shoes off now and I'm sitting here on the floor in my bare feet. There's a slight breeze, just enough to stir the leaves on the trees outside, and there's a beetle crawling along beside me, and now he's reached my toes – a lovely slim-bodied beetle with blue wings. Father would identify him as *Calosoma sycophanta* and lift out of his way a peach pip that someone had spat out, and solemnly tell him, "Go in peace, little traveller."

You really would have loved my father. I've never talked about him much. If I haven't done so it's because I never say much about anything, not about you or anyone else; as a child I was so quiet I never learned to talk very well. What it says on my CV is a pack of lies, the things people say about me are all lies, I lie so easily I could have made a career out of it. I have come to realise that if I can't bear to speak the truth even to you then I am beyond all help.

But it is true, for example, that he would have chatted to the beetle and told him, "Go in peace, little traveller," and that he would have squatted down next to him to say the words. It's interesting: whenever I think about him I always see him squatting down like that, with his thin grey hair tousled over the dome of his beautifully formed forehead, gazing from behind his glasses at some insect or flower. I see a kind of dew on his brow – not horrible and sweaty, more like condensed steam, like when you breathe warm air onto a glass and it stays there for a while. When he died the moisture was still on his skin; I wiped it off with the palm of my hand; I had washed the handkerchiefs the night before, but they were still damp, it was winter and the wet washing was hanging in the attic and making cracking noises when it moved (all our best handkerchiefs came to us from Auntie Irma). Later I dried them over a coal fire for mother to wipe her tears on. I've never told you about Auntie Irma, and yet I wore her shoes for two whole years.

Have you ever noticed how, whenever we're bathing somewhere, when I get out of the water I always put my sandshoes on straight away? I put my left foot on the pier and quickly bury the right one in the sandal. At Szolnok, when we went up to our room and you came in to join me, I wasn't sitting normally on the bed with my legs stretched out, I was squatting on my heels. When you left me early next morning you laughed and said I was such a prude, because when you switched the light on to pick up your watch and your wallet, I pulled the bedcover over and hid my foot under it.

Pipi will have told you that I am certainly no prude. When the weather's warm I am perfectly happy to go about undressed. But Pipi also knows that I have two large corns on my right foot, and they never go away, even when I have shoes specially made. You were so cross when I wouldn't let you come with me to the shoemaker to try on the red ones with straps! I didn't want you to see my right foot, and I didn't want to tell you about Auntie Irma.

Yesterday it was my right foot that was swollen; I was wearing slippers when I showed it to Gyurica; today I'm wearing Gizi's shoes, and it hurts every bit as much as it did when I was growing up, in the ones I had from Auntie Irma; her feet were as small as a child's, and she took a childlike pride in their being so incredibly tiny.

One summer, when I was at secondary school, my foot burst out of one I was wearing. That evening I went to see Ambrus the bootmaker, to ask him for some thread to sew them up; he gave me the thread but wouldn't let me do it, he sewed the soles to the uppers himself. "What do I owe you?" I asked him, and he said I should feed the pigs. So I dragged the swill out for the two great brutes and nearly broke my back lifting it over the fence; if I had gone inside and stood at the trough they would have knocked me onto the ground. I also had to sew a tear in his blue trousers, the ones he wears to the orchard on Sundays, and only then were we quits. I still thought he had put me to a great deal of work for a stupid bit of thread.

When I got home I was still barefoot, carrying the shoes in my hand. Father was in the garden. "We must get her some shoes," he said, and Mother sighed. "That's true." I just went into the kitchen to see what there was for supper. "We should get her some shoes!" Well of course we should. But I finished the school year just as I was: still no shoes.

That evening Auntie Irma called round. Father was already in bed, so Mother took out the cherry wine that he wasn't allowed to drink; she didn't drink it either, she just made a show of doing so, and when the guest had left she carefully poured the untouched contents of the glass back into the silver-plated carafe, drop by drop. Auntie Irma was very fond of me; she would hug me and stroke me, and give me lumps of sugar. I put up with the caresses like a little whore, watching her to see if she was going to give me money. She didn't often do that – almost never, in fact – but she almost always gave me presents. That evening it was a coral necklace, because I was a big girl now, a pupil at the gymnázium, and she hung it round my neck with a kiss. I stared at her in amazement. If we sold it to the jeweller he might put it in his window and she would know. Clear coral! I didn't even have a decent skirt. I slid down out of her embrace; I could no longer bear her petting and her intimacy.

I was still standing beside the table in my pinafore, with pigswill smeared on the hem, my toes sticking out of the front of my shoes – and this coral necklace glowing around my neck. Irma looked me up and down, then asked what I would be wearing to the school start-of-term ceremony. Mother gave another sigh. The school specified three sorts of uniform and I didn't have a single one of them. She avoided answering, she just stammered out something. Auntie Irma's stupid little eyes brightened with pleasure; she stretched out her foot, compared it with my bare one, then pulled off her shoes behind the tasselled tablecloth and tried on one of mine: it was slightly too big for her and she was filled with pride and joy. She asked Mother not to be offended, because they were relatives – first cousins in fact – and she loved me like her own child, but since we happened to be so very similar in the size of our feet she would like to send me some of her shoes to wear at the ceremony; she got bored with them very quickly, she was forever buying new ones and the old ones were left to dry out in the wardrobe. I looked at her feet; she was wearing beautiful yellow shoes with slightly raised heels, they were very small and very showy, like toy shoes. Mother lowered her eyes and looked away.

The next day I received a pair of black ones; they had buckskin insoles and were done up with buttons on one side. I wore a plain white dress to the ceremony; it was a windy, rainy September afternoon, the rest of the class were in their regulation dark blue uniforms, buttoned up to the neck, and even then some of them were cold. I was well hardened, like a little bear, but on the way to the church I felt thoroughly fed up, limping along in my horrible buttoned-up shoes. My form mistress called me to one side; she had a message for my mother: she should buy me a pair of proper girl's shoes and not this flashy sort designed for grown-ups. I asked her if the school was prepared to provide me with a pair, so she asked me my name, and when I didn't answer she turned bright red and dropped the subject. The school had been founded by my great-grandfather, it's named after him, Moses Encsy Gymnázium; I went there on a scholarship, in my side-buttoned shoes.

After a year it became apparent that Auntie Irma's right foot was half a size smaller than her left. At the start it had simply hurt when I walked in them; after a while I could only hobble along, and then not even manage that. Mother was in tears every evening when I washed them and she saw my toes growing twisted and swollen. By then I had four pairs of the shoes, each one smaller than the last. When my aunt died, my first feeling was one of relief that she would be sending me no more of them. Mother had always believed that she would leave everything to me – the apartment, the furniture and her clothes – but she died without making a will and her younger brother packed it all up and cut us out completely.

The next day I went back to Ambrus and got him to cut the fronts off. Open-fronted shoes were not in fashion at the time; Father went white when I arrived home in these butchered ones with my toes poking out in my torn stockings. I carried on wearing them to school for a while, then the form mistress bought a pair with money from some religious foundation and showed them to me after school. I kissed her hand and asked what I should do in return. From then on I was allowed to go to the boarding school and help the third-years memorise their lessons.

By the way, that rehearsal that had been arranged at the china factory was cancelled. I didn't mind one way or the other, the whole thing was to have been very short anyway; I walked home, Pipi went with me as far as the theatre; I felt perfectly contented, looking at the displays in the shop windows, and on the ring road I bought an ice cream cornet. When I got back Juli wasn't there; I had no intention of asking her to leave her flat and come over, so I took out a book, lay down for a while, then got up in some agony to make a cup of coffee. I was grinding the beans when I caught a whiff of the aroma and then suddenly I didn't want any . . . You were sitting there in front of me on the kitchen stool, working the grinder and laughing:

I had remembered that time when I had to do a two-night show in Pécs; when I arrived I had to struggle across the snow to get to the taxis, I hadn't seen you since the morning, and I hate working when you aren't somewhere close by; when I got to the rank I saw you standing there, next to the driver, eating a croissant; you sat beside me in the cab and announced that it was time to go and have a cup of coffee.

I left the kitchen, sat down at the desk and started to draw up my CV, it was the ninth time I had been asked do this since I joined the theatre. I wrote down my name, started to doodle and drew some fish and a goose; then I needed to blow my nose, so I went to the wardrobe and took out three hand-kerchiefs. I pulled out the medicine drawer, because once again that stupid catch had caught one of my fingers, and behind the boxes of medicines and rolls of gauze I discovered some liqueur cherries with the word "aspirin" that you had written on the label; I had no idea when you could have done that. I immediately got dressed and set off for Margaret Island.

The CV should have been handed in today, I had been called in by the new Personnel Manager. He could have recited everything about me without looking at it. "Dezső Encsy," he would begin, "so your father was a lawyer . . ." And what would have happened if I told him that, properly speaking, in the commonly understood sense of the word, he wasn't? What sort of lie would that be taken for? Of course my father was a lawyer. My mother spent the whole day sitting at the piano turning over the sheets of music, there was music in our house from morning to night, exotic plants grew in the space between the windows in the office and my father sat gazing in awe at the chalice of an epiphyllum.

My mother had a triple-barrelled surname: Katalin Marton von Ercsik von Táp von Szentmarton. In the middle of the music stand there was a shiny porcelain miniature of the young Mozart, in his little wig and sky-blue costume. I once stole some eggs from a peasant.

During the war the house we lived in was destroyed by a bomb; I've always wanted to show you the place without your knowing that – I would have loved to watch your face and hear what you said when we turned off Greek Street and headed down towards the reedbed. Our street didn't have a name; we called it the Barrage. It was right on the edge of the town, on the floodplain, where people came to cut the reeds and carried them away in great bundles on their backs. The huge blocks of stone were put there after the great floods of 1803; it was the part of the town most at risk, and they were piled really high. Down below, in the hollow beneath the barrage itself and all the way to the far end, the houses clung together like birds' nests; and weeds grew between the stones – some sort of labiate, with lush petals. One of the houses, the one right at the end of the barrage area, leaned over towards the reeds, another one crouched down on the stones, as mean as a hen coop; ours sprawled in the elbow of the barrage, fenced around by the huge stones. I looked out on the world from behind it as from behind a parapet. Father had inherited the house long before

I was born, and when we had to move out of Templomkért Street that was where he took mother and me.

Our courtyard was in the shape of a triangle; our front windows looked out onto the street and the garden onto the reedbeds; the front gate of course opened onto the street but we always went in from the garden, straight into the kitchen, which served as the main entrance. The single bedroom was on the left of it and Father's office on the right; mother had divided the kitchen into two sections with a lilac-coloured curtain to hide the oven and the washing tub, but every time we lit the fire the smoke got out under and over the partition. We had three apple trees, some Japanese shrubs crouching on the barrage side, a jasmine bush and a lilac tree, and beds of dark tulips, a few old roses and all sorts of sweet-smelling flowers. From early evening until early morning, from spring through to autumn, the scent of flowers seemed to cling in the nose.

Our neighbour on the left was Ambrus, the bootmaker; on the right was Kárász néni, the confectioner. She had levelled her garden and constructed two little cabins and tables under multi-coloured umbrellas; you couldn't see into our garden from hers because it was screened off by greenery. In the evenings I used to sit at the top of the fence, clinging to the trunk of an old jasmine bush that had grown as thick as a tree, and watch her customers snogging. Next to our front door there was a bell that you rang by pulling a cord, and a plaque on the wall: *Dezső Encsy, Solicitor*. The last time I went there a new family were living in Ambrus' house and Kárász néni's patisserie had been replaced by a hostelry, with a radio blaring in the garden and people drinking beer and Spritzer and eating pigs' trotter stew – you could no longer buy proper meat. They had cleared away the rubble of our little house and the communal garden wall had been taken down; they had even dug up the flower beds. All that was left was a single apple tree and a few bushes, and now a green wooden fence marked the boundary on the side towards the road. There wasn't a soul to be seen. I ate an omelette, drank a glass of beer and left.

During the night Gizi asked me what news I had of Emil. She had hesitated a long time before she finally spoke, after much tossing and turning in the bed and clearing her throat. It was pitch black; the windows looking out onto the gallery were wide open and the building was completely silent, apart from the occasional tram rattling past in the street; I hadn't dared ask her where she had sent Józsi, I would have much preferred to hear the sound of him breathing somewhere close by; I would have felt much more relaxed with him here on the premises than I would have at home with Juli. It occurred to me that you never knew Emil, and I remembered a childhood photograph of him beating a drum, or then on his motorbike, racing by with his jet-black hair flying above his unusually white face.

I had never realised that she loved him. When I told her what had happened to him she turned away; I felt her back under her thin nightshirt as it brushed against me in the narrow bed. She sobbed for a while, then got up and took out her rosary. I lay in the bed smoking a cigarette and imagining her getting married to Emil: Auntie Ilu would be holding her head in her hands, the way she always did, and screaming and screaming, and Uncle Domi would be running to the telephone and asking József how much money he wanted to keep Gizi away from their villa. Gizi got to the end of her rosary, stroked my hand and snuggled back into the bed beside me; the water on her fingers was ice-cold. She always believed he was still alive somewhere, in a peaceful meadow where the Choirs of the Elect sang, and that they would one day meet again and never again be parted: I had never before realised why she had never married.

With the CV I had to fill in a sheet of paper answering God knows how many questions. One of them asked if I had any relations or close friends living abroad, currently interned or in prison; that would have needed a whole ream of paper: Gyurka Palma, arrested at the border; Évi Dolhay, who stepped on a mine and lost both her legs; my uncle Béla, thrown down the steps of his castle; Alexandra, in prison for all these years now, and all my other relations sent to live on farmsteads and in villages between Kövár and Kutasi, not to mention Juditka, probably now in America. When I had finished, I signed my name: Eszter Szentpáli Encsy, member of the Lendvay Theatre, Kossuth Prize winner. Then yesterday I remembered Auntie Veronika: I should have told the Personnel Manager to stop the pension she was still drawing because all she did now was walk about the whole day with a stick and her dog, despite the fact that her husband had been an adviser to the law courts. But he wouldn't have taken me seriously; he would have thought I was lying or trying to make my point in a really stupid way. The fact is, I loathe all my relations.

Our house was destroyed in a bombing raid on the town. When the sirens went off we were out in the timber yard; Gámán néni and her family were at the cinema. After the thirty-minute bombardment was over we made our way back to the Barrage, wading through piles of bodies and rubble. Our home between Ambrus' house and Kárász néni's cabins had simply disappeared. It was as if something had simply blown it away; in its place there was this horrifying deep hole, and the scattered remains of what was left of our furniture and the building itself; later the reed cutters found our pots and pans lying in the reedbed. At the time, Mother neither wept nor blanched; we slept the sleep of the contented in the main hall of a school, along with everyone else who had lost their homes; I felt like the nation's favourite child, everyone seemed to want to look after us, and the whole city shared our grief. Now that we had nothing we no longer had to be afraid of losing everything in the next raid. I never saw the piano again. Something was finally over – something that had ended a long time before, with the death of Father.

Father was orphaned at an early age. His father's land had been managed by his guardian; in his hands it brought in little revenue, but it had been enough to pay for his travels abroad and his university course. When he married he sold everything, furnished his new home and had half a dozen suits made for himself. Mother brought nothing into the marriage, and none of the Martons – apart from Auntie Irma – went with her to the church. Her parents had just left the town and moved back to their farmstead near the village. While she was still at school, and later as a young woman attending society balls, they lived in their house in the city and went to their country seat only in the summer. One day, if you remember, we had to change a wheel on the way between Lovaskút and Marton; you were squatting down next to the driver and I was lying on the grass beside the road with my face plastered with suntan lotion; you pointed to a chateau that you thought a remarkable example of the Hungarian Baroque style. I was sceptical at first, then I noticed the hammer and sickle underneath the flagstaff, and that the staircase leading up to the main entrance was swarming with Korean schoolchildren; I burst out laughing, and you looked round and asked what I was laughing at. It was where my mother was born, and the place where my uncle Béla was thrown down the stairs by the peasants.

My father was a clever man, refined, easy-going, exceptionally cultured, and he had a delicate, rather touching beauty to go with it. He had fair hair, blue eyes and a slender nose and lips; when she stood beside him my mother's strikingly dark-haired beauty blazed like a glowing coal. I have no idea how I could have been born to such handsome people as they were; I don't have the same looks, the same facial contours; when I'm not made up my face looks almost featureless; I wear a series of masks rather than a head. I am one thing in the morning, another at midday, and something else at night. Last night, when Gizi got up and put the light on I glanced at myself in the mirror: I looked like a ghost.

*

The day I stole the eggs we were in such straits that we had nothing to give Father for his supper. All we had left were some dried peas and beans, which he couldn't digest. That afternoon a peasant woman happened to stray into the house. I say "stray" because our legal and musical clients only ever found us by chance. She set down her basket of eggs in the kitchen to show we could trust her. I took five of them. Father of course turned her out and she left. That evening I produced the stolen eggs. Mother wept for a short while, but she broke them all the same and made an omelette. We absolutely adored Father.

At first the Martons kept their distance from us, but when our poverty became really desperate they made some effort to help us, if always in such a way as to make the offer unacceptable. My uncle Béla offered him some work; Father turned him out of the house. I don't know what it was about, because nothing was ever said on the subject, but it must have been something underhand, some matter relating to the county where he was employed in the Lord Lieutenant's office. Father would not accept any brief that he did not believe was absolutely above board – so of course he earned almost nothing.

We must have lived on the ring road for about a year, and then moved to Ferenc Deák Street.

In our part of the world moving home was always considered shameful: it meant that there had been some disaster, or bankruptcy, or divorce; gossip and scandal always trod in the wake of the removals van. Very few people came to visit us, and no-one from the city or county councils who did ever repeated the visit. Father was a member of the Gentlemen's Club and the Chamber of Advocates, but he never went to either; he found the company boring and he couldn't drink or smoke because of his bad lungs.

From Ferenc Deák Street we moved on to Muzsaly Street, from there to Vicarage Street, and from there to the Barrage. Every removal brought another loss. First it was the maid, then the cook, then some of the furniture, and finally the oven and kitchen fittings; there wasn't enough room in the new house for them. Luckily we had very few things left.

Father rarely went out into the street; he preferred watering his plants with water that had been left to stand and burying his head in botanical tomes. The tropical plants behind the window brought passers-by to a halt. When a rare example of a bud appeared on one of them, he never left it, he didn't move from its side, he was like an anxious family doctor tending to a woman in childbed, gently stroking its chalice and praising it as it slowly opened. One winter, I remember, the epiphyllum came into flower; its long, slender petals cascaded down like a scarlet waterfall, they were like shiny porcelain.

Father stayed beside it the whole night, gazing at it and singing little songs to it.

I was never bothered by the fact that this made us the laughing stock of the town. We acquired a certain celebrity – "the mad lawyer's people" – and his acquaintances at the Chamber circulated stories about him. Every time the doorbell rang I stood listening with a beating heart to see who had come. When I heard the usual rambling, hesitant voices I shrugged: yet again Father would be handing out professional advice free, gratis and for nothing, before gently sending the person away, telling him it wasn't worth pursuing the case because there was no hope of winning. "Don't you even want to try?" the disappointed client would reply. I wanted to scream in despair: once again he was turning away the goose or the capon that had been lying there in the basket with its feet invitingly trussed. But I quickly cheered up again: as soon as the man had gone, Father would go out into the courtyard and feed crumbs to the ants; his dear face, getting thinner by the day, would now be calm and lit with a gentle happiness, and I would heave a sigh and go back into the kitchen. When he died I never for a moment felt that I had lost a father. My heart was broken, but the bitterness I felt as I stood by the coffin was that of a mother who had lost a child.

"Why don't you like music?" you asked me one day, when we were in Pest. Eric Willmer was going to play Beethoven and Bartók and you wanted to take me; I wouldn't go, and you were quite offended. I said I was tone-deaf and started to sing the national anthem in a put-on voice; then you got really cross. I decided you were angry with yourself because you loved me so much and yet I was tone-deaf and couldn't appreciate serious music.

My mother was a housewife, it says in my record and all my CVs, but she wasn't one in any sense that the Personnel Department would have understood. She worked like a slave from morning till night. You once brought me a biography of Mozart, with a wonderful portrait engraving in the baroque style on the first page, and you asked me three times after that if you could borrow it, because you had never read it yourself. I said I didn't know where it was – Juli must have put it somewhere, or I had left it behind when I went swimming. Your face flushed with anger, then you roared with laughter. I think you were always happy when you caught me out in some act of irresponsibility, some act of supposed negligence. You thought that I hadn't noticed, or even suspected, that I had given myself away. I hadn't lost the Mozart. It's still there, hidden away behind the works of Shakespeare, but the engraving has gone. I tore the page out and burned it in the kitchen.

When you asked me about the book, did you remember the engraving? Saint Cecilia sitting at a celestial organ surrounded by angels singing and making music, haloes and smiles on all sides, a line of little holes over the angels with the violins, the fair hair of the saint flowing down to her ankles and her hands raised to the heavens – even though she was already up there. The whole image was filled with the sound of music. I couldn't bear it. Saint Cecilia took the bread out of our mouths, and that is why I have hated her since I was a child.

We were a public disgrace, as I said before. When it became clear that Father was not going to be able to support us, Mother put a notice in the window offering piano lessons; Father had bought the instrument for her as a wedding present to replace the one she had left in the house at Marton. It was a beautiful old piano, with a miniature of Mozart between the two music stands; it was actually too large to bring into the house in the Barrage, but Father preferred at the time to take down the front door frame rather than lose it. Mother loved music with a passion; whenever I think or dream about her I always hear her playing it. I never see her face, I can only hear her, playing Mozart, or Handel. In Handel's music everything is bright, self-confident, ordered, perfect; and Chopin's too – when he isn't moaning and groaning and raging in a frenzy. In my dreams I always feel what a brave woman she was, pounding away tirelessly at the *Études* so that she could greet her husband with a smile.

At first no-one responded to the notice; then slowly, one by one, a little following began to form. When I was a child there was no music school in the city, the mothers sent their children to elderly spinsters who damaged their ear and their sense of rhythm. I think my mother must have been wonderfully gifted. Her family, who followed our successive hardships with anxious disapproval, soon heard about the advertisement, and Uncle Sándor came to see us about it. When he arrived

Mother was giving a lesson to her only pupil at the time, the son of Kárász néni; he had fingers like sausages, and he stared in hopeless wonder as her hands flew lightly and at great speed over the keyboard. She simply laughed at her visitor and informed him that she had no intention of taking the notice down. The next day Gréti, the German governess of one of our relations, arrived with little Judit and some music by Czerny. Within six months Mother was teaching the piano to all the children in our wider family, at a far lower rate than she charged any of the outsiders.

We were now quite the fashion. Every summer young French and German governesses would sit in our garden reading their novels under the lilac trees; in winter they took shelter in the living room and sat on the sofa, perching there as if it were filthy, listening to the children's dogged tinklings. Father greeted the girls in faultless, exquisite French and exchanged little jokes with the German governesses; no-one could resist his gentle charm. They told him everything they had picked up from each other about what was happening in their families; I had no time to sit and listen while he joked and chatted to them, but then one day, when I happened to be in the kitchen with my hands empty and everything spotlessly clean, I did stop to listen. They were talking about Elza.

For me at that age, a married couple should be inseparable, even if they were not as close as my mother and father. I knew, from books, that people had lovers, but I had no idea that you could have one living in the same house, that the spouse might be aware of it and accept the fact, and that everything would carry on as normal; people would continue to visit, you could raise two children, and behave as if no-one had noticed. To me it seemed both bizarre and unimaginable. The idea occupied my mind the rest of the evening.

Six months after the appearance of the advertisement it had become "the thing" to be taking lessons from my mother, even if you did have to come to the Barrage. Her name gave status to her pupils from outside the family as well: after all, she was a Marton. Responsibility for the housework fell on me. I was twelve years old, in the third year at school; Aunt Irma was the only member of the family who kept in touch with us – socially, that is: in her timid, old-maidish way, she was a little bit in love with Father, and she had never forgiven Uncle Béla for some ancient adolescent prank. Mother had to take special care of her hands, so I did the shopping, I cooked the supper, I chopped the firewood and dealt with the laundry. Every afternoon I prepared the meals for that evening and for the next day, put them into earthenware pots in the cold hatch, and surrounded them with roof tiles to stop the rats knocking them over. At midday, when the lessons were over, I went to the market when the traders were starting to pack up and everything was cheaper. We rarely ate meat, and not very much when we did: Father lived mostly on milk products.

And all the time, whether I was studying, doing the cooking, laying the fire or washing up, I could hear the Czerny. The last lesson of the day was from six till seven; at seven we ate,

Father went to bed as soon as it was over, and I set about my lessons or my reading. I began to loathe the music. It went straight through the cotton wool that I stuffed in my ears on the days when I had so many lessons to do that I couldn't wait for the teaching to finish. But the music was what we lived by – or rather, it helped us not to die from starvation, it paid the bills, bought medicines for Father (all that milk!), allowed us to heat the house as instructed by the doctor, and not have to borrow from anyone.

The fees for the last of the lessons also enabled me to enrol at the university. That autumn the Music School opened and my mother found herself with no more pupils. Kárász néni's son remained loyal until he was old enough for military service; in all that time he had made no discernible progress, but every Sunday he came with a slice of cream-filled pastry and two slices of Turkish cake.

When the first public competition for young people was held, Mother persuaded me to go along with her. We made our way up the imitation marble staircase and took our seats at the back of the semicircular concert hall; with her shock of black hair and long eyelashes she looked wonderful. There were lights in brackets around the walls, a huge chandelier hung from the ceiling and wooden shutters blocked out the morning sunlight. Above them there was an enormous fresco: a fat Cecilia with a bulging neck, in a saffron dress with her mane of blond hair tumbling down her back. It was the start of winter and we had no more pupils.

Mother gave herself up to the music; she sat there with her eyes closed, enjoying even the most plodding interpretations; whenever it was the turn of one of her former pupils she leaned forward in her seat, paid rapt attention, and when the applause came she glowed with pleasure. I sat and stared at Cecilia. I had no desire to look at the other people present, the women's dresses, not even the coiled locks of the girls or the young men in their silk cravats. To me the Cecilia up there looked like an ecstatic cow.

*

Angéla was my mother's second pupil who was not the daughter of a relative.

Emil conducted the negotiations with her with great diplomacy; that such a thing as money might exist was not mentioned by either of them, yet somehow they came to an agreement. I remember the day he called. It was in September, Angéla wasn't in town, she was expected back at any time from her holiday with Auntie Ilu and her younger sister. Father had spent almost the whole day lying down; I had placed the flowerpots on shelves next to his bed so that he could reach them more easily. I was in the second year then; the larger shoes that the school gave me hadn't yet appeared and I was still wearing the ones from Auntie Irma when I went out and slippers inside the house. Angéla's family had moved to Szolnok that summer, from Budapest. I had walked past their villa in Köves Street, where all the lawyers lived, but it was still empty at the time. I didn't yet know Uncle Domi, though I did know that he was a judge. Angéla's brother Emil was a law student in the big city nearby. Angéla had been enrolled in my class, and at the start of this September her seat was still empty. Every morning we heard the teacher say: "Angéla Graff, absent yet again."

The first time you undressed me I was wearing a lilac-coloured dress, the same colour as the curtain that hid the stove in our kitchen. I lay there in silence, waiting. We had been living in a state of intolerable tension for so long that I could hardly bear the time you took over it. I have never since taken so much pleasure in the house I live in as I did then; it seemed so wonderful and magnificent to live up there, high above the town, in the winds that blew, the rain and the storms, like the one that was raging that night. I had wondered for weeks what we would say to one another when you did speak at last, and we stopped circling around each other.

"And what should I say to you?" I kept wondering, as I lay gazing out through the clear blue rectangle of the balcony door at the stars beyond, with a cool breeze blowing from Eagle Hill. I would have loved it if you could have known everything about me without my having to say anything, yet at the same time, creaking rustily somewhere down inside me, the words had already taken shape – about the Barrage, and Father, Ambrus and Auntie Irma's shoes, and everything . . . and I was afraid that I would start crying, though there was no reason to cry because I was at last happy, as happy as I had ever been in my life.

You were sitting a short way away from me; I couldn't see you and I didn't know if you were naked too. I felt as if I were slightly drunk, but also tired and ready for sleep. You were already so much a part of me that, even with my eyes closed and in the dark, I could see you from inside myself if I chose: your hazel eyes, your sensitive mouth, your long muscular limbs. You felt around for a cigarette but didn't find one – the case was under my shoulder and I didn't move because I didn't want you to light up again; I was thinking of Juli, that she would have reached Máriabesnyő by then with the other pilgrims, and I wondered if she would be praying for me, and what she would have said if she stepped through the door, turned on the light and found us like that.

But what you said was, "I know you love Angéla." That was all. Not that you loved me, or that you knew that I loved you; you made no attempt to define the nature of our love, though it had been so blindingly obvious for the last several weeks. I raised myself up and pulled out your cigarette case from under my back so that you could have your smoke. You took a quick pull on a cigarette, then threw it out onto the balcony. I lay in your arms with my eyes wide open, not moving but near to despair; when you fell asleep I went out onto the balcony, in my bare feet and naked as I was; the cold bit into my skin, so I moved back from the railings and the stone floor and stood, with my teeth chattering, looking out towards Pest and the mountains beyond, and the big street lamp at the head of the Chain Bridge; then I came back in and snuggled in beside you. You had taken my pillow and slipped it under your neck; I didn't want to disturb you – I can sleep anywhere, even on the ground or on stones – and I rested my head on my elbow.

And suddenly the Barrage was there before me, as if there had never been a war; Father was coughing quietly among his flowerpots, little Judit was with my mother, working her way up and down the scales, and I was dealing with the dirty dishes. Mother had cooked a honey cake in the morning, because Father was supposed to eat plenty of honey and he could only take it cooked in a pastry; the pastry had stuck to the pan and my fingers were raw from scrubbing it; I drew back the lilac curtain so that I could see better and the kitchen floor was instantly flooded with water. I was drenched, my apron, both of my arms, and my feet were covered in dishwater and muck – I had been scouring out the baking tray with stone powder but it just wouldn't clean – and at that very moment the bell rang, and the little window in the kitchen door darkened; someone knocked and I called out for them to come in; my hair flopped forward over my forehead, I pushed it back with my elbow, the door opened, and in stepped Angéla. She stopped for a second, staring at the rivulet of dirty dishwater advancing towards her and stood there speechless. She had a golden-brown tan from the seaside, she was holding a ball in her left hand, a beautiful sky-blue ball with a gold ring around it, and in her right hand, in a snow-white glove, she held a lacquered music stand covered with red hide. Elza was standing behind her. "Good afternoon," she said to me.

You stirred and were suddenly completely awake, as if you had been sleeping for a whole night and not just a quarter of an hour. You drew my head down next to yours on the pillow, murmured some lines of verse, took a lock of my hair in your hand and fell asleep again. I wanted to wake you up straight away, get dressed, and inform you that I have loathed and hated Angéla from the moment I first saw her, that I have ever since, and that even when I am dead, if there is any life after death, I shall hate her still.

2

There are lizards here too.

I have always loved animals, even, to be honest, Ambrus'
pigs. When they were slaughtered I cried even though I knew
we would be given some of the meat; I never ate it myself, but
it had a wonderful smell. Father lived on honey and butter and
eggs, Mother and I just ate whatever came to hand; there were
never any leftovers in our house so we couldn't keep a dog.
For a while I kept silkworms, then I was put in charge of the
laboratory equipment at school and they gave me an old unused
aquarium and I got some guppies, but they died off one by
one. Angéla had a fawn. I went to the house once to see it
after I had finished my afternoon housework.

Angéla is no longer beautiful. The wonderful oval of her face
has sagged. Yesterday when she was sitting with her mother
it was like seeing two versions of Auntie Ilu, only one was
thinner and more sickly-looking than the other. When I spoke
to her she never answered. She looked up but you could see
in her eyes that she had no idea who had spoken to her or

what they had said – Elza must have pumped her full of drugs. I took a good look at her, I had plenty of time for it, I was thinking that she had lived all this time like someone completely detached from the real world. At one time I would never have believed that she could lose the self-confidence her beauty gave her; she had worn it like a suit of armour. I often used to think that if any real trouble came into her life, something that really dented her confidence or frightened her, she would have only to go and look in the mirror and her courage would return.

I have seen her with Emil, and with Uncle Domi and her mother and holding on to Elza's arm, and I have also seen her with you: there is always someone taking care of her, someone holding her hand, someone stroking her arm or showing her the easiest way forward, and whenever I have seen her on her own, out shopping or with a book on her lap in the garden, she has never looked lonely or isolated because of her wonderful physical beauty. It struck me yesterday that she has never in all her life learned how to handle money, or fill in an official form, or do any real work or understand anything properly. The reports and accounts for the orphanage have always been done by you, not by her; her role is to be benevolent and wonderful in all her ways . . . and now she has lost her beauty, and any money that she gets runs through her fingers like water; soon she'll be poor, and her body will turn to dust and she'll simply disappear; for a while she'll be nothing more than a name, and then not even that. When I die they will make a film about my life and a statue will be put up in the Barrage. It will stand in the restaurant garden looking out towards the reedbeds.

Yesterday, when we were sitting opposite one another, she didn't glance at me for a single second; she just can't look me in the eye. I almost laughed out loud, thinking what she would say if I told her that my whole life had been a preparation for the moment when I saw her finally setting off down the road to death, defenceless and beyond help, like any ordinary human being, and how funny it would be if that day were to prove the happiest day of my life.

She really loved me. She loved all my mother's family; she loved our house, even the lilac curtain in the kitchen and my shoes with no toes; she once asked if she could try them for an afternoon. To her we were exotic beings. She attached herself to me as sincerely as I hated her. I have never asked you what she told you about me and my family; I am sure it can't have been anything that would have made clear to you the true extent of our poverty, or that we lived in the Barrage in the sort of house where you went in through the kitchen. I sometimes had the feeling that she almost envied us. On one occasion the school organised a picnic outing; she hovered around me despondently, with some slices of paper-thin pink ham in her hand and her eyes fixed on the pot into which I had scraped some toasted semolina from the previous night's supper; I was hiding behind a bush gobbling it down with a large spoon to finish it off as quickly as I could. She asked me for some and offered to swap it for her ham, and when I snapped at her she turned bright red and her eyes filled with tears.

Everyone in the class loved her, because she was so generous and always so willing to help. On one occasion I really could have strangled her: she had done a Latin translation for Gizi. Gizi was on the verge of failing and I was terrified that she might actually pass as a result of this last assignment of the year and no longer need me as a personal tutor. I never once saw Angéla eat a whole orange by herself; she always brought one for the mid-morning break, but as soon as she had peeled it she shared it around, segment by segment.

You were the only person who knew how much I love good food. My mother and father believed to their dying day that I wasn't very interested in it, that I saw it simply as something to fill my stomach with; you were the only person who knew how excited I get when there is crab salad on the menu, and how greedily I gobbled up those dates that you found for me, guzzling every single one, one after the other, as I went up the stairs. Only you knew how gluttonous I am and how miserable I get if I have to wait to be served. During the last days of my mother's life I never moved from her side, I took my meals sitting next to her bed and she smiled in wonder at how much I ate and how much I enjoyed it; I had only recently started to have any real money and I ate voraciously. But I don't think about food so much anymore. Among the many, many things that you have been to me in these last two years, you came to mean to me what food had meant before; it is all part of the time we had together, that you would be sitting there, raising your glass or pulling my plate towards you and finishing off the last morsels. Last night all I had for supper was a cup of tea and a slice of toast.

This lizard is sunning himself on the stone. I moved my leg a bit closer to him but he wasn't scared and he didn't move. Animals aren't afraid of me. The fawn wasn't frightened either; it sniffed my hand and licked it; it was salty because before I left home I had been mixing bran and feeding Ambrus' pigs.

You have never been to our part of the world; all you have seen of it is the forest on the outskirts of the town, and that was from the train. When I was little there were plenty of deer among the trees, and the hunters shot huge numbers of rabbits; when it got very cold they came right to the edge of the town.

It was Emil – the one who rode the motorbike – who got the fawn for Angéla. He was the only member of her family I could stand. He hated Uncle Domi and Auntie Ilu; Angéla was the only one of them that he loved. If he were still alive he would be with her now, tucking her up in bed, fussing over her and telling her little stories. How lucky he's no longer alive to do that.

Our city was so proud of the new concrete motorway – there were articles in the papers about it for weeks – but it runs straight through the forest. Emil ran into the fawn's mother by accident, he didn't mean to, you know how animals freeze when they are caught in the headlights of a motorbike. The young fawn was sniffing around its dead mother, so he tied its hoofs together and took it home. For days it was all the class could talk about, nothing else: *Graff has a fawn.* When the bell rang for lunch she would race down the front steps in her hurry to get home; on one occasion the music teacher caught her and made her walk down again nice and slowly, in the approved manner. She was in floods of tears, the poor thing, while I sang all the way home, and nicked a string of garlic in the market on the way. I didn't need it, I was just so happy at what had happened. When I got home Mother pointed to the aquarium with her chin: the two guppies were floating belly-up on the surface. I threw them in the waste bin, washed the aquarium out thoroughly, ripped out the plants and emptied out the gravel. Father said something about our getting a cat, but I just shook my head. There were pigeons flapping about in Ambrus' garden all day and we couldn't possibly keep a cat; Ambrus was an essential part of my life and he hated cats because they were a threat to his birds.

Angéla kept inviting me to her house – half the class had already been there – and the more reluctant I was the more she cajoled and stroked my arm. When the guppies died my resistance broke; I now desperately wanted to see the fawn. When I finally went, one Sunday, she was standing behind the fence clinging on to the bignonia with one hand and beckoning to me with the other as I came down the road. As soon as she caught sight of me she spat the flowers out of her mouth. Elza was in the garden reading her book; we barely acknowledged one another. She always accompanied Angéla to the music lessons and had seen me washing and scrubbing, so I had no standing in her eyes. For my part, I knew what everybody in the town except Angéla knew, and what Emil and Uncle Domi knew better than anyone else: that she was Uncle Domi's mistress. Whenever I saw her I just pulled a face. As you know, children think that love lasts until the grave and adulterers should be thrown into boiling tar.

She must have shown you a picture of the villa. At the back, where the vegetable garden and the orchard are (no house was ever built at our end of the town without its kitchen garden), Uncle Domi had converted a little shed into a hutch for the fawn. When I set eyes on it my heart simply broke. It was already used to Angéla; it would eat oats and little bits of cabbage out of her hand and let her stroke its back and fondle its ears. I stood there for ages, unable to speak; she was ablaze with happiness. She bent down over it and put her arm around its slender neck and kissed its muzzle. I put my hand into the hutch to feel around for some hay; I wanted to try and tempt it with some, but it pulled its head out of my hand and sprang away. "It's afraid of you," she said, and she assured me that it had been afraid of her at first too but it would get used to me in time.

With our tea we had foaming hot chocolate; a table was laid in her bedroom and I sat there nibbling at it without any appetite. I felt thoroughly hostile and ate very little. Towards the end of the meal Auntie Ilu came rushing in, her nose was bright red and she didn't even see me; she began to shower kisses on

Angéla and mutter something unintelligible, then Uncle Domi came dashing in and the two of them went out together. I looked at Angéla: she was still eating. Then Elza came into the room – her nose was bright red too. Angéla poured some more hot chocolate into her cup. A little later I saw Auntie Ilu again, through the window. She was walking in the garden with a towel wrapped round her head like a turban and she was smoking a cigarette; Uncle Domi had his hat, his gloves and his walking stick in his hand, and he strode on ahead to the end of the clinker-covered path to avoid speaking to her. "Mother's nerves are bad today," Angéla said, and she followed her with her innocent, compassionate gaze, as Auntie Ilu tottered doggedly round and round between the beds of flowers.

I dreamed about the fawn night after night. You don't know what it's like when a person longs so unspeakably for something. I was still angry and bitterly ashamed – of the shoes, of the clothes I wore, and the food we ate. I loved oranges, but I would rather have choked than accept a single segment of one from Angéla. I wasn't interested in their house, the illustrations of fairy tales in her room, or the contents of her little bookshelf: only the fawn. In those days I often fell asleep crying about it.

At first I thought I might steal it and take it home; I took the thought really seriously. Of course there was no way we could have kept it in the house, but I hoped that perhaps Ambrus would give it a home and not tell anyone, and at least I would be able to go across to wash it and clean up after it had eaten; he had plenty of fodder all the year round, and in the summer it would eat hay anyway.

One morning I climbed over the fence and looked inside the pigsty, but I could see that there wasn't anywhere in it to make a separate compartment for the fawn. I had also begun to realise that Ambrus might not agree to the idea – and worse, that sooner or later everything would come out and that would be the end of my place in the school. If they threw me out there was no other school in the country that had been founded by my grandfather and what would become of me if I couldn't get in on a foundation scholarship to pay the fees? I forced myself to pay close attention in class. I was an outstanding student; I took no interest in the lessons, and I had not the slightest spark of ambition, but I had a wonderful memory, I never forgot anything that I had heard and understood, and I listened attentively whenever the teachers explained anything because at the end of the year there was a prize for diligence, thirty pengős, and I won it every year.

How you laughed that time at my place when you kept coming across money hidden everywhere – in among my night-dresses, in the sweet tin, between the pages of books and tucked into my shoes! And that Easter, when you spent the whole day with me and you bet me that you would find everything I had hidden, I laughed myself silly, watching you hunt high and low. The only money you didn't find was stashed away above a pelmet – Juli found it later, when she had an uncharacteristic attack of diligence and set about spring-cleaning the house; she reached up with her brush and the cigarette box came crashing down at her feet. It was full of hundred-forint notes. "You are a real hamster!" you said, and you laughed so much you had to sit down. "You are a real hamster, Eszti, the way you hide your money away." You pressed a two-forint coin into my hand, saluted me with a deep bow and kissed me. My fingers opened and the coin rolled somewhere under the bed. How little you knew about me! At one time, when I was about thirteen – about the time when Emil took the fawn home – if someone had offered me money to go with him I might have felt bad about it but I would have slept with him without a moment's hesitation.

From that day onwards I went to Angéla's regularly. After a while the fawn would take food from my hand and even let me lead it by the collar out onto the street, though if there was any loud noise it would tear itself out of my hand and run back inside, panting frantically. Angéla was very happy with me; it was almost as if I had given her some special present; every so often I would help her with her maths, because neither Emil nor Elza knew the first thing about the subject; she did so well in exams only because, as everyone knew, at the end of every semester Auntie Ilu would go to the school and make a great song and dance and insist that "good" just wasn't good enough, and they would give her the top mark just to get rid of the woman – and the headmaster and his wife dined at her house every month. Gizi had her own reasons for disliking Angéla; again it was because of the maths. Juszti too had gone to the school on one occasion, shortly before the Latin teachers met to agree the marks, and they showed her the door. Gizi had got into the school only because Józsi paid for the building of a new chapel and they had taken her on that basis.

When Aunt Irma fell ill it was Mother and I who nursed her – I by day and Mother by night. I sat there beside her bed anxiously calculating how much longer she would live: she was taking me from my work, I had to do everything in a rush, and I was aware that looking after her night after night was wearing Mother down. What with teaching the pupils all day and nursing her all night, she just sat slumped in a heap beside the piano while Judit and her ilk hammered out their scales. Father and Mother slept in the larger of the two rooms, where the piano was; I slept on my own in the office. In the period when Aunt Irma was ill I would go and check on my father five times a night to see if he needed anything. As soon as my mother came to release me from nursing Aunt Irma I would make a detour to Angéla's to see the fawn for a few minutes. It was wonderfully clever. It had learned how to open the inner latch by nudging it with its head, and by the time anyone spotted that, it would have got into the garden and be nibbling the young shoots on the fir trees. Uncle Domi had had enough of the fawn and would have liked to get rid of it, but of course he did nothing, because Angéla worshipped it.

I don't know how it is in the countryside these days but I think it must be very different from when I was growing up. In those days people went to bed very early and the streets were empty by nine. The theatres operated only in summer and the last films ended by ten; the showings that did end late had very sparse audiences and those who did go were always in a rush to get home. After nine the city centre and the streets in the Barrage were deserted; the only life was in Smelly Row, next to the tannery, where they worked a night shift. There were people still singing in the Three Hussars, but that wasn't the sort of area you would want to walk through. Gizi always slept with her rosary around her wrist because she was frightened by the racket made by the revellers.

I never meant to kill the fawn.

The servants in Uncle Domi's house slept in the basement, and the grounds were walled in on only three sides; on the fourth side, at the rear, there was only a fence, as was usual in our part of the world, where the plot ended in a vegetable garden. It stretched a long way back, and the hedge was a barrier in name only. If anyone really wanted to get in they could do so by climbing over the grille between the concrete posts and pulling the fence to one side to create a gap. In our part of the world everyone grew all the vegetables they needed round the sides of their houses and it wouldn't have been worth breaking in just for a sack of potatoes or a basketful of sweet corn. Any thief would be after something more valuable, and if he were out to steal anything it wouldn't have been from Uncle Domi's place or from Köves Street, where there was a watchman on duty day and night.

Just beyond Köves Street, a couple of hundred metres away,

was the new railway station; it wasn't one that the townsfolk thought much of. When they came home by train they preferred to go the whole way round and get off at the old station: it was considered more proper, more genteel. That night when Gizi was changing my cold compress a train standing in the goods yard gave a blast on its whistle and I heard it clattering away. I had an immediate vision of the new station, with its rails like ribbons and its superfluous trains jolting and jerking along, trains that were only ever used by itinerant workmen and countrywomen bringing goods to the market.

Father went to bed at eight, and by nine he was fast asleep; it was only in the later part of the night that he would call to me in the office for anything. Mother was away, tending to Auntie Irma. It must have been about eleven when I climbed out of the window and onto the street, then pushed the window back, leaving it very slightly open.

It was a moonless night in May, at the end of the school year. Every house in the town had its own yard or garden, and as I walked the air was thick with the scent of acacias and olive trees. I went past Ambrus' house and round the whole area. I couldn't see the reedbeds down below but there was a slight breeze, a warm night-time breeze, and I could sense their presence. Have you ever heard the sound of reeds moving in the wind, the way their stalks rustle against each other? Dogs barked, not too loudly, just for form's sake, as I passed the fronts of the houses. It was dark everywhere. Whenever I think of the town I once lived in, the sky seems lower than anywhere else. That night in particular it felt like a thick black cloud hanging over me, not the usual taut sky stretched out above us by day but somehow softer and lumpy.

A thousand thoughts were running through my mind, about whether Auntie Irma would die that night, and about school – there was going to be a maths test and Angéla wouldn't be coming in because every time there was one Auntie Ilu kept her in bed with a scarf round her neck in case she failed, and that would be the end of the special mention; and I thought too about Gizi, that perhaps she would fail her Latin after all, and that while I felt dreadfully sorry for her, if she passed it would mean the end of my coaching her, it would carry on only if she failed – and it occurred to me that I might give her a few misleading suggestions; it seemed appalling that I should be helping Angéla with her maths and not Gizi. All sorts of things went through my head as I walked. I was perfectly calm, I didn't hurry, I just strolled along as if I had all the time in the world. A lilac tree had burst out over one of the fences and I broke off a little branch. I was going to let the fawn out on the road to the forest, so I would have to avoid taking it as far as the end of the street. Sometimes you feel you really know that what you are about to do will turn out well, and I didn't bother to make up lies to tell anyone who saw me – why should anyone? Mother wouldn't be on her way home from Auntie Ilu's yet, and if she had found her dead she would stay there, she would never leave the body in the care of a servant. We all "knew" that servants will steal anything, even from the dead.

The only thing I had to fear was meeting the odd drunk, and they can hardly walk straight, let alone run.

I parted the hedge at the point where I knew the branches were thinnest and made my way down the path in the middle of the garden; it was surfaced with pebbles so that you could walk between the vegetable patches in wet weather; I was barefoot and the gravel cut my feet horribly. When I got to the kennel the fawn snorted loudly, but it recognised my hand when I held it out. I could barely see it, it was more a case of just knowing it was there. Ever since it had worked out how to lift the latch it had been tethered overnight, but all it had to do was to lift the round end of the strap off the nail; my only moment of alarm came when the door made a loud squeak. I crouched down for a few seconds beside it, it sniffed at me insistently and restlessly, but when I stood up and started to lead it away it came with me obediently; I could still barely make it out but I sensed the same wild joy in it that I was feeling. It was an extraordinary night. I had some trouble dragging it through the fence; at first it refused to go in it and I had to widen the gap for it and then pull it out with the lead wrapped around my wrist.

In Szolnok once, you and I went down to the river after dinner. It was threatening rain, and the water was no longer sparkling but dull and brown; we stood there and I leaned my back against you. Every sound seemed to come from an immense distance: frogs croaking at our feet, the smell of the water, of fish and of flowers, and I felt that I really was in the countryside, where I naturally belonged, and not in the capital.

In all the years I have been in Budapest I have never ceased to be astonished and to look in wonder at the people, the shop windows, the hubbub – everything. To me it all seems at once comical and deeply unsettling.

As I stood there, leaning against you, you asked me what I was thinking about; I said about the dinner, but I wasn't thinking about the dinner, I was thinking that the night was so like the one when I stole Angéla's fawn.

I led it to the end of Köves Street, towards the new station, with the clouds threatening rain from that soft lumpy sky, knowing that I was about to set it free; I would never see it again, it was going back to the forest to be happy – and once I had set it free Angéla would never get another one and all Uncle Domi's money could never replace it. I wanted to see it running off into the woods, flying along on its dear little hooves and vanishing into the darkness.

It began to rain, large, slow drops falling on my hair. The fawn became extremely skittish and started tugging on the lead; I had great difficulty holding on to it, the strap bit into my wrist and it sprang forward; it was now a case of it leading me rather than me leading it. Then, as we turned into Viola Street, where the road bends off to the forest, a cattle train came out of the station. The fawn tore itself out of my hand and ran straight onto the rails.

Despite that, Angéla came into school the next morning. She buried her head in my neck and told me that the fawn had run away during the night: old Mr Sokoró, the new level crossing guard, had found it dead on the track. Then we did the maths test. I finished in twenty minutes and spent the rest of the time doodling on the spare paper. I was desperately wishing I could feel the fawn's muzzle in my hand again, sniffing the bran and lifting its eyes up at me. Gizike looked at me hopefully and I caught her glance. I was seriously wondering whether she might fail her maths too. Angéla was sitting in front of me, her back was shaking and I could tell that she was crying.

3

It is now midday and a siren is wailing in a nearby factory. Back at home, they went off in the morning, at lunchtime and in the evening, because the factory operated three shifts a day. Our region produces a lot of maize, but the cockiest of the working girls were those whose fathers were tanners, even though they themselves went to the state secondary school and not to a gymnázium, as I did. They mixed with us in the communal playground, we whispered and laughed together and they addressed us in the polite third person, but I always detected a hint of mockery in their attitude towards us. We wore navy-blue sailor suits; their uniform was a darker blue, embroidered with folk motifs, and in summer it was a spotted cretonne. The blue material straining over their fine, rapidly developing bodies was adorned with tulips. They lived apart in Tanners Row, near the tannery; you could always tell where it was because the smell of the tannin hit your nose as you drew near.

People called the street "Smelly Alley", but you could never say the name aloud in the shared playground because if any of the "tanning girls" heard they would lay into you. Gizike was especially afraid of them because of her father's pub; workers from the factory were regulars there, and they and the tanners had hated each other ever since the factory had gone up. The workers in the factory were the only ones of their kind in the town: the rest of the labouring poor worked on the land. Ambrus' younger brother was one of those employed in the factory and I could always tell when he had been to see Ambrus; even several hours after he had called, the thick, pungent smell still hung in the workshop.

It took me a while to discover what the distinction between the workers and the tanners was all about. It was Ambrus who put me right. At first he didn't want to tell me, but his hatred of the tanners made him break his silence and he was the one who explained which of them was the man and which the boy, the tanners or the factory workers. Up until then I had always thought that the only difference between us and the tanners' daughters was that they didn't go to our school. I was shocked when I discovered how well off they were. Every one of the master tanners on Tanners' Row had far more money than the most affluent of my fellow pupils' fathers. The factory workers hated them so much that they preferred to take jobs elsewhere than work with them, and the tanners were forced to recruit fresh labour and take on apprentices from outside the region.

"Who was your first love?" you asked me last spring, and you stared at me with hostility and suspicion: in those days we used to torture each other with pointless questions like that. "A worker from the tanning factory," I immediately replied, and I pushed my lower lip out the way I do on stage. You rushed out of the espresso bar and I delighted in the fact that you were out there on your own, choking with anger; you thought I was lying again and playing the fool. But this Károly, Ambrus' younger brother, really was my first love. I was hopelessly in love with him.

Károly couldn't stand me. Ambrus couldn't either: he put up with me only because I was useful; when the rheumatism in his back was playing up really badly he would force himself to be nice to me because I chopped wood for him, but Károly never hid the fact that he loathed me. At first I didn't understand why, but of course I do now. At that age I didn't know why Károly only ever went to his brother's house after dark and never during the day, and why he always brought other people with him . . . and why, if I went into the workshop for any reason, to bring something or to ask for anything, he yelled at me that I hadn't been invited and should stay at home. I fancied him desperately, because he had two large dimples on his face that came out for a second when he smiled – which wasn't very often – and his face took on a bright, gentle, childlike look, like clouds suddenly opening in a stormy sky and flooding the dark land in light.

For a long time I dreamed about what it would be like when Károly married me. Mostly I thought about the two pigs, Ambrus' pigs, and how he would send us more of the food that Mother liked to share with her little circle. At first I thought he was so grumpy with me because he loved me. Then one evening, when I was up in the loft above the workshop, lying face down with the scattered maize seeds pricking my skin, I eavesdropped on their conversation; I hung on to his every word. I never told my parents that he had beaten me when he found me there. Cursing and swearing, Ambrus shook his head and tore me out of his grip. I was so frightened I didn't even cry. Why had he beaten me like that? I could have listened to his voice for ever. If I'm in a read-through and Hella launches into a tirade to persuade her companions not to show fear, or when Pipi starts grumbling and complaining, I always think of Károly and his angrily muttering voice as he spelled out how unnatural it was that there should be both rich and poor in the world, and I feel the maize under my limbs once again, and a wild happiness flashes through my mind at the special memory of that time, up in the granary, when I was able to conceive of a time when the poor would take everything from the rich and there would no longer be any difference between one person and another.

Károly certainly knew where to hit. I told them at home that I had fallen from the loft and that was why I was black and blue all over. All the time he was hitting me he kept calling my father names; I had no idea why but it made me weep all the more – I couldn't bear it when anyone got at him. "Little madam," he spat at me, when he finally let me go – and the way he said it! "You clown," Ambrus told him. "She's no little madam. She's a beggar."

He had beaten the love out of me, and something else too. I stood there in my bare feet, in my filthy apron, my hands coarsened by housework and my nails cracked and chipped, and if I had been capable of speech I would have told him how much I loved him, and also how hungry I was at that moment, and that if he married me perhaps our lives would be a little easier; but at that same time I sensed that when he had been ranting about some distant world in the future he had left me out of it because I was an Encsy girl, and my father was a lawyer, and that mattered more to him than the crumbling plaster on our walls and the endless hours of piano teaching that went on. The things I heard that day up in Ambrus' loft I have never repeated to anyone.

Károly never went there again, and I didn't dare ask about him. To this day I can still remember what he said: I repeated the words to myself over and over again, lying in bed watching the light from the gas lamp filtering into my room before I fell asleep, as it threw its soft yellow glow over my father's bookshelves and the gilded bindings on his law books. I would dream for hours about the workers from the factory coming first to the house, then marching on Köves Street and throwing Uncle Domi out of his home; Angéla would run away screaming, leaving her shoes behind in her panic, and I would make her wear Auntie Irma's and I would go and live in the house on Köves Street myself and everyone who was poor would also live in fine houses like it, and Auntie Ilu would be forced to work, hoeing the ground or lugging mortar all day long, and my grandmother would give music lessons on our old piano, and she would teach me too, because I was the only one of the grandchildren my mother had never had the time to teach. I'm trying not to cry now – it's just that siren going off on the other side of the fence . . .

Gizi loved the sound of it too. She would go into a reverie about it, gazing up through the bedroom window. Whenever she did, I would slap her on the hand with the lid of a pencil box because she was wasting time and I was afraid to go out onto the streets after dark. I was terrified of meeting Károly, though I never saw him again. The siren was so loud that it drowned the music of the gypsies in the Three Hussars and Juszti's high-pitched laugh. Gizi never could make her Latin nouns and adjectives agree. The Three Hussars is still there, only it's now called the Rose Garden. Józsi will never know how much I longed for his presence last night, and how good it would have been for me if he had been at home – not speaking to me, just lying there, breathing heavily in his sleep.

Yesterday, when I went into the kitchen to put the note I had written to Juli on the pan of the scales, my eye happened to fall on the calendar and I noticed that the twenty-seventh had been underlined; I stared at it in a state of shock, realising that it was your birthday. Juli had told us that she would cook the supper herself so that we wouldn't have to go out. I left the kitchen at once; there was no point in standing there staring at the wall.

You have reproached me so often about that calendar. You

were furious when I refused to buy another one for Juli, and that I could actually bear having a sheet of paper nailed up on the wall with such ridiculous pictures round the edges. I didn't dare tell you that I was the one who had bought it and not Juli, that I had found it only after a long and wearisome search, and that every time I went into the kitchen I took every available opportunity to look at the posy of dancing pigs and chimney sweeps with gleaming white teeth.

You have no idea how humiliating it is when January arrives and the greengrocer hasn't sent you his calendar or the chimney sweep brought you one. The one at Gizi's had a dusting of glittering white powder around the edge and little boys and girls racing round it on sledges; beneath the list of days and dates there was a suckling pig with a sausage in the shape of a heart around its beaming pink face. It was beneath that calendar that I taught Gizi; every time we came to a halt she looked up at the silver-dusted frame in despair, as at a religious painting. The room smelled of lard and paprika soup and other mouth-watering odours. I liked teaching Gizi; Juszti always brought me a plate of something and I ate it during the lesson. Gizi never asked for any: living with the permanent smell of cooking had deadened her appetite. I just sat and gorged myself regardless.

On the very few occasions when she came to visit us she always kissed my mother's hand, mumbled something to Father and immediately sat down and gazed at his books and the ghastly lilac curtain in the kitchen, and her eyes were filled with happy wonder, and if one of the pupils arrived and started to torment Mozart she would open her mouth wide and raise a hand to me to tell me not to interrupt. As she sat there with her pretty little head tilted slightly forward listening to the awful music, I had the strong impression that she envied us. I exploded with inward laughter to think that someone who lived amid the aroma of lard and paprika soup, and whose father was as strong and healthy as a bull, should envy *me*, whose shoes had no toes and who lived as we did in the non-stop flow of mutilated music.

By the time I started going there one of Gizike's uncles had retired from the business but the sign outside still bore the image of three hussars puffing out their chests and raising the key aloft, as if the three Huszár brothers were still running the place and not just her father Józsi. You know how I always shout at the radio the moment it starts to get boring, or if my monthly salary arrives half a day late. Józsi was the one person I insisted should pay me only when I specifically asked. It was a game between us.

On the first of every month he would furrow his brow, shake his head from side to side, slap his knees, swear that he was ruined, that he would have to close the pub the following month and he couldn't possibly afford to pay me, and anyway I had already had the value of the lessons in what I had eaten. Then I would ring my hands and start to weep large tears all over the table, and declare if I left without my money I would die, and I kept that up until Józsi collapsed on the bench purple with laughter and had to undo the buttons on his shirt. He was the first person to realise that I was an actress. The ritual also involved my going into the tap room for the money; it was wildly entertaining, but I never dared tell them at home, because the drunks used to grab at my skirt, and Juszti herself didn't approve of the game, standing behind the counter shaking her head.

When I got to the counter Józsi would count the money out pengő by pengő – he always gave me a little more than was due – then he pulled my hair, slapped me roundly on the bottom and bundled me out of the door. Father had no idea I was teaching at the Three Hussars; I told only my mother. Juszti's suppers helped me put on weight.

Angéla never went there, but Emil regularly stopped there on his motorbike on his way home. There was no university in our town; the students went to the nearest one in the regional capital some twenty-eight kilometres away, travelling by train or bicycle. He never sat at a table, he just stood at the counter drinking a spritzer. He always arrived at the same time, around seven o'clock on a Friday – Angéla once told me that that was when he came back from a seminar on the history of law. At around seven we would draw the curtain aside in the window – Juszti's magnificent curtain, on which she had crocheted angels cavorting on swings and holding bunches of roses in their plump little hands. "*Ad rivum eundem . . .*" Gizi would mumble, and I would correct her scansion and repeat it for her to memorise. The herd of cattle had turned into the street from the market square and a great cloud of dust and a clanking of bells told us that they were now very close; *"Ad rivum eundem . . ."* Gizi always stressed the *"um"* as she pronounced the words; I rapped her on the knuckles and she tried again: *"Ad rivum eundem . . ."* The evening breeze sent a tremor through the angels on their swings. The cattle were now passing outside the window and crossing the plank thrown over the ditch on their way to the barn, before nudging the doors with their foreheads and lowing while the women opened them – they were the half-height type; Juszti ran out to join them, her slippers flapping on her beautiful slim feet; Rózsi the cow licked her arm and moved off towards the barn, and the odour of warm milk reached the table where we were working – a smell of warm milk flavoured with chamomile and cockshead sainfoin.

When the dust had finally settled, the horn of Emil's motorbike would be heard. Gizi's face would light up, but she carried on mumbling the Latin text. On one occasion Emil brought a girl with him, but he left her outside on the bike and took her out a glass of beer. At that point Gizi closed the curtain and was subdued for the rest of the evening.

When the tapestry was pulled back from the glass door into the room, we could see into the restaurant. I always paid attention to what Emil was doing: I really wanted to see him get drunk, fall over and do something outrageous, because Angéla loved him so much, but nothing like that ever happened. He finished his spritzer, paid, thanked them and dashed out to his bike. My mind was so tied up with Angéla as I watched him that it was only yesterday that I realised that Gizi was in love with him. The picture is with me still: the herd of cattle, the motorbike, the spritzer, Juszti's angels, Rózsi's udders smelling of milk and cockshead sainfoin, and Emil himself. If he hadn't gone to the Three Hussars I would never have realised that Juszti was deceiving Józsi.

You have seen Gizi often enough; she is very like her mother but that won't tell you what Juszti really looked like. Gizi is blond, and Juszti was too, but her hair wasn't a pale gentle blond like Gizi's, it was much richer; Gizi's eyes, under their long thin eyebrows, are blue tinged with green and narrow, like a cat's, almost invisible; Gizike is quiet and timid, withdrawn and extremely diplomatic. When you first saw her in the Swan she and I had already met and chatted together but she never let on that she knew me. You ordered paprika chicken and she brought mine garnished with potatoes and not dumplings, or "gnocchi" as it said on the menu. "What a clever girl!" you laughed, but she just stood there with her hands under her apron, and the impassive smile on her face never wavered for a moment. She then brought me a soda water, and you laughed even louder, shook your head and said she must be in league with the devil to have known what to bring – but again she didn't laugh herself, she just glanced at me, warning me with her sad eyes not to give her a hug, and that we shouldn't let on that we knew each other; so I sat there in silence, eating my potatoes and drinking the soda water. You suddenly became very serious and obsessed about how often I had been there before and who with, seeing that the waitress knew me so well and knew that I hated dumplings and never drank alcohol.

"What's that to you?" I asked, as I stabbed my chicken breast, and you fixed Gizi with a hostile stare. You thought that she had been witness to some infamous episode in my life, something I had never dared tell you about, and you never warmed to her even though she brought us our food for years after that, and if you said something really silly she would giggle, then blush furiously and look thoroughly ashamed of herself. She showed real pleasure every time we went there, but you just scowled when you saw her rushing on ahead to offer us the last table in the room. I shrugged and was glad that you were suffering, and I thought of Józsi and his mighty laugh and Juszti's wonderful looks, the fine turn of her ankle, the elegance of her roughened fingers that always smelled of wine as she wiped the foam from a glass of beer. If Józsi was like a bear, Juszti was a water nymph. In those days no-one ever wore their hair long, but Juszti kept hers in a bun, a bun of copper-coloured hair held in place by a white comb encrusted with glittering stones; at night, whenever she went into her room for anything she would brush out the parting, singing as she brushed. She very rarely laughed out loud and yet she seemed to be laughing all the time. Did you ever see me as Anna in that French play? Of course you did. That's exactly how Juszti was.

I always thought that Gizi had no idea why Mr Trnka – he was the greengrocer – went there so often; but she and I both watched the development of that liaison through her door. It was a ground glass door with the image of a bowl of fruit etched into it: apples, apricots and bunches of grapes, surrounded by a transparent ribbon through which we were able to see Mr Trnka arriving, greeting everyone and ordering a drink. In the early days Juszti would tell Józsi to take him his first glass of wine; later she took them to his table herself. Józsi held him in high regard – he had a high respect for anyone from abroad and Mr Trnka's relations lived somewhere near Prague. They always talked politics together. One Sunday afternoon I was sent to the cemetery to tidy up Grandpa Encsy's grave, and I saw Juszti and Mr Trnka walking along between the tombs ahead of me, with the fake gemstones glittering on the comb in Juszti's hair.

Józsi began to lose weight; Mr Trnka came no more. Gizi never spoke about him. When I asked her why, she simply frowned and didn't answer: *Fame coacta vulpes alta in vinea* – a case of the fox and the grapes. One day they were walking in the Barrage and popped into Kárász néni's confectionery for an ice cream. I spied on them over the top of the fence and had to suppress my laughter. Then Józsi's behaviour became abominable. He waved his arms around and shouted at Juszti, not of course about Mr Trnka but because the glasses were dirty, or about why the tablecloths wore out so quickly. Juszti just smiled at whatever he said and shrugged. Then Teréz néni, the cook, announced she could work there not a moment longer and handed in her notice. It was a difficult time, that spring.

When I was a child there was a grand fair in our town every

three months. You know only the Spring Fair here in Budapest, but even there you couldn't stop yourself buying everything you saw. Did you really need that clay pipe, the year before last – or that children's rattle? For me those occasions were pure torment. The vendors squatted in the reedbeds, the richer ones put up tents and the travelling comedians followed; a carbide lamp blazed on top of a contraption consisting of a plank erected on a table and there were all sorts of useless things on offer – multi-coloured sugar, gingerbread men – for anyone who had money to buy; for twenty-four fillér they could have whatever they wanted – dolls, pearls, little wooden birds – only I never had that much money; but I went there all the same and gazed at the stalls from afar; I marvelled at the strong man wielding his hammer and ogled the sword swallower and the man who ate red-hot iron bars; there were people cooking doughnuts and frying steak, there was even a roundabout and a second, much larger one, shaped like a hoop skirt, that went up and down under the people sitting on it and spinning around, like a ship waltzing on the sea. You once took me to the funfair in Budapest; you bought me popcorn and a stick of barley sugar and we sat in a gondola and you kissed me on the haunted train. When you touched my face it was running with tears and you couldn't understand why, and I couldn't tell you that for me it was far too late for that sort of thing. I could now see, for the first time in my life, how stupid Snow White and the Seven Dwarfs were, and I didn't like the barley sugar because it smelled like paint and made me feel sick.

That year the fair was held the weekend before Easter, on Palm Sunday. On the Saturday night, on my way home from Gizi's, I went to the end of Kút Street to watch them putting up the stands. The circus tent was already up and there were lovely, gentle horses eating straw behind the van.

It wasn't a very savoury area; it was a bit like the market was in Víg Street in old Pest, where the road turns off just beyond Görbe Street, and there is a hotel with eight windows. Naturally it isn't the same sort of hotel as the Turul in Market Square; it was a hotel only in name: at the time I didn't know what the words "brothel" or "garrison hostel" really meant, but I got the general idea, and when I spotted Juszti hurrying through the general throng out of Görbe Street, and Mr Trnka turning into the same street on the other side of the road, I knew exactly where they were going, and why, and what they would be getting up to there. As I was following Juszti with my eyes, my heart suddenly stopped; I had seen what neither of them could have: Józsi was standing in the stall selling sheepskin coats, concealed in the darkness behind a row of them. It was a Saturday evening and I knew what it would be like at the Three Hussars. Gizi told me on the Monday that her father had been summoned by the police after a confrontation with a vagrant who had eaten there the day before, and her mother had been called away to her Aunt Mariska, who had sent a message that she had had a heart attack and was very ill, and Gizi spent the whole evening dashing back and forth between the kitchen and the dining room, she and the cook.

I also saw Angéla at the fair. She was allowed to go there and look at the stalls, but only in the evening – Auntie Ilu had forbidden her to mix with the crowds in the middle of the day. Elza was at her side, holding her hand. Angéla had her purse and Elza a basket, and as they went along Angéla would point to something that took her fancy and pay for it, and Elza put it into the basket. There were workers from the factory there too, tired but high-spirited girls and young men; you didn't have to look at them to know where they worked, you could tell from the way their clothes smelled. Angéla wanted to go into the circus tent as well, but Elza stopped her. In the glare of the carbide lamp I could see how sad and subdued her face was, and I was so happy I sang all the way home. Ambrus was sitting on the bench in front of his house and he told me off, rather rudely, for singing: it was Palm Sunday the next day and I should be singing something religious. It was his idea of a joke and he was grinning all over his face – he had little truck with religion. So I sang about the mulberry tree and he mumbled tunelessly along with me; then I went home and washed up the pots and pans after supper.

Holy Week had begun on the first of the month, so it was now the Easter holiday; we didn't have to go to school, and in fact Gizi and I weren't supposed to have our lessons either, but I still continued to go to the Three Hussars every day for supper. The pub was closed for Good Friday so I walked round the side and tried to go in by the garden gate; Gizi had only just shut it and was locking it as I arrived; she had a prayer book in her hand and her hair was tied in two pigtails with blue ribbons – she had been sent off to church. My face fell. She told me to go with her and we could say a few prayers; dinner wasn't ready because her father had sent Teréz néni to the vineyard: she would be back late and perhaps not even that night since there wouldn't be any customers, but that didn't matter because her mother would cook something for us. Overhearing our conversation, Józsi stuck his head out of the window; I went over and told him he needed to pay me because it was the first of the month, but he didn't answer; he just looked at us, and I suddenly didn't want to pursue the matter, because I had the impression that he wasn't in the mood to play the usual game with me, in fact he didn't care very much whether he paid me or not; perhaps he hadn't even heard what I had said.

There was no sign of Juszti anywhere. I really wanted my money, but I didn't want to ask again, I was afraid it might undermine my right to stay for supper. So I went with Gizi to the church. With her ivory-covered prayer book and pigtails tucked under her round hat, she was the image of a good Christian girl; I was just as I always was, in my apron and shoes that had no toes. I found it rather boring. Jesus lay there stark naked in his mother's arms and the whole altar was draped in black. I particularly disliked going to church on Good Friday; I preferred the Masses when everything was red – the great services when the Monstrance was on display and it was bright and colourful, showy and theatrical; I found the grieving atmosphere of Good Friday oppressive and disheartening.

On the way home we said little at first: the gloomy atmosphere in the church and its all-pervading blackness still hung over us. Then our mood suddenly lifted, we began to giggle and romp about and run hand in hand; Gizike dropped her beautiful prayer book and we washed the ivory cover at the fountain on the corner of Török Street. I was already looking forward to the smell of Juszti's Lenten supper, my stomach was rumbling at the thought of it and I was buoyed up by the idea of getting my money: if Józsi threw in only two extra pengős I would be able to buy a pair of stockings.

The house, as we drew near, was strangely silent. Usually at that time of day you could hear the gypsy orchestra, lights would be blazing everywhere and people carousing in the garden area. This was a real Good Friday, the sky heavy with cloud and the streets deserted. But it was still a Friday, and the herd suddenly appeared out of the gloom. I thought of Emil, though of course Emil wasn't about to appear on his motorbike because the university was closed too, but Rózsi was there, and Gizi called up to the window for someone to go and open the gate, and when no-one answered, we dashed after the cow, tugged the half-door open, and I led her into the barn. I started to sing, then I thought better of it and stopped, because Józsi was very devout, like Gizi, and because he was about to play the game with me and hand over my money; perhaps if I made him laugh a lot he would give me three extra pengős, so what might I do to make him do that? Gizi tugged on the garden gate and frowned, because it was locked; her face was alert and her eyes narrowed; she seemed almost suspicious – I don't know what was in that face but there was something. That, and the silence in the garden, the absence of voices outside and in the empty garden area, seemed brooding and ominous.

"My money," I urged her, speaking, I don't know why, in a whisper. "You must tell Uncle József that I would like to have my money!"

She just stood there, staring inside; there was not a sound to be heard; she put her hat and the prayer book down on one of the garden tables and the two of us stood there, at the foot of the steps, listening. It was already getting dark, and very quickly; Rózsi was banging about inside the barn because she needed to be milked. "That will be Juszti," I thought, but it was all very strange, it was as if I had been thinking aloud, and I suddenly looked at Gizi. We took each other's hands and went up the steps. The dining room was in total darkness; Gizi switched the light on . . . and I no longer wanted to joke and dance and make light of the nameless something that had suddenly enveloped us. It was all so bizarre: everything was perfectly in order, it was just that József, the pious and devout József, was slumped over one of the tables in his shirtsleeves, with a bottle of apricot brandy beside him. He had drunk himself into a stupor on the day of Jesus' Passion. I burst out laughing and turned to look at Gizi, but she wasn't laughing at all; her previously pale face had turned bright red, as if she had been physically struck, and the veins on her kindly, delicate temples started to pulsate. I thought she was feeling ashamed to see her father drunk; I went over to him, shook him and asked him for my money. He didn't move, he just snored on, in his solid, unshakeable drunkenness; he certainly didn't look like someone whose head would soon clear. I looked at Gizi, she had now opened the door into the kitchen, she called out, very softly, "Mother?" But there was no answer. The fireplace was cold, there was no smell of fish or of poppyseed bread. What about our supper? And my money? "I need my money," I repeated to her, and again my voice was a whisper.

She just stood there. Where on earth was Juszti? In the kitchen, the yard, the empty barn? She must be in her room, in bed and asleep. I didn't like asking her for my money because she never added a fillér more than we had agreed, but I had decided that at least I would be paid; there wasn't going to be any supper anyway, or if there was it would be almost nothing, these people were so much more religious than I was that they might even be fasting. To hell with supper! I went to the door, but Gizi was there before me. There was such a look of horror in her eyes that I didn't dare follow her in. She went inside for only a second, then she came out immediately and closed the door carefully behind her; again her face was white, so white that I became so frightened I almost screamed. She didn't look at me; she just went over to the cashier's desk and opened the till.

As she opened it the bell of the till rang, and rang again and again, so sharp and shrill in the silence that I almost shouted; I looked at Józsi to see if he had moved – normally he had the hearing of a lynx; Gizi reached into the till and picked up a wad of notes, far more than I was owed, perhaps five times the amount. She pushed it into my hand and went on ahead of me, like a sleepwalker, out into the garden; I followed her obediently, holding tightly on to the money; she opened the little gate and turned towards me; there were violet shadows under her eyes. "Go home, Eszti," she said quietly, and she folded the notes into the pocket of my apron. I clutched it with both hands to stop it falling out and ran back up the garden, back through the dining area – Józsi was still snoring – towards her bedroom, I pulled the glass door open and saw Juszti; she was lying face downwards, her strawberry-blond locks had slipped out of the teeth of the comb and I saw the axe under them, still impaled in her neck. Neither of us said a word. I was still holding my money, Gizi came and stood beside me, took me by the hand and opened the door. "Go home," she said; she raised her eyes for a moment to look into mine and we kissed; I was still crying, she wasn't. I started to run, I didn't look back until I got to the corner of Török Street; she was sitting on the steps, her white churchgoing dress glowed in the dark, her head was buried in her knees and she was whimpering like a dog.

When Juszti died Angéla fell ill and was confined to her bed. It was from her that we learned that after the funeral Gizi's two uncles had sent her to Budapest; Uncle Domi presided over Józsi's trial and gave him fifteen years. While Angéla told the story, trembling and with tears in her eyes, I kept watching Elza; she was darning Angéla's white socks and she never looked up once.

4

The print of my bare foot has left an impression in the soft sand – the firmer initial hollow left by my heel and five shallower ones for the toes. When we went out walking together, in the sunshine or by moonlight, I always loved to watch our shadows, two silhouettes linked arm in arm stretched out and bobbing on ahead of us, or slanting off to the side, or wobbling behind our backs . . . this single one looks so abandoned . . . I'll make another one next to it, so that it won't seem so very alone . . . and now there are two, side by side, like twins . . .

I've rubbed them both out: there was something frightening about them – they were like some grotesque monster; your footsteps were always there, next to mine. When we came into the house together after it had rained Juli would wipe our two pairs of muddy footprints off the rubber floor in the foyer with a towel. "Feet like horses!" she would grumble; but if you had looked back as she knelt down to deal with them you would have seen how reluctant she was to wipe yours away. She adored you.

She didn't adore me, she only worked for me; I paid her too much for any personal bond to form between us, and I always asked too much of her. I have worked so hard in my life I just don't have the patience to praise other people's efforts. She worked well for me because I put up with her mania for pilgrimages and the museum of plaster statues on her bedside table, but she would have worked for you for nothing. You used to sit down with her on the kitchen stool to chat about her village, and you gave her that pressed flower someone had brought you from the Garden of Gethsemane when you were still at school.

It bothered and baffled her that I should still need to do things for myself, like cleaning and scouring and cooking meals for the paupers; I was much stronger than she was; when we were spring-cleaning I wiped everything down in a flash and hoisted the heaviest carpets up onto my shoulder. She hated Angéla and she was deeply suspicious of me. She could never understand why I had her work for me when I could clean and dust just as well as she could, and I was quicker and stronger than she was anyway: there must have been some terrible earlier poverty in my life, or how else would I know all those secret little tricks that only the really poor are wise to? Every time she brought me breakfast in bed and set it down beside me I almost burst out laughing. She brought it in on a silver tray, with a jug of cream and black coffee, and gave me a hard, critical stare as she set it down on the bedside table – as if to say that she too was going to go and loll about in bed under a striped duvet, in her *respectable* nightdress, the one with embroidered hems, and I should get up and take her coffee for once, so that she could have a chance to see what it was like to have your breakfast served in bed – if she could bring it to me, then I could equally take it to her, and she at least would be dressed decently and not lolling about in bed like I was. She held my profession in very low esteem – acting was immoral and thoroughly stupid – and she never went to the cinema or the circus; when she came and dressed me in the theatre she refused to look either to left or right, and when the hairdresser came she would turn her head away and page ostentatiously through her prayer book. The only time I ever saw her cry was over you.

I didn't care whether she loved me or not, and why should she? The truth is that apart from you no-one ever has. The last time I went to the cemetery to look at my father's and mother's graves I felt that it was all utterly pointless and irrational and I promptly left. As for the Marton tomb, I can't bear the sight of it. They only let my father in after endless begging and pleading. There is a kitsch angel kneeling at the head of the grave holding a cypress branch in her two hands; I had intended a separate grave for him in the shade of a mighty oak tree, I imagined myself planting some of the bulbs and nourishing herbs that he had loved so much there, but I couldn't afford it – all the less so because Mother wanted to buy another one next to his at the same time. So I had to go to Uncle Béla and ask for him to be buried in the family tomb. When they opened the crypt and lowered his coffin into it – it was the only wooden one among all the lead and silver ones – the Martons stood around in mourning dress to pay their respects; my grandmother even had a veil over her hat. I couldn't bear to look at them.

I had planned to bury my mother next to him, and when she died I took her there. As soon as I saw the angel in the crypt I had the feeling that there was no-one inside it and I went back home. I thought what a stupid idea it was to have gone. On the way home, as I sat in the plane staring at the river and the peaks of the faraway mountains, and the long strips of green and brown fields below, they were both strongly present in my mind and I knew I would never be able to think of them lying beneath that ghastly angel, only of their faces as they had been in real life. They were now so far away from me; while I was there in the crypt they had been total strangers to me; I shrugged and wondered why I had gone there, like some sort of pilgrim – getting on a plane and travelling as if to a sacred shrine. On the way there I had stopped and stood for a moment at Juszti's grave; it felt much more real there than it had with my own dear departed. The city too had changed a lot since I lived there; the whole neighbourhood had altered – new houses had gone up and a woman in uniform was directing the traffic in the High Street. I didn't know a single soul.

I gave Köves Street a wide berth, but I did go to the Barrage. I bought a drink in the restaurant, but there was nothing left of the old house that I could see apart from a couple of fruit trees; as I sat there, with the radio blaring, the image of my father finally appeared to me, he was crouching down between the branches, tending to an underdeveloped and malformed seedling, and at the same time I sensed the hovering presence of my mother, standing there rubbing her weary wrists; the memory was so fresh and vivid that I immediately paid and left, I felt that I had seen something I shouldn't have – the two of them were so close, both in death and in my memories of them, that even to think about them was an intrusion and there was absolutely no point in going back to spy on them.

When my father died it was already something I suspected, but when my mother went I knew for certain how utterly insignificant I had been to them: the only important people in their lives were each other. I could sing and recite poems to them, but however desperately I tried to attract their attention I never succeeded for more than a moment: they were interested only in each other, they had no surplus feeling to share with anyone else, and certainly not with me.

Had she wanted to, my mother could have been alive today: I got her all the medicines she needed, the latest and best ones from abroad; she was treated in the University Hospital in Kútvölgyi Street, in a private room, I spent long days sitting by her bed, I took my meals beside her; on one occasion I acted that scene for her that always drew wild applause in the theatre, but whatever I tried I felt that her reaction was merely polite; she didn't mean to offend me, she simply had no interest in anything I did. I could take her all sorts of things, all her favourite things to eat, she had a new piano – a better one than the old one – and there was no world-famous performer who would not have come and played the piano or violin for her if I had asked them to. But there was nothing she wanted, and I knew it, even though she never said as much. All she wanted was my father. He had been dead for some years by then, she was measuring the distance he was ahead of her down that path, and the best thing for her now would be to follow him.

This ant is now attacking that peach half for the sixth time, the silly thing. She should have realised long ago that she would never be able to carry it away, but she keeps trying, over and over again. She reminds me of Erzsi Csóka: she has just re-appeared, in the role of Judit for Ványa; every time she comes into the theatre he sends for me, and we listen to her speaking the part and try to persuade her not to take it on. A waste of time. "I never wanted to be a typist," she murmurs, and her sweet, innocent face clouds over. "It was always the theatre, the theatre." Whenever she starts on her lines I shut my eyes and hope that the music of the verse, the rise and fall of the phrasing, will help me forget her stiff legs and her skinny, sad little arms . . . "Come civil night, / Thou sober-suited matron all in black, / And learn me how to lose a winning match / Played for a pair of stainless maidenhoods . . ." It's hopeless. The moment she opens her mouth the verse dies. She is always in her best dress, her party frock, and she has obviously excused herself at the office and gone to the hairdresser because her hair is crisp and firm. When the speech is over she turns to us with that frightened, hopeful, timid look to ask if it was alright this time, and she smooths her dress down, her nice party frock; every time she does that I see myself standing in my nightdress on the stone floor of our kitchen.

It was my father's birthday, and Auntie Kárász had taught me a birthday greeting song. It was early morning, an early morning in May, and I pressed my ear to their bedroom door to hear if they were up yet. My feet were cold on the floor, I could hear whispering inside, but I didn't dare go in, I just stood there holding the nightdress around me; eventually the door opened and my mother came out, her face was flushed, her hair was all over the place – she was still very young and wonderfully beautiful. We went in; my father was sitting up in the bed, I stood in the doorway and my voice rang out: "This is the poem of a pretty little bird, rising in the rosy dawn of a new day, the name day of Dezső. May the Lord grant Dezső long life, and may he always love his daughter Eszter!" My father kissed the top of my head – he never kissed me on the cheek – then he put on a solemn face and asked me to recite it again. I was five years old, perhaps six; when I finished I lifted the two sides of my nightdress and curtsied. My father looked at my mother and said, "Katinka, were there ever any actresses in your family?"

Erzsi Csóka came to see me once; she gave Juli a present, a mixing bowl and a strainer. She had worked in the office of a factory where they made pots and pans and she got discounts on that sort of thing. Juli exploded with rage and threw them in the back of the kitchen cupboard. That was the day I wouldn't let you in and you were wild because you had rung the doorbell and I didn't answer; then you phoned me and I didn't pick up the receiver, so you didn't come the next day – you thought Pipi was with me, and I was thrilled to see you jealous. It was Erzsi who was in my bedroom, sitting opposite me, dutifully sipping the cognac I had served. She had varnished her nails bright red for the visit, her skirt was so tight I thought it was going to split over her bum, and her wonderfully youthful skin was plastered with red grease; she looked like an old-fashioned whore from the provinces – and she was such a nice girl, the poor thing. I sat there in my grey trousers and black pullover, with my hair in two short pigtails as usual, wearing my flat-heeled shoes and no make-up, gazing at her and smoking. She looked at my books, and my collection of plays, and the copper comic mask you had given me – she even lifted it off the nail, tried it on, laughed, and bleated out, "I always wanted to be an actress." The front doorbell rang; when I shook my head Juli turned her face away and clamped her mouth shut. "Always," Erzsi repeated and sighed. As for me, I never wanted to be an actress; the idea never once crossed my mind.

That first time you and I were together with Angéla was also the first time she told you, so enthusiastically, that I had been given parts in all the big ceremonies at school; I was the shining star, the one who recited the prayer before the exams, the one who gave the speech when the Minister of Culture came to visit, the one who welcomed the Bishop at confirmation services and Zoltán Kodály at the school's Jubilee Concert, and I was the one who gave the vote of thanks to the Head-master. The last was one of the main reasons why everyone hated me. I was also a bad classmate, sour, irritable and riddled with envy. I never joined in their little whisperings and I never gave anyone any help: when it came to the school-leaving exams I did do one or two things for people, but only for money: they had to slip a ten-pengő note into my palm before I gave them the answer. Neither the teachers nor the pupils liked me; I wasn't a very nice person and I wasn't very friendly, and when Gizi left town I became even sulkier. But when it came to these public roles, it always had to be me. I didn't know what stage fright was, and I never forgot a word: prose, verse or song, it was all fixed in my brain instantly, I never had to learn anything twice, including what I had to do with my hands or my feet; if the role was a solemn one, I howled like a thunder-storm, and if it was a merry one I laughed so much and kept on laughing until the audience split their sides. I also declaimed patriotic and religious verses, though they weren't part of my usual repertoire; I was always chosen for roles that didn't require costumes, or ones that could easily be run up. I would be a peasant, or an old woman, or a servant – but it was all the same to me what I played, male or female, young or old; I preferred to be anything other than what I was in real life, and I enjoyed it all the more for that. Angéla also told you that the parents came to these school events just because of me, and it really was true. I was given the leading role only once, and then they never wanted me to leave the stage.

On the afternoon of Easter Sunday, the Sunday after the Good Friday when Juszti died, I was supposed to play the Wicked Stepmother in *János Vitéz*. Angéla was to be Iluska, a lovely, adorable Iluska in artificial pigtails, utterly without talent; she had no idea how to act or move, she simply whispered her lines in embarrassment. She was always given the leading role because she was so wonderfully decorative, and every time she acted Uncle Domi brought the entire judiciary with him – it was very good for the takings. But she became ill after what had happened to Gizi; she caught a violent cold and couldn't stop crying.

I went to see her; she was lying in bed with a face blighted with weeping, and Elza was sitting beside her reading her one of Grimm's Fairy Tales in German. She was thrilled to see me. She sent Elza away, threw her arms round my neck and whispered in my ear that she kept seeing Gizi's mother in death, though she had never met her in life. I wasn't impressed, and I paid no attention to her chattering: I had come for her costume. The stepmother was now going to be played by a girl in year six and I had been given Iluska. Auntie Ilu handed over the coronet, the fairy dress and Iluska's tiny red slippers – with a very sour look on her face. I was a huge success; total strangers came up to me with presents of chocolate from the buffet. That evening was the first time I hadn't thought about Gizi; they had all been constantly on my mind of course, only this time I wasn't thinking about Juszti but of her. She was sitting in the foyer huddled up, hiding her face from me.

"Say something," you used to say when you woke up, and I would recite poetry – something from Shakespeare, or the second song in *Toldi*, the one you loved so much. Ever since I knew how much pleasure it gave you watching me act, the roles I have played have taken on a new significance for me. You remember that time you made me do a dog, a tiny little new-born puppy, and I went down on all fours on the carpet and yapped and yapped and emptied my face of all human under-standing and gazed up at you with innocent trusting eyes, like a tiny puppy, and uttered imploring little whimpers, and then sneezed because something had stuck in my throat? One Christmas I dressed up as an angel; we had a lot of trouble getting the wings out of the building, until old Mr Szalay smuggled them out to the taxi through a side door; I didn't have time to lengthen the straps that attached them to my shoulders, so they were too short and they cut into me, but I made a true angel all the same, a really beautiful one; and the cloud I was standing on was even more glorious – it was an enormous bowl of whipped cream that came up to my ankles, and you had squeezed little decorations onto it with an icing bag. I stood next to the table with the Christmas tree on it, in the bowl of whipped cream, absolutely still and with my eyes shut, and all the time I was thinking of the angel in the Marton crypt, and what my father would have said if he had seen me there, draped in a huge white sheet with absolutely nothing on underneath and you playing Christmas carols on the piano. When he was alive I never knew what to buy him – whole milk, ordinary milk, or just the skimmed version, the poorest, thinnest kind – and there I was up to my ankles on a great cloud of stiffly whipped cream . . . and what would Mother have said when you immediately plucked off the wings and the sheet? Juli had gone off to church for Midnight Mass, and I wanted you so much I didn't dare look up; the sight of you would have made me jump out of the bowl and hide somewhere where you couldn't see me; and you had absolutely no idea what I was thinking, because all I did was stand there and smile the eternal smile of the angels, with my hair tumbling down on my shoulders, all very virginal and chaste and sexless, an *angelos* – not a mere sweet little angel but a messenger, a truly celestial being, come among the shepherds to announce the birth of the Saviour. That night I almost told you where my mother and father were buried, but I couldn't bring myself to speak the words.

It wasn't a proper Christmas, there wasn't any snow, just a raging wind tearing at the trees; I snuggled up against you in the bed – after I had hidden the wings in the cupboard in case Juli saw them and handed in her notice. Another time I pretended I was a fish; it was in the summer, I had been swimming, my eyes were screwed up and I was moving my fins; you gave me a deeply serious look and told me that the whole world should see me, and you talked about Reiner, the Austrian actress who died so young. I slowly rolled over onto my stomach on the carpet, I held my head back and the fins faded away and I thought how I had never seen the sea and I didn't know any of the great cities of Europe, but you had travelled over half the world and your head was filled with just as many memories as mine was, and I suddenly saw Angéla again, the way she used to be, in her garden, pouring sand through a little sieve; even when she was in her teens she used to play stupid games like that, with sand and a little spade, burbling away and laughing and saying how Vienna was such an amusing city – from the giant Ferris wheel in the Prater you could see all the way to Hungary, and there was even a Papal theatre, and her father had once seen Reiner, who was a very famous actress.

I sat up and asked for a cigarette. You looked at me and burst out laughing. You said that once again I had no face, I looked like a corpse.

5

Now I must go and find the nest.

The ant was calling for help but even fifty others wouldn't have been enough, so I hobbled off with the rotting peach and took it to the nest. I waited a while to see what would happen to it, and when it had turned black with ants I left and came back here. I was lucky that no-one came past; what would have happened if they had stolen my shoes and I had had to walk home barefoot?

Why did they teach us at school the stupid idea that a good deed will always find its just reward? You take everything so seriously, you work so very hard and cling to your hopes – and then nothing happens. If I were still a child, I would have noted down in my scout diary that "today I helped some ants". Huh! Apart from the time I rescued Béla I have never done a good deed in all my life, not for anyone; I had neither the time nor the inclination. All I ever wanted was to make you happy. On Saturdays, when I was little, I used to dip my pen in venom and stir it around while I was filling in my Diary of Good Deeds.

It was horribly difficult to find something that grown-ups could understand, I could think of nothing a mere child could do, and I moaned and groaned and scratched my leg in torment.

Have you any idea how hard it is to think of some credible good deed that costs you almost nothing? "Today I helped an old lady lift her bundle onto her back. I helped an old blind man across the road . . ." Angéla was always told off when she showed her Good Deeds Diary to the leaders of her Scout Family at school: it was always full of gaps. She certainly shared everything she had and helped people, anyone she knew, but thoughtfulness and giving were so natural for her that two seconds later she forgot what she had done, so she stood there in shame while everyone else was able to show what a splendid week they had had – especially me and Ágnes Kóvácsi. Whenever Kóvácsi got stuck I told her what to write: twenty fillér for every good deed.

I have always distrusted good people. I never believed as a child that goodness came naturally. I always suspected that beneath it lay some sort of payment for services past or still to come. If Ambrus was kind enough to send us that leg of pork, it was only because I chopped the wood and picked up the pigswill for him, and the Turkish cake was simply compensation for Béla's sausage fingers and tin ear. My aunt hung gold and jewellery round my neck so that no-one could say a granddaughter of a Marton didn't even have a necklace. It was so much simpler to close the clasp on a necklace than to help my father, when a bit of money would have prolonged his life. When you first started to "take an interest" in me, and tried to find out not what my desires were but whether I had any desires at all, I watched and waited, I was waiting to see how it would turn out with you, and if it would prove to be with you as it was with everyone else – that you were evading some responsibility, or there was something you wanted from me, something you were paying for in advance, a seed you were planting, a score you were settling; the first presents you gave me, the ones I took from you with trembling hands and tears streaming from my eyes, that were thrown in the bin. When you first took me on that rainy evening to show me the view of the mountains in the fog, and we walked along the Fishermen's Bastion, I let you go on ahead so that I could follow a little way behind and pull my tongue out and make faces at you, like Puck. I hated you.

I remember when I caught the flu, it was the first time I'd had it in my life, and you sent a medical professor to me, one of your friends; I was at home, I had an apron on and blue ribbons in my hair, I was barefoot and wiping my hands on the apron when I opened the door, and my cheeks were burning with the fever – I must have looked like a servant raw from the country. I told him the lady actress had gone out and nobody in the house was sick and his journey had been wasted. Then I washed my feet, lay down, took a couple of aspirins and spent the day in bed reading the new play from Romania. I used to watch you talking to old Mr Szalay, you sitting in his porter's lodge listening to the stories he never stopped telling about what his grandson was up to, and looking at those dreadful snaps in which everyone is screwing up their eyes in the sun. I've seen you throw children's balls back up to the balcony for them, and lend money to Pipi, who, as everyone knows, never pays anything back.

In the early days I just laughed at you, and pulled faces at you as soon as the door closed behind you; I laughed at you for being such a "good" person, who always paid your way, and paid up before everyone else did; I wasn't the least interested in your goodness or your considerateness, I wanted something else from you. I didn't want you to "be good" to me, and certainly not that you should "really love me". That was out of the question.

Then one day I went to a lecture you were giving in the university on *Hamlet*. You had asked me to go, I said I wouldn't because I had a test coming up, but the real reason was that I didn't want to meet Angéla. I wandered along the inner ring road looking in shop windows for something to buy – I still used to catch myself looking at things I thought of as children's toys, and warm things to wear, and sheet music; there was a west wind blowing, heavy with the scent of rain, a typical early evening breeze; the details on the posters were tinged with yellow, and there were even coloured eggs, and I thought that perhaps, because you are so thoughtful and good, you might come to the theatre afterwards and leave something in the costume cupboard – chocolate or a porcelain egg; I was so worried about it I started to kick the asphalt, and I went on as far as University Street; despite everything, I had decided to look in on your lecture.

The hall was packed; I had to elbow my way through the entrance. You know how no-one ever recognises me when I am not on stage? Well, everyone muttered and told me not to push. Then your face turned in my direction, our eyes met, and I knew you had spotted me; your voice instantly changed, but you kept on reading the passage and I stood with my back against the wall to hear you better; I closed my eyes – all those faces distracted me, all I wanted was to listen to the text, to your voice, to Shakespeare. I was there for about ten minutes, then I slipped out into the corridor and looked at all the busts in their recesses in the wall – Plato with his bald head, Tasso with his laurel crown, gold ones of Lenin and Stalin – and wandered through the teaching rooms looking for yours; I pushed my bus ticket into your brass keyhole so that you would know that I had come, and been at the lecture, then I went out onto the street and stood admiring the displays in the shop windows again. Next to a supermarket there was a dog tied on a lead, a fox terrier; I squatted down beside him, as I bent over him I felt the breeze blowing on my bare neck, he sniffed me all over, I patted him on the shoulder, then stood up so quickly it frightened him and he started to bark; I ran into a side street and sang, "Wake up, Sleepyhead, the sun is shining on your neck," then I stood and let the tears pour from my eyes and roll down my face. One of the houses had an iron door, the knocker was a circular one, made of brass, with a lion shield in the centre with a ring in its mouth. I didn't know whether I loved you or not and I didn't know if you still loved me the way you used to, when you used to look at me the way my father did at my mother all those years ago – it was all so overwhelming and so confusing that I started to tug at the ring and squeeze it and twist it about, sobbing and whimpering. The street was in darkness; there was just one other person making their way along the other side, otherwise I was alone with the lion; there was a shaft of light coming from the square, from a shop window, yellow, then violet, then flame-red, the colours of the Easter Bunny, and they had the Easter Bunny himself in the window, a Bunny the size of a young child; it was as if he had taken over from the Lamb; his face was as expressionless and simple as mine had been as a child, only mine wasn't so impudent and pseudo-benevolent, as if he were a little bit drunk.

I set off back towards the square and then on to the university. "Why oh why? Where has his little wooden horse gone today?" I quoted to myself, the way Pipi said the line in the second performance; an elderly gentleman stopped and asked me if I was alright. The windows in the university were still lit up, I stood staring at them for a while, then got on a bus and went home. I made myself some bread and dripping and stuffed myself up to the ears; the phone rang. "Hi," you said, and I said, "Hi." The tears came pouring out again and I started to munch the fried bread next to the receiver. "Are you eating?" you asked, and I mumbled, "Yes," and there was grease all over the dial and on my nails and my face. "Can I come round?" you asked, and I said nothing, I just munched the crust a bit louder, then went and sat next to the window in the darkened room; only the outside lights were on. I saw the taxi when it was still far away, turning into my road; you still had your briefcase with you, and your notes on *Hamlet*; you had come straight from the university.

I let you in, then went back into the living room and sat on the floor in front of the stove and raked the embers; it was a very cold spring that year and the heating was still on. You sat down, the two of us like china bookends, back to back. For some months you had been bringing me presents. You always took them out of your right pocket. I would glance at your hand as you produced them, then quickly look away and say, "Thank you." Now, sitting with my back to you on the rug, I reached behind me and your waist stiffened as I slipped my hand in your pocket. There were three tiny hothouse tomatoes in it, firm, shiny, yellow-red globes. I wiped one, bit it in two and pushed one of the halves into your mouth. We didn't once look at each other, and the fire crackled and spluttered away.

At home we had the heating on from early autumn until the summer; even in the winter, when it was at its coldest, my father slept next to an open window and all our money went on keeping the house warm; during the day, when the pupils were practising, he lay on the bed in the office and only in the evening went into the main room, where the piano and table were, and the two beds he and Mother slept in. We used to bake potatoes in the embers in the grate, and sometimes apples, and after supper my parents would settle themselves down next to each other as if they hadn't just spent the entire day together but had been far apart and were at last meeting to talk about all the exciting things that had happened in that time. "Shall we talk?" my mother would say as she took out her darning, while my father followed her every movement, in the dancing light of the flames, and moved closer beside her. I stumbled awkwardly around them like a sulky little servant girl, bringing them water, going to the cellar for firewood and staring at them morosely and enviously from a corner. I was utterly superfluous to them, and at the same time so essential; they needed me so much, for my hands, and my muscles and my quick feet. I hovered around them like a voyeur, or a grumpy genie let out of a bottle, an innocent witness to the still undiminished passion that bound them together. Whenever I say the word "marriage", it is they who spring into my mind; every time you have seen me on the stage or in a film, under a long veil and wearing a bridal coronet with that sweet and nervous smile, you haven't been looking at me, you've been looking at my mother; she put on that same sweetly diffident smile every time she took her wedding coronet out of the tissue paper and settled it into her hair.

The love between Elza and Uncle Domi was rather different; there was something restless about it, something twisted and dangerous. I often watched them in church; they sat across the aisle from us; it was the only place where they were all together, Auntie Ilu, Uncle Domi, Elza and the two children.

My own father never went to church, it was too cold for him even in the summer, and my mother didn't go very often; but I had to, the school insisted on it. Angéla didn't sit with the rest of the pupils, she sat with her parents; our school party filled one side of the nave, the rest of the congregation, mostly parents, sat on the other. I spent a long time studying Uncle Domi at Juszti's funeral service – he looked like a man under a death sentence. I imagined it finally dawning on Auntie Ilu what she would have to do – pick up an axe one evening and kill him. Juszti had at least gone away from the house, but he and Elza lived with the rest of the family. Back home, I acted the scene out in Father's office, but I immediately decided not to use an axe, I chose poison instead; Auntie Ilu didn't seem to be the sort of person who would be capable of killing someone with an axe, there just wasn't the strength in her fat soft body. Everyone was talking about Juszti at the time – at school there was no other subject. I thought that Józsi had been fully justi-fied in what he did, however horrible it was seeing Juszti lying there on the floor; I thought she deserved it.

During the Mass I kept my eyes on the prayer book; I was simply amazed that nothing had happened between them. Auntie Ilu continued walking in the garden with the wet towel wrapped round her head like a turban, Elza laid the table, did the shopping, went over Angéla's homework with her and took her to the dentist; Emil still went off to the university – he was now almost at the end of his course – and Uncle Domi went to the court, discussed points of law and passed sentences.

And every Sunday, there they were in church. When the service ended the married couple would leave arm in arm, with Angéla and Elza in front and Emil bringing up the rear. Everyone greeted them warmly, with solemn, respectful faces. If anyone did ever turn to look at them, it was because of Angéla's remarkable beauty. I always watched her closely, as if she were an animal in a zoo; I was trying to see what made her so beautiful. It wasn't her face, or her hair, or her mouth, or her short retroussé upper lip – it was the whole ensemble of her body that was so harmonious and perfect. She was never adolescent and ungainly, with big knees; everything that was beautiful about her as a child and a growing girl simply reinforced and deepened the perfect and assured beauty that radiated from her arms, her legs, her narrow little shoes, her long neck and her glowing shoulders.

One day, after her lesson, we were together in the yard; Elza had gone to the market and wasn't yet back, so I tried to tease out from her what she knew about the issue everyone was whispering about.

We were sitting on the ground under an elderberry tree making daisy crowns; I was chewing a bitter elder leaf and leaning over our collection of delicate, absurdly pink flowers, waiting to hear what she would say. She knew nothing about any of it; she hadn't understood my question; all she had gathered was that I wanted to hear her secrets and she was thrilled. She obviously thought we were going to be real friends now. I was taking an interest in her family and what went on in her home. She put the half-finished wreath on her shapely knee, sat closer to me and whispered – as if she were afraid that someone other than myself and the bumblebee droning above our heads might be around in the garden – that there was some sort of problem with Emil. I spat the leaf out. Who in God's name was interested in Emil? What interested me was what I had heard the German governesses whispering about on the bench, that day I left the kitchen door open when I was inside doing the washing-up, and if they really were saying that Józsi had murdered Juszti, then why didn't Auntie Ilu do the same to Uncle Domi, as he was deceiving her with the governess? Inside the house Judit was working at her scales, appallingly badly as usual; then she started to batter a cradle song, getting the tempo all wrong, so that Mother had to set the metronome going. Angéla seemed to know nothing of any of it and I began to lose heart: perhaps it was just gossip after all.

So I took little notice of what she was gabbling about Emil: that he wasn't studying, he wasn't going to take his exams and he wanted to leave home; he was saying strange things that made his father so worried that he had yelled at him that he should never forget that he was the son of a judge; that all these rumours were damaging the family reputation and he should choose his friends more carefully. Judit was hammering away at the keys; Angéla snuggled up against me and put her arms around my neck, still blathering on about Emil; I raised my head and gave her a look of such extreme astonishment that she actually noticed and pulled her arms away and stopped speaking, and I mouthed a few appropriate platitudes. The gate opened and Elza came up to us; her basket was overflowing with apples for making strudel. I took a good look at her; she looked old, of course she wasn't, only a child thinks that every woman of about thirty is old, but she had lost her youthfulness: she was a stiff-bodied, dark-skinned young woman with a severe mouth; she looked quite Spanish, but without the excitability you see in pictures of women in Spanish paintings, her expression was too guarded. What she needed was a ruff round her neck and a red velvet dress, like the one worn by the maid Eboli in *Don Carlos*.

Angéla got up, brushed down her dress, said goodbye and set off with her half-finished daisy chain. Elza took her hand and led her away, gently and with affection; there seemed something unnatural, even indecent, in the way they walked out of the gate hand in hand, because as I watched Elza I knew that everything I had heard about her was true; she was deeply unhappy, she had no place in the world, whereas Angéla was exceedingly happy, the path before her was cleared of every stone, and it was precisely for her sake that everyone in that house presented such a stiff, unvarying front: it was all so that Angéla wouldn't notice anything.

That night before I went to sleep I began to act out what it would be like to be Elza, but I quickly stopped. I had begun to wonder whether my own mother would keep quiet for my sake the way Auntie Ilu was doing for Angéla. I sat up, with my heart pounding: I had realised that neither of them would show me the slightest consideration; if either of them wanted to leave they would nonetheless keep the relationship going and try to save it . . . Or, I wondered, if she did ever find out that my father was deceiving her, would my mother, the mother who loved to talk of nothing but Mozart, who would occasionally put on her bridal wreath, and whose arms were as strong as a man's from all that piano playing, would she too have picked up an axe, butchered him, then taken herself off somewhere and spent the rest of her days on her own?

I started to eavesdrop, but all I could hear was the dripping of the kitchen tap. I was filled with a sudden urgent need to see my parents, so I opened the door and stood in the entrance to the central kitchen area, deliberately eavesdropping. Silence, apart from the low murmur of intimate conversation behind their bedroom door, something I had heard so often; I shut the door again, feeling every bit as ashamed as if I had actually seen what they were doing.

A candle was still burning in Ambrus' house. My bedroom window was just underneath a street lamp, so I never had to turn the light on if I wanted to read in bed. I loved looking at the law books, especially one, a history of the law in French, that had beautiful coloured pictures of the old Roman lictors and *tesserae*, a portrait of Theodosius the Great and some of British judges on their woolsacks. I took the books to the bed and spent a while playing out what it might be to be those people, then I lay back and imagined that I was a judge sentencing Angéla to death. That brought back the greatest of the revelations of the afternoon, which my thoughts about supper had made me forget earlier. "What sort of a world is it?" she had whispered in my ear. "Emil keeps saying, 'What sort of world is it where people like Papa can be judges? Why doesn't he pass sentence on himself, and who is he to sentence anyone anyway?' That's the sort of thing he's been saying," she whispered to me under the elder tree; and he didn't want to study law, he wasn't going to be a lawyer, and he had these friends their father thought really dreadful – everything was falling apart and the poor people were going to come and sort it all out.

I sat up in the bed, bolt upright, and the book fell off my knee; the light from Ambrus' candle flickered on the wall opposite me; he started to move around the room, the light followed him and I caught a brief glimpse of his head and the shadow of the candleholder moving across his hand. Once again I felt the ears of corn prickling under my limbs, and I heard the muttered whisperings through the hole in the ceiling; Angéla's whispering had merged with Károly's. It was as if the dust had blown away from the front of the Three Hussars, the dust raised by the cattle every Friday, and I saw – it was all so vivid – the motorbike, Emil's motorbike, the one he had just arrived on from the main road, the curtain in Juszti's window fluttering, him running into the bar then out into the street again, with his normally pale face looking flushed . . . and then, without my having to bolster the memory in any way, I saw that girl, the one that had been sitting behind him on the motorbike; she wore a red skirt that she kept tucking under her thighs and she never went into the inn – he brought her beer out from the taproom and she drank it outside. That night I knew I had seen that girl's face before, only I hadn't paid attention to it because I had other things on my mind; that evening when Juszti and Mr Trnka came out of that house in Görbe Street she had been at the market, with those loathsome workers from the leather factory.

"A very unlucky family," you once said, as you stroked my hair. You were stroking me the way a zookeeper caresses a tiger. "The father she adored is no more, her mother is a clown, Elza is nursing her injuries, and the brother who would have been a support to her was killed in the war."

I looked at you and saw that you were sad and feeling sorry for her. I didn't respond; I closed my eyes and the pressure of your hand increased. You were thinking that I might be less harsh and more understanding that evening, but I just snuggled into your arms and closed my eyes; behind my eyelids I could see the house in Köves Street, and the kitchen garden with the now disused kennel that the fawn had vanished from, and I saw Emil rising from his chair on the verandah, stretching himself, kissing Angéla, then going out of the house, knocking our German language textbooks off the table as he went past . . . and no-one, neither Angéla nor I, knew that we would never see him again. He had gone to the station without a change of clothes, as you would on a quick trip to the tobacconist. The detectives looked for him all night, but the only people they found were Uncle Domi and Auntie Ilu and Elza and Angéla; it was months later that he was arrested in Budapest. He hadn't "fallen humbly" in battle, as it says on the statue of the young soldier in the university chapel – he had been hurled into the air and bits of his body scattered everywhere by the explosion across the minefield where his punishment squad was working . . . and the next image I had was of Károly. I started to laugh, you took your hand off my forehead because you thought I was laughing at Emil, but what had occurred to me at that moment was that if it had been Emil lying on his stomach in the loft and Károly had shaken the breath out of him and yelled in his ear that he was a "young toff", he might still be alive today.

6

There's rosemary somewhere around here – I can't see it but I can smell the scent. An old woman has just crossed the road, she looked at me, but she must be short-sighted because her glance just slid over me without realising that I was sitting on the ground. I ought to run after her with a sprig of rosemary, I could still catch up with her by those ornamental plants: "Here's rosemary, that's for remembrance; pray, love, remember; and there is pansies, that's for thoughts . . ." She would think I was mad, I wouldn't be able to run anyway, my foot is so painful, I could sing out to her, at least she would hear me: "How should I your true love know / From another one? / By his cockle hat and staff / And his sandal shoon." She would ask me what the song meant, the way Hella does in the play. My throat is so sore I uttered a little cry a moment ago, very softly, the way you do to test a microphone – I thought I might have lost my voice or even the power of speech, but no, my voice is perfectly clear, I'm just imagining it.

I've made a brioche out of the mud, a really fine one, right here where I am sitting, in a damp little spot of earth still wet with the morning dew – a fine brioche with a plaited top. I'm good with my hands; if anyone passes this way tomorrow it will be a little surprise for them, if the rain hasn't washed it away. I've always loved working with my hands; Kárász néni and Ambrus were the same; I had planned to leave home and take an apprenticeship somewhere, after the fourth year ended at school, that way I would be independent, I would have a place of my own and I wouldn't have to live like a student anymore. My mother burst into tears at the very idea: the university was another Encsy foundation, my grandfather had given all the family wealth to educational institutions, and in her eyes teaching was the most secure and socially respected of all the professions, so what if I became a teacher and taught the children all I knew? "A diploma," she murmured reverently, and my father nodded gently; I glanced up at the wall, where his framed certificate hung under the Encsy coat of arms, and indignantly set about my lesson again; I was trying to work out what the winged Mercury had whispered in Iarbas' ear, and what Dido's sister Anna was urging her to do.

I was really interested, and it wasn't otherwise particularly difficult. Our stupid teacher had made us draw a picture of Fama because he was so simple-minded he thought children were as simple-minded as he was, and that we couldn't grasp anything by simply reading about it. He made us draw pictures of everything before he would accept that we had understood it. I created a hideous monster on a sheet of drawing paper;

it was swarming with mouths, eyes and ears, it was covered in feathers and it perched on top of a tower; it was very detailed and truly terrifying; at first I thought it rather amusing, then I started to find it repulsive; I didn't dare leave it exposed, so I put it away in my folder to avoid having to look at it. "*Interea magnas . . . Interea Fama . . . Interea Lybiae magnas it Fama per urbes . . .*" You see, I still know the passage, just as when we were taught it. We were taught it after Angéla had left town but I thought of it at once, during that lesson; I was angry with myself for that – I would much rather have forgotten about it. Your early memories must be very different from mine. You were born in the capital, in the great city; here an acquaintance or a stranger would never dream of tapping on your window with some news that was being gossiped about in the market.

This woman – she was a complete stranger – knocked on the office window, greeted me when I opened it, said, "The judge is leaving town," and then carried on towards the Barrage. I watched her as she went, to see if she would knock on Ambrus' window as well, but she ignored the workshop and turned instead to a reed cutter who was walking beside her and repeated exactly what she had said to me, that Uncle Domi was leaving town.

It upset my father very much, and that did make me angry. But he was the only one of us who really grasped what had happened; I for one couldn't comprehend why a totally innocent man would have to resign from his position simply because his son was wanted by the police. "You don't understand,"

Father said, shaking his head sadly, "you simply don't understand." I didn't. It seemed to me perfectly natural that they should pack up and go back to Budapest, people who felt unsettled always did, people who didn't really belong in the town, who hadn't been born there – those "newcomers" always went back, sooner or later. Uncle Domi's family were "newcomers" too, they hadn't been born there so at some point they would have to leave, it was obvious that they couldn't stay: the locals would point their fingers at them, the way they did at Jóska Vízféjű, the boy with hydrocephalus who wandered around the salt barrier with his mother who begged and smelled of apricot brandy. That Angéla couldn't come into school again was natural and understandable, but that Uncle Domi couldn't continue working as a judge somewhere else was something I just didn't want to accept.

After supper Father began to think about what Uncle Domi might do when he was back in Budapest; he thought he would probably open a lawyer's office and earn even more than he had before. I shook my head and carried on construing the Latin. Uncle Domi wasn't the sort to become a solicitor. Not him! He would never bring himself to run about drumming up business and practising little wiles, he would have been ashamed to do anything like that. I suddenly looked up and gazed at my father as he swirled his medicine about, took the bottle to the lamp and began mixing drops of it in the water, and I had the sudden feeling that, for all their differences, he and Uncle Domi were very alike. It was a silly idea, because they were of course in every way the opposite of each other: Father's hair was blond and Uncle Domi's black; father was sickly and Uncle Domi in good health; Father was no good with his hands, Uncle Domi very capable. And yet one of them was simply not cut out to be a lawyer, only I couldn't say why. But I could now.

I pushed the book to one side, picked up my teaching diary and looked up the number of lessons Angéla owed me for. It came to eight: twenty-four pengős. I glanced at the clock: seven-thirty – rather late but not too late for me to get to Köves Street; they never dined before eight, it was only we whose day ended early, so that my father could go to bed in good time. I took my apron off, brushed my hair carefully and announced that I was going to ask for my money because they would have left by the time I got there the next day. Never before had my father behaved towards me the way he did that night.

Back in the office I got into bed and settled down to sleep and wept, not because he had scolded me – something he had never done in his life before – but out of rage at how stupid it was to let twenty-four pengős go, pengős for every one of which there was a ready need: to pay the doctor and buy medicine. Once again, the whole business was utterly incomprehensible, it wasn't exactly going to make beggars of them, but it wasn't the "done thing". It was fine to get ill, and perfectly acceptable to earn nothing while your wife gave piano lessons from morning till night, and make a small child cook and wash up and scrub and skivvy – that was perfectly acceptable too. In short, every-thing was fine and dandy except for asking for some money you were owed. I sat on the windowsill howling with rage and making the latch squeak. I was angry with my mother too: why hadn't she at least shown some sense and spoken up against it? I racked my brains trying to think how I could make up for losing my pupil, and what I could do to get hold of another twenty-four pengős. I picked up the law book and took it to bed; I smudged the pages with my tears, I poked out the eyes of the judge with a needle, and then the eyes of all the other judges too, and finally fell asleep.

The next day Elza came round. My father was polite to her as he never had been before, and my mother, who had always previously addressed her in the formal third person, despite the fact that she was a relation of Uncle Domi, now rushed out to greet her, held out her hand and said a friendly "hello". Elza blushed and her eyes filled with tears. That I really didn't understand, I just stood there feeling hostile, and I only brightened up when I saw her hand my mother an envelope; I thought it must be my twenty-four pengős, but, as we later discovered, there were also the full thirty-six due for a full month's piano lessons. That did cheer me up. After Elza had gone my mother told me that the family would be leaving in two days' time and Angéla had sent a message to say that she would like it very much if I went there so that she could say goodbye to me; they were leaving at dawn the day after next, on the six o'clock express. I said all sorts of things about having too much homework, but my father fixed me with his eye and replied, in an unusually sharp tone, that I had to go. What had come over me these past few days? He just didn't recognise me. Hadn't I realised that something very bad had happened in Angéla's family? But we should condemn neither Uncle Domi nor Angéla because of Emil, and I had to go. Propriety demanded it. "Yes," I said, and went to do the cooking. Those people had not visited us once since they had moved into the town, they had never once invited my parents to the receptions they held for their circle of judges and lawyers, but I had to go, my father wished it. Fine. Another example of something I just didn't understand.

The next afternoon I put on my Sunday dress and brushed my hair carefully. At five my mother sent me on my way with orders to stay for a full half-hour and be on my best behaviour. She had made a little bouquet of red roses from the climbers on our wall for me to take to Auntie Ilu; they were floppy and had no scent. I flung them into someone's front yard in the Barrage and wandered through the reedbed, following the narrow path used by the reed cutters; in the centre of the reed-bed there was a series of small square-shaped clearings, as if part of the ground had been shaved clean; I carefully tucked my skirt up, sat down and started to whistle. I could see the church tower that looked down on the reedbed from the top of St Anthony Street and watched the long hand of the clock moving slowly. There were swarms of mosquitoes, I never managed to drive them off, but there was no-one about, the reed cutters had all gone home, and it never occurred to me to be afraid any more than I would have been had I been sitting beside the main road at the war memorial. When the clock hand reached six I waited a few more minutes, then made my way home, this time not from the Barrage end but from the other direction. I told them Auntie Ilu sent her love and Uncle Domi his greetings, and I added that there were boxes everywhere, everything was topsy-turvy and there were no visitors apart from me. And Auntie Ilu had shed a tear when she saw the roses.

We had supper, I washed the dishes and pots and pans; after I had gone into the study and got into bed my mother came to ask me if the mood there had been rather gloomy; I told her they were all deathly pale and found it hard to talk. After she had gone, Ambrus passed by my window, I called out to him to stop and asked him to wake me early the next morning because I had washing to do. "At five?" he grumbled. "Five," I replied. But there was no need: when he pushed my window open a crack and pushed it shut again, as he always did when I asked him, I was already awake.

I had had bad dreams that night and was awake by four; I dared not wash, I was afraid I might wake Mother if I splashed about in the kitchen. I went out into the courtyard on tiptoe and put my shoes on only when I reached the gate. I heard Ambrus moving around outside and the pigs grunting, but I knew that he could see nothing through the high fence. First light was already breaking, the sky above the reedbeds was a pale grey, then greenish behind the church tower, and ahead of me, to the east, the narrow, irregular strip of dawn blazed red. People were already up and about, the cows were being taken off to be watered, and it was only as I drew near the city centre that the houses were still deep in silence. I turned off towards the newer part of town feeling so happy that I started to sing; a servant girl came towards me, carrying a can of milk, and she smiled when she noticed me and I whistled the tune again; she stared after me when I had moved on, but I broke off because the policeman was standing in Köves Street and it was too early to be making a row.

In our town the tram shelters were made of steel, not glass, and their sides were covered in advertisements. This little booth was very rusty. I withdrew into a corner and peered out through a hole. A carriage was waiting outside the house, not the official one that served the judiciary, with its plump white horse familiar to everyone in the town, but one of those for hire. The garden was empty, every shutter that I could see was closed and everything was still. The coachman's face was turned towards me; he was smoking his pipe as he sat waiting. OLGA SCHŐN, OPTICIAN, I read on the side of the booth, and underneath it KORDA, DEVOTIONAL OBJECTS. The adverts were covered in obscenities scribbled in chalk. Meanwhile a tram had stopped; an old man and a youth were standing in front of me and they gave me a long look when I didn't get on it with them but carried on reading the adverts and peering out through the hole. I was very near the house, about twenty metres away. The verandah door opened and out came Elza and the two servants; my heart started to pound so loudly I thought they surely must hear it. The trunks were brought out and lifted up onto the roof of the coach. It seemed that Elza was staying behind, because Auntie Ilu kissed her and I noticed her wiping tears from her eyes. I would dearly have loved to see more of her face, but it wasn't possible. Uncle Domi was standing very erect, holding his hat; he shook Elza's hand, but he didn't get on the coach immediately. A conversation seemed to be taking place, but I couldn't hear what was being said. Then, last of all, out came Angéla.

I had spent much of the previous day wondering what she would be like. I had imagined her with a red nose, stammering and stuttering, tenderly stroking every bush along the way, crying and visibly distressed. I was so desperate to see her suffering I was positively trembling. She raised her eyes to the sky, which was now flooded with the light of dawn. She was wearing her hat and gloves, her beautiful hair was done up in coils in the usual way, and she had a cage in her hand, one I had never seen before; it was shaped like a lute, with flashy lattice-work, and inside it an absurdly green bird swayed back and forth on a swing. Her gaze passed from the sky to the bird and she smiled. Elza kissed her, and tucked something into the pocket of her coat: chocolate, Lucky brand – I recognised the chocolate-coloured lettering on the yellow pack.

Uncle Domi helped Angéla up onto the coach and seated her beside Auntie Ilu, who had now put her handkerchief away. Angéla settled the cage on her knees, said something, probably to the bird, then looked up at the sky again with deep and undisguised delight. That was a dagger through my heart: I had imagined that it must be the first time in her life that she had been up so early – they always travelled at the most comfortable time of day – and that she would still be half-asleep, and there she was, sitting gazing at the sky in this wonderful chilly dawn, seeming to have forgotten or be simply unaware of the despondent thoughts that she should be having. That bird, that miserable little bird, the parrot inside the cage that she was clutching on her lap, wasn't one she had had before; she must have been given this one because Emil had run away. They knew that if they simply put a new toy in her hand, she wouldn't notice how bad things were. It was even possible that she didn't know what had happened to her brother, that they had told her some lie or other, and that was why she wasn't upset; she just thought that they were moving to somewhere else. She said something to her father, who was looking very tired and old at that moment, and she took his hand and pointed at the sky. Everything was aglow, like burnished copper; the dawn light breaking through the unmoving leaves was so wonderful that her lips half opened and she laughed in delight, as if almost intoxicated by their beauty.

I screamed. A woman standing next to me shook my arm and gently brushed my hair from my face, which was now sodden with tears; she started to say something, but I didn't answer. The tram rumbled again, but I just stood there howling and pushed her hand aside; I only quietened down, and suddenly wiped the tears from my eyes, when I noticed that the carriage was turning round and not coming in my direction; it was avoiding the main square and lurching off to the other end of Köves Street instead, towards the woods and the new station, the one that was never used by respectable people; by now I was standing outside the little shelter, I didn't want to lose a single second of the action. The coach turned off at the corner and only the policeman was left – the policeman, the still-humming tram and the sky, its early rays falling on my face that glittered with tears and was sodden with weeping.

7

The sunlight is filtering down.

When the rain reaches the house I ought to take off all my clothes and lie stretched out naked on the ground; the leaves above my head are already quivering, there isn't a proper wind yet but one is approaching; every individual bush is soughing and sighing as if it had taken hold of everything, trees, bushes and flowers – though a real storm would tear them all off, and detonate and rumble over the city like a bombing raid.

Back home the winds that blew over the river were really wild; in the summer they came sweeping across the Great Plain bringing clouds of dust; in the winter they almost scraped people's noses and ears off. In spring and autumn the town was like an air balloon: it tossed in the wind, the houses and chimneys rocked, their doors and windows could never be secured properly and almost everything inside jittered about. Angéla was really afraid of the wind, it made her anxious, and she was also afraid of the storms – she would hide her face and cross herself. But how I loved it! And the rain, and fire, and even mud! Sometimes I go out onto the balcony and look down at the city below and I want to laugh and shout obscenities and sarcastic words at the people living down there. How can they bear to live so stupidly like that, in those impossible blocks of mass dwellings?

When a storm threatens and I see the streets emptying, people dashing into espresso bars or sheltering in doorways, women gathering up their skirts and looking anxiously up at the pouring rain and then stepping awkwardly around the puddles, my heart sings. When I am here at home, on the road that circles the foot of the mountain, and the rain starts, I take my shoes off and run through the water and the mud and the pools that swell out at the foot of the gutters. I have never been able to adapt to the city, with its multi-storey houses and narrow little courtyards. You have come to terms with it somehow, but I have always rejected the idea of spending the greater part of the day seeing only a tiny square of sky, with no wind between the buildings and people peering out at the streets from behind panes of glass, or buying little bunches of flowers in front of the National, apoplectic-looking roses kept gasping for air in iceboxes.

Nor could I accept the way people were always on the move in the capital, until the first time I saw it under rain, that is: the sky turned black, everything up on the mountain started to crash and bang, I saw people fleeing before nature, the hateful car-smelling streets emptied rapidly and the streets shone in the rain. I finally started to feel at ease with myself here when the dog days of summer arrived – everyone closed their shutters and went and lay down or ran to make themselves a drink of beer or spritzer, the tar started to melt and high-heeled shoes left little holes in it. When that happened I just laughed and quietly jeered to myself, then I too sprawled out on the chair in the garden, stark naked, and wallowed in the dry warmth of my skin in the sun; but there's no hope of wallowing in the sunshine now; the thunder has started. Let it come on, then, like the Great Flood itself! At this moment Elza will be shutting the windows in every room in Angéla's house and making the sign of the cross on her forehead.

The light is closing in, the sky has become as lumpy as a sack of potatoes about to burst; the clouds are swollen and have started to rumble, the leaves are sighing and the flowers flattening themselves down.

It's like the booming of heavy gunfire.

I am so glad my father didn't live long enough to see the siege, and that he never heard the sound of those guns: my poor dear would surely have been terrified. If a mouse squeaked in the wall he looked so miserable – miserable and ashamed, because he was frightened of the mouse and he must have felt sad about his inability to protect us from it. By the time they spread out the collecting sheets to pile the gathered reeds on we had already buried him; it was a comfort to me not to have to think of him standing at the window, trembling and trying to avoid looking at the flames.

That evening everyone gathered outside, in the centre of

the Barrage; I am told I was still awake and studying when the attack started; my mother snapped out of her dream and ran out into the courtyard in her nightgown; the blaze from the fires was reflected in the whites of her eyes and her white nightgown was tinged with red; Gámán néni knelt down in the office and started praying at the top of her voice. That was the night when I made Béla leave our attic, and I did well to, because he would have perished along with the house a few weeks later.

The pumps under the barrier were squeaking and the water was being taken away in buckets. Kárász néni's three German shepherd dogs were jumping up and down in front of the reedbed and the Barrage stones were being hosed down with water from above. Palla bácsi, who rented the reedbed from the Council, was dancing around, shouting and weeping; I went out myself, with a notebook in my hand, and I bade him, "Good evening"; he just stared at me, still weeping, with a face that suggested he suddenly had no idea who I was, so I gazed back at him and patted him on the arm to encourage him to cry, which he did, then I turned my mouth down and peered out at him from under my eyelashes, but his stupid fat face was already quite distorted enough.

Palla bácsi had been a classmate of my father's; he was the only one whom my father occasionally asked for a loan, but he never gave him anything, he just sent a message that we would have to provide some security. I patted his arm for a while, studied his face as he wept, then I ran back into the house and started to sing the *Dies Irae*, only it turned into

"The Little Hut is Burning"; I lifted up the hem of my skirt and studied myself in the mirror to see how odd I looked in the red light of the flames, dancing and singing, ". . . *solvet saeclum in favilla* . . .", then I suddenly stopped, went out and sat on the ground; from down there the sky looked even more spectacular.

When the war broke out I was just fifteen, but I immediately realised that, though it would be horrific for other people, terrifying in fact, and the cause of endless anxiety, it would make little difference to us as a family, and it might even turn out well in the end. My uncle would hide his silver, the horses at Marton would be taken away, and Angéla would be very frightened. When the reedbeds caught fire in 1944 my face brightened up as I watched Ambrus shouting through the fence that this was the end of our neutrality. Well, the day came when every one of my cousins would fall to their knees in terror, and no governess or father – and certainly not my dear father – would be able to save anyone from anything. It struck me that we should phone Juditka from the pharmacy right away and tell her to come to the piano and give us the *Magic Fire* music from *Tannhäuser* while I held my hand over my mouth to stop myself laughing; my mother wept and whispered something about "our poor country". I picked a mug full of gooseberries and cut a very thin slice of the rationed bread we were having for supper and took it up to Béla Kárász – he was now a cuckoo nesting in our loft; he had been there ever since he had run away from his military service, and I took him a spoon and a cook's hat and a packet of cheap cigarettes.

My mother had no idea he was living with us; Kárász néni didn't know either, we didn't dare tell her, she was such a gossip she might blurt it out in front of the Germans, or it would at the very least arouse suspicion if she were seen making up food parcels and running around howling and in a state of permanent anxiety. Béla had buried his uniform in the reedbed and climbed up into our garden between the Barrage boulders; he tapped on the glass pane in the door into the kitchen, where I was doing my schoolwork at the time, and asked me to hide him. He was in his shirt and underpants, so I gave him my father's gardening clothes; they hung down over his wrists and ankles. His hands were as white as snow, they looked wonderful, like knuckles of veal; the sedge had left its mark on them and time in the army had made them rough and coarse.

You once remarked, about confectioners' hands, how very white they were from handing all the milk and butter, and how strong from all that mixing of ingredients; Béla gobbled up the gooseberry and would have asked for more bread if there had been any, but there wasn't, I had wrapped it in my apron, and we just sat there together in the armchair with the stuffing hanging out, my father and I had lugged it up wrapped in a blanket from the cellar, where the House Clearance Committee had dumped it. We kept watch through the hole in the ceiling, but I kept having to laugh when I saw how pale he was after almost four years in the army, and how fat and pudgy he looked in my skinny father's clothes.

The next day Árvai was outside my door. For a while he hung

about unsure whether he should have come or not, then when he saw that I was just standing there calmly, turning the house key over repeatedly in my fingers, he immediately went and stood behind my back and whispered that he had accepted the job, then suddenly reached out and dabbed his eyes with a handkerchief. I didn't say anything, I just nodded that I had understood; I thought that you would be prepared to move heaven and earth with me for his sake, and how very good it would be for him if you were to coach him in the rooms at the music publishing house rather than rehearse him at the Opera House, and I kept twisting the key in my fingers and staring at my shoes; my ears noted that some nattering was going on, but the sound wasn't connected with words and made no sense. I started thinking about the question he had failed to answer at the last Socialist Development session, and I began to intone the answer, over and over again, like a catechism: "The psychology of relaxation of effort is inimical to peaceful development . . . The psychology of relaxation of effort is inimical . . . The psychology of relaxation . . ." I kept repeating at the top of my voice: "The psychology of relaxation . . ." and Pipi, who was sitting beside me, turned his head and asked me in a whisper what it meant. "The psychology of relaxation," I said. He looked at me in astonishment. Why would anyone ask that of a busy répétiteur, who has no idea what the phrase means, let alone what it means in the context.

Árvai may not have known what the words meant, but every atom of his being is musical – and on that subject, his vocabulary is certainly growing and he is finding his voice. But I should have told you why I was late at the Swan. It was because I had gone to the Workers' Educational Institute for him.

It's started to rain again. I can see a sort of shelter over there on the left; those two columns have a bit of roofing over them . . . The marble still feels warm so I won't get cold; I'll stick my foot out into the rain, it will do it good if the water runs over my ankle. How strange that even marble gives off a smell if the sun is on it for long enough. This one isn't the usual white, it's more of a yellowish pink – that was the colour of Angéla's skin. She caught a rash from some strawberries once and she kept staring at herself in a hand mirror and crying. She certainly knew she was beautiful; she took a timid, innocent pleasure in the fact. Yesterday, when I was standing there mouthing "the psychology of relaxation", I noticed some wrinkles on her neck. Árvai was still hovering round her, he somehow thought she might have had a hand in the fact that he hadn't been thrown out for "showing such passivity in the professional development session" and had not been re-assigned. But she didn't offer him her hand, she just listened to him in silence, like a deaf mute.

"I was in love with Angéla," you told me once, not with any great warmth, you were just sharing a fact, and I nodded the way I always do when I have fully understood something. And of course you were. She was the sort of person anyone could fall in love with, she was barely adolescent and already half a dozen young lads were hanging around her. I was drinking a cup of cocoa when you said that, its sweetness suddenly made me feel sick and I just swirled it around in the cup without wanting any more. What I should have replied was that I'd had lovers myself, about four or five of them – just for the pleasure of knowing that you too would be having the same bad taste in your mouth that I had, and just as stupidly and disappointingly. But I was never in love with anyone the way I was with you. When someone falls in love with me I watch their face and their gestures; I am interested in all the different ways these things reveal themselves – the trembling of a hand, the way a mouth widens; I pay no attention to the words, but I always look at the face.

Béla was older than I was; by the time I was going to the gymnázium he was at the apprentice school. He was the best thing that ever happened to them. Kárász néni tried to compensate for his stupidity with terrifying quantities of cream buns and cakes. He was so stupid there was nothing to compare him with; he was certainly a lot more stupid than Ambrus' pigs.

My father noticed that he was courting me. One evening he started to tease me about him and the idea that if I became a confectioner's wife I would be forever eating layered cake; I should be sure always to look at him when he came – he never arrived without bringing flowers, even if they were from their garden and Kárász néni had had all her seedlings from us. After supper my parents had a good giggle over him, but I was putting the laundry in to soak and was only half paying attention. The next day, when he came for his piano lesson, I stayed inside the main room with a basket of darning and kept looking up at him, something I had never done in my life before. If my father had said he was courting me, then I would have to do what was expected. He played "O sole mio" and "Mia bella Napoli", both of which he was still having to be taught. At first my mother tried to explain some music theory, then she suggested the Czerny-Chovant, but all he wanted to play was "O sole mio" and some gypsy-style Hungarian folk songs: he mugged up a little programme of these every year. He was so completely tone-deaf that my mother, poor thing, could barely restrain her impatience, but her face lit up again when he at last managed to hammer out a faultless rendering of "Santa Lucia" and "Whose Little Farm Is This Poplar On?" that reduced the listener to sheer pity. And yet his hands were magical: he rolled the strudel pastry with such skill that after inviting him only once to try doing it his mother always entrusted the job to him. At school his inability to remember a historical date or the biography of a writer was matched only by the assurance with which he could tell you how many grammes of sugar or butter went into the various pastries. He quickly grew into an awkward, hairy teenager; he bought me one of those heart-shaped cakes at the fair with a tiny mirror in the centre, and one Easter, when he came round to our house with the traditional bucket of water to throw over me, he blushed to the ears when I tucked a daffodil into the lapel of his jacket.

Kárász néni, like my father, had seen what was in his mind, but despite the fact that she could expect little more than a pair of pillowcases from me as dowry she did not oppose the idea. Sometimes in the summer, when I was out in the yard doing the laundry, she would pop round on some pretext and lean against the washtub with her huge bosom resting behind the brush and soap and, after watching me in silence for a few minutes, nod as if to say, "Well done, my girl, this dirt isn't going to bite you. I can see you aren't afraid of work." And it was she, not Béla, who came to ask for my hand, a few weeks after my father had died. I was in my sixth year at the school at the time and Béla had finished his apprenticeship. They didn't discuss it with me, which was just as well, because if I had known about it I would have agreed instantly; it was only much later that my mother told me what she had come for and that she had sent her packing at once. I was furious with my mother but I just shrugged and muttered to myself. I knew perfectly well why Kárász néni had chosen that time to speak – while I was still at school, we were still in mourning, the new music school had now been built and I was doing a great deal of the housework. She found it harder to accept the difficulty of my lot than my mother seemed to and she was looking for a way to help us both; the cake shop was doing very well and there would be plenty of work for all of us there. My mother took it as an insult; she kept glancing up at the family crest and wiping away her tears.

*

It has now started to rain and I can no longer see you. It is still warm, though the rain is slanting down and swirling around between the stones. Now I'm really happy. Everyone is scuttling along the streets and people are dashing to their windows and closing them. What would it have been like if I had married Béla and never met you, if the only kiss I had ever known was the one he gave me when he was called up, on that last evening, when he climbed over the fence to see me? What if I had never known you and your gentle touch, the smell of your hair, the unvarying coolness of your skin? I told him not to worry, he could go off to the army and I would bring my mother round to the idea, there was plenty of time, and when he was discharged he would have what he wanted. He smelled of flour and caramel; I was eighteen, I waited patiently, with my eyes open, for him to kiss me; I was calculating how long he would take to get home from the army and we could take down the wall between our houses. I would have loved it if he had given me a ring; I had sold the jewellery that my grandmother had given me years before.

It was a pitch black, moonless night and it was impossible to see through the wartime paper linings in the windows of both our houses, so we kissed undisturbed.

Béla sighed and moaned, then he suddenly started to croon. My head was on his shoulder and he was singing straight into my ear: "The corn is ripe and bending over." As he kissed me I felt such an unbounded excitement I briefly forgot that the smell of flour on his skin was like that of a miller's cat, but when he began that tuneless yowling I shuddered and pulled myself away from him. At that moment I really loathed him; I tried to reassure myself that Kárász néni was earning so much that if he really wanted to sing to me I would let him, but I was also starting to realise that if he was going to croon like that I really wouldn't be able to bear it. He said that when the war was over my mother and I would be welcome to come over and have our meals with them; the days of hardship would be over, they would expand the cake shop and he would apply for permission to have music and play the piano every night – it would be just like the musical cafes in Budapest. I could see myself running back and forth between the tables with cream cakes and ice cream, and it was an attractive picture . . . But with Béla at the piano, and doing the singing? I had to smile.

Despite the darkness he noticed the smile and was strangely annoyed. I felt his hand grow hot and I wanted to go back inside, but then we kissed again; Kárász néni called out for him so, like the bride-to-be I was, I stayed there; my mother would have already gone to bed, and I could hear the wind sighing down in the reedbed. Ambrus no longer kept pigs, he no longer bought fodder, he was getting steadily older and he was riddled with gout – and because he had no more need for my services he never so much as greeted me now. All around me was silent. I started to think about the fact that I was now a bride-to-be, and I thought about Gizi in Budapest, and I wondered what had become of Angéla. Juditka had been in Budapest at Christmas and had spoken to her once at Mass; they had gossiped a bit about the theatre and she had told me that Angéla was about to be married. I thought, "But there's a war on – what if her fiancé were killed?" and I realised that I was making a terrible mistake, I should never have let Béla go back to the army: when his training was over he might be sent to the front and he would die, but if we were married by then then I would be his heir anyway. I started to worry and walked around restlessly; how soon might he be back, and how could I raise the subject with my mother when she wouldn't hear a word of it? She still hadn't realised that once the music school was ready to open she would have no more pupils, and that unless some miracle happened I wouldn't have enough to buy even my weekly ration of bread and sugar.

Árvai was a prisoner of war with you. The two of you slept together, and he looked up at you the way a dog looks at his master, so how odd that I actually did something for him, it isn't my way and I would never have thought of doing it myself if you hadn't asked me, I would have just let them kick him out, it would never have occurred to me that I should try to stop them. With Béla it was like Elijah fed by the ravens: I supplied him with food for three whole weeks simply because I was living in the hope that something would come of our marriage. As the Russians drew nearer and it became clear that they were about to cross the river, I tore up one of our three sheets to make him a white chef's cap and apron and sent him off with our large wooden spoon for making jam; that was the night the reedbed caught fire.

While he was up in our loft he never once tried to kiss me or speak about what it would be like when we were married. That evening when he appeared in our yard in his shirtsleeves and underpants and knocked on the window and I burst into laughter despite the fear I was feeling, something of his love for me was destroyed. The letters that we had exchanged by then now seemed childish and stupid. He had written that he was worried that one of them sent from the camp might accidentally fall into my mother's hands, and I was also worried that they would be censored in the post, and about his appalling grammatical mistakes; I was at the university by then, in my second year on an Encsy scholarship, apparently on course to become a teacher, a "real teacher", when I would earn enough money for the two of us to live with my mother.

When we were setting off to Budapest with Pipi I went to say goodbye, first to Ambrus and then to Kárász néni. She was very kind. She immediately dashed into the shop to pack us something for the road. I found Béla in the workshop. He was singing a bitter little song, but he stopped as soon as I went in. Neither of us knew what to say. I was already worried that he would tell me not to forget our old plans, but he didn't, he just stood there, he didn't ask me to sit down, he just kept stirring his bowl of dough from time to time, and when I was about to leave and had got to the door I looked back and saw him glaring at me with a suspicious, even murderous, look in his eye. I wondered what the matter was, and straightened my shoulders while Kárász néni put two little flour-covered paper bags in my hand. Was his problem that I had concealed and fed him for all those weeks? The idiot. I picked up the packets: there was a savoury scone in one of them and some bread flour in the other, and I felt that I really shouldn't have laughed at him that time I saw him at the kitchen door, and I should never have told him to lower his voice because he sang so badly out of tune it was unbearable. Then Pipi tooted on his horn, my mother and I climbed up into the truck, and I forgot all about Béla.

*

Árvai was in tears yesterday. He went on and on sobbing. I stood there turning the key over in my hand and looking at Angéla; I was thinking how utterly expressionless her face is. Árvai was stamping his feet and weeping as if annihilated by his gratitude and sorrow. The people at the Centre for Folk Art wouldn't let me in at first, even when I showed them my papers; finally someone recognised me and the performers started to dance around me in excitement; one of them told me immediately that Árvai's case had been considered and there was probably nothing that could be done about it, the matter had already been dealt with and they had no-one there capable of teaching the relevant party material; they had decided that he was a deliberate saboteur who had been making fun of the Forward Development meeting with his deliberately stupid answers; the new group leader would no doubt take the same view, and if I still wanted to see him I would have to wait for a while.

I was taken to a room where a woman with an unusually broad head sat at a desk; she sent me away to wait outside a green door; I smoked a cigarette, looked out onto Kálmán Square and studied the pictures: a foundry worker firing up a Father Christmas-red chimney, portraits of Mussorgsky, Borodin and Erkel – musicians of the first order. So the new group leader must surely be Maté Örs, that wise and agreeable man; he would have been in his new office for about ten days now, but there was probably no need to be worried about him. I had read about him in the theatre magazine: he was a worker, part of the movement since his early years, he had fought alongside the Russians; he had had a difficult childhood and had no family to help him, and had got where he was by his sheer humanity. I felt a boundless trust in everyone who had no family behind them, and I hoped that if he had been a longstanding member of the movement he wouldn't still have to prove himself step by step, unlike some intellectual who had been a Party member for only two months, so he would surely be open-minded and understanding. I hoped so anyway. I had always thought of myself as one of the workers and that too would surely help Árvai's case; it would make him think that I was stupid as mud and so be well disposed towards me.

The broad-headed woman came back and asked me to be patient. I lit another cigarette and waited for almost an hour – which was all the more surprising as the Group Leader had received no-one in the interval and the broad-headed woman put his visitors in a queue. I was really quite surprised: no-one, anywhere, made me wait once they had heard my name. When at long last the buzzer summoned me in, I rearranged my face to look alluring while at the same time radiating innocence, and brightened my face and flashed my teeth to look like a good fairy. Árvai. And you. I wanted you to be happy. I wanted to get a result. Árvai had given you cigarettes in the prison camp, he had looked after you when you were sick, and during the nights he hummed whole symphonies to you from memory.

The broad-headed woman shouted, "Next!" and opened the door. I went in and stood there gaping, as the radiant look slowly vanished from my face. The whole thing had been pointless. Behind the desk sat Béla Kárász.

8

In front of me there's a statue. I've only just noticed it; it was raining so hard I could only make out the outlines, but now I can see it's a copy of Michelangelo's *Descent from the Cross*; the rain is still dripping from Joseph of Arimathea's hood and Jesus' knees are wet and shining.

It's a long time since I last saw this statue but I have always loved it. At school we studied art history for two years and it was the only subject that really interested me apart from literature and music. In the evenings in my father's office I used to hold the illustration in my hand and play at being the people I saw on statues and in books. I used a scarf and a pillowcase to decorate my head and a sheet for the robes. The Michelangelo was one of the statues I mimicked; I was Christ, I had a real struggle trying to see myself in the mirror and what sort of likeness I had achieved, and I almost broke a leg because there was no-one else with me to play the Madonna and I had to kneel on a stool, half-supine, with my limbs looking limp and helpless and my head tilted to one side.

I never did Joseph of Arimathea, he was too easy a challenge, standing there like a gloomy overgrown dwarf, but the face of the dead Jesus really did interest me. I half closed my eyes and studied myself in the mirror to see if I looked sufficiently corpse-like.

If I had been allowed to choose my university courses I would have chosen art history, but of course that was out of the question because they only let you do it if you could take courses abroad for two years, at one of the German or Italian universities: Kázmér Cheh, the professor, refused to examine anyone who could not produce a record of study abroad. How you laughed when you fished my record out from my other papers and discovered that I had taken a foundation course in Hungarian and Latin! "What in God's name made you take a subject like Latin?" you asked. I said that it interested me a lot at the time, then I plucked the record from your hand and threw it back with the other papers. I never enjoyed my time at university as much as my years at school.

I recently read a novel about the way students in the old days used to dance and carouse, how it was understood and excused for the duration of those four years, and I kept nodding my approval. Of course it would be like that. But me? I could just see myself, the first time I went to the Dean's reception, wearing the same sailor suit uniform I had worn to school, looking thoroughly sulky and glancing every few minutes at my watch because I had to get to a lesson with one of my new pupils. The boys all took note and grinned, and went over to the other girls.

We were at our very poorest at that time. Can you imagine me, at the age of eighteen, in the blue sailor suit I had outgrown and with that grim scowl on my face, standing apart from everyone else in the bay window in the Dean's office bristling with impatience, then dashing out of the building, running off to my lesson, on foot of course, because I had no money for the tram?

And the Latin authors, how I hated them! Of the Hungarians I somehow came by the *Comicon Tragédia* and the *Debreceni Disputa*, Bornemisza's *Magyar Elektra*, *Bánk Bán* and of course Petőfi. But the Romans! *The Roman Army under the Emperors* was the theme of the first course; in the first lesson I thought everyone had gone mad. I was to spend four years studying the way they developed their military techniques – how they learned to shoot arrows backwards from the saddle from the barbarians on their eastern borders! From the age of thirteen I had drummed the declensions and conjugations into my pupils' heads; before we got to read any literature I tortured the ones who were at risk of repeating the year by going endlessly over *Integer vitae . . . / Dulce ridentem Lalagen . . .* How I hated Lalage and her stupid smile! Where was that "sweet smile" when I got home every evening? I majored in Latin, along with Hungarian, because it was one of the subjects you could study without having to go abroad.

When Ványa was first made our Director, Pipi and I always pretended not to understand the Latin words in Shakespeare's plays. I would ask Ványa for advice on how to pronounce the names, and Pipi would put on a special idiot voice and ask, for example, why the River Lethe was supposed to be amusing. Ványa was so young, so big-headed and so stiff he could hardly bear it. When he had had enough of us and our stupid questions and innocent faces, he would call for a break, leap out of his chair and rush out of the room. You were present on one of those occasions. We were doing a first reading of *Antony and Cleopatra*. "Agrippa?" Pipi muttered. "Who is this Agrippa?" I nearly choked; Pipi had a bust of Agrippa in his bedroom that he had bought in Verona at the Shakespeare Festival more than twenty years earlier, and I had just explained to him in some detail the role Agrippa played in Octavian's circle, how clever he was at all sorts of things, his passion for maps and aqueducts and public shows with staged sea battles. Ványa scrolled down his *Shakespeare Director's Notes* and read out who Agrippa was: a military leader and high-ranking officer, and a true son of the people. I had to run into the bar to finish laughing.

I had instantly conjured up an image of Agrippa – with the same head as the one above Pipi's bed, but barefoot and wearing a sea-blue tunic and trousers to signify that he was a son of the people. Pipi came racing after me, then you came in as well and you gave us a look that wiped the smile from my face; I started to worry and became upset, and Pipi grew very serious: he had realised what you would be thinking and that it had done neither of us any good.

At that point I should have gone up to you, shaken you and yelled that it wasn't true what you were thinking, but I kept quiet because I realised that you were deeply jealous of him, and you thought some sort of wild delight had taken hold of me, some malicious pleasure, but instead in fact I was so merry I started to sing Mark Antony's song at the top of my voice, "In thy vats our cares be drowned, / With thy grapes our hairs be crowned," and then it was Pipi who didn't understand: he didn't realise that I was singing about you and me. When you didn't come to see me that evening that also gave me pleasure; I was counting the hours to see how long you would hold out, and I had a real shock when the doorbell rang. The sound of that doorbell ringing was like someone coming at me with a knife in their hand and I flinched. At the next rehearsal, when Pipi saw you in the viewing gallery, he didn't dare touch me. You mustn't be upset, he was a long way away from my thoughts; but I'm sorry. I didn't mean to talk about him.

I know an awful lot of things about the ancient world, and about its people and institutions, down to the tiniest detail; you remember how amazed you were that evening when I told you about the way the theatre grew out of pagan religious practices? Of course I know only about the things that I had made a special study of. I spent two years of my four writing five separate dissertations about the way they lived; it was a much easier way of earning money than teaching, only riskier.

You never wanted to believe that I had no admirers at the university. But why should I have? I didn't have a single decent dress, I spent my whole time swotting to make sure I kept my bursary, and whenever I caught sight of one of the richer boys I went up to him and asked if he needed any help with his dissertation, though none of them ever did. I kept well away from the girls; they were far too dull and cowardly, never the sort to risk disappointment. Poor Karki Sziki – he was the first of our year to die in the war. He was more than happy when I handed him his dissertation on Agrippa, but he never took the trouble to read it before he went into the exam and I kept my fingers crossed in case the professor should slip in a question about the actual content – he would have had to sit there helplessly: he couldn't have quoted even the chapter headings.

But don't get me wrong, these were not masterpieces. I have no idea what real scholarship is about; the books I liked were hardly the weightiest, but what I did learn in my first year was to gather all the facts so that I would have an easy time in the final exams – it was much more fun than teaching pupils. I had very little time for sleep, I spent the whole day gathering information in the library and writing it up at night, in the ablutions block when everyone else was asleep – the dormitory lights went out at eleven, so that was the only place I could work. When I think back on my university days the image that comes to mind isn't of the main building, the chapel or the examination hall; instead I get a sudden sensation of warmth, the warm, dry heat of the bathrooms. I always wrote in there because it was warm even in the winter; I shut the door behind me, wiped the bottom of the bath clean, sat down in it with the folder on my knees, and wrote; no light leaked out to betray me – the windows were all blacked out. It was good living in the hostel, much better than at home. Father was no longer alive. I never got used to the fact that there were just the two of us now rather than three.

We were on a tour of the provinces once, with Pipi and Hella; you were standing with me outside the university hostel and you had no idea why I kept looking up at one of the windows on the second floor. We were in the city where I had been a student, preparing a performance of *Bánk Bán*. It was your first time there, and you kept looking around all the time; I was constantly amused at how tiny this little city in the Great Plain seemed to you and how enormous and glittering it had seemed to me when I first went there. My hometown was on the other side of the river, about twenty kilometres beyond, and people there spoke about this one, with its university and hospitals, as a metropolis. When I first arrived as a fresh high-school graduate, with my things tied up in a belt inside a wicker basket, I gazed up at it in wonder. That evening I played Melinda, and after dinner we went for a stroll around the houses; you kept standing on your toes outside people's windows peering into the rooms and pointing out the kitsch chandeliers and dreadful pictures; you barely glanced at the hostel, you said it was a barracks for students and there were even guards on duty – the two soldiers on the war memorial – but nothing of the least interest, there was plenty of that sort of thing in Budapest. "Naturally," I said, I removed my gaze from the windows of my old room in the hostel and stepped around a puddle. You had now "shown me" the university and you turned back under the arcades; I was walking more and more slowly and thinking what it would be like if I suddenly changed back to the person I had been then, in my blue coat that reached down to the knees and my old skirt worn out by constant ironing, clutching a pile of books under my arm and racing off to the canteen.

And how appreciative I was when I got there! I didn't have to cook, they served different dishes every day and every evening and the portions were generous, everything was always tasty and gave me pleasure. The evening we were there together we dined at a fish restaurant beside the bridge; there was hardly anyone there, just an old fellow drinking in one corner, a red-faced old boy with a huge white beard and as tubby and well built as Father Christmas. "That's St Nicholas sitting over there," you whispered over your glass of beer, and I instantly saw myself again in the hostel corridor in red dungarees and a cotton wool beard, with a sack on my back, a bishop's mitre on my head, and the janitor's daughter squealing with joy at the sight of me. The girls inside were getting worried, then I hammered on the door, the prefect opened it and in I went, a very old, very weary, benign old bishop, calling out to everyone; I was having enormous fun being that man, that antiquated fellow full of bonhomie, so deeply thoughtful and even a bit reverential; the janitor's daughter clambered up onto my lap, stroked my arm, took a fig from me and ate it, while I watched her like a burglar or a sneak thief from under the bushy white eyebrows I had put on to deceive her, and realised that I had succeeded. That child had been to see me every day: she had had trouble learning her alphabet and I was teaching her how to read and write; we had extended lessons poring over her exercise books, with me guiding the pencil in her hand, and she hadn't recognised me in my Father Christmas outfit, neither by my voice nor by the touch of my hand.

Don't think for a moment that it bothered me when I opened the sack and found that no-one had given me anything, not even the usual little red bag with my name on it; I have already told you that none of the others liked me; if they hadn't been too proud and too ashamed to put those boots on and stick cotton wool on their faces they would never have let me be St Nicholas. But they thought it beneath them, and certainly none of them was prepared to wear a comic mask, so it was left to me. And it was because of that Father Christmas that I later was given Iphigenia. I should have told you earlier why I had flowers from Pipi on every seventh of August. Again, it isn't what you thought. He and I were very fond of each other but in all our time together we were never actually in love. Can you understand that? You never have. And now you never will. August the seventh was the premiere of *Iphigenia*.

The thunder is still rumbling, but the storm has moved a long way away now. It's like a roll of kettledrums or distant cannon fire. You once told me that when you were at the front your greatest fear was the thought of the bombing back at home, people having to shelter in the cellars and Angéla having to go out into the street after every raid and bandage people up because she had taken a first-aid course and was then on duty. It was some time ago that you talked about it, and you never once noticed that every time you mentioned her name it went through me like a knife, like an electric shock, and that I struck back, not always according to the rules, but I really wanted it to hurt. Why did you think I did that? Because I felt shamed by her? Or guilty? Why did every mention of her name drive me almost mad?

Poor little Angéla, with her first aid box in her dainty little hands unrolling the bandages, bending down like a Sister of Mercy over the wounded and smiling her beautiful smile. Poor little Angéla, the timid little thing, picking her way through the terrible ruins on her dainty little feet. My God, how it hurts me still! You thought the worst thing of all about the war was the bombing of the capital? For me that was the best. Whenever the radio announced another raid I became like a hunting dog. I shook with expectation. What harm could it do me? I stood at my window in the hostel like a voyeur – wondering if the bombers would get to us as well and not just Budapest. If the rich people here took fright my mother would be able to rent out the office and I would be able to stay in the hostel – and at least she wouldn't be so lonely. I never went home on Sundays, like the students who lived locally, and I didn't have a season ticket.

In fact I never went home, I really didn't want that; every time I saw my mother we just burst into tears, and it made us think of Father. What was the point of going? What would I do with myself when I got there? What would I have gone back for? My mother just played her piano and read and starved herself; she had sold everything she no longer needed. I only went home in the long vacation when the hostel was closed. I once asked her whether she was afraid of living on her own. She just smiled and turned away, and I bent down and brushed my shoes: what stupid questions we sometimes ask! My mother would never be afraid of anything again. After the night my father died there was nothing left for her to be afraid of.

Poor little Angéla, stepping along on her dainty little feet with her first aid box in her dainty little hands, what beautiful little bandages and dressings she must have made! Everyone had been so wonderfully attentive to her since the day she was born, so of course the wounded and the dying would be thoughtful too and not trouble her with their internal bleeding. I was still in the university when the first bombs finally reached us; almost four hundred people died that morning, but where my mother lived there was nothing. Bolvári bácsi, the NCO of our seminary, set off to the city straight away to see what had happened before the all clear had even sounded. He was a sour, wrinkled old bachelor who wouldn't give you the time of day; he sneaked out of the basement door when the guards were elsewhere and there was only the odd-job man at the front door. For some obscure reason he and I had formed a close bond; he sometimes brought me a loaf of bread that he had cooked for me himself – he had been a baker in his youth. I saw his uniform lying on the grass on the riverbank when I was still some way off. I thought I would undress and use my slip to bundle it up, but there was no point, his head had been split in two like a melon; he made a really ugly corpse. I didn't know how to feel sorry for him or even look at him. I had gone out to try to find a tenant. I knew the time had come for me to put Father's office out to rent and by that afternoon Éva Gámán's mother was on her way with her two children in a country cart. I charged her an awful lot of money for the room, a really fantastic amount.

Just listen to the thunder! The bombs made a high-pitched sound, a sort of protracted hissing or whistling, then bang! I took my final exam in the university cellar. The professor, Klement, smoked non-stop, his hands were shaking so much he kept dropping the ash everywhere; Sztukics, from the Teacher Training Department, paid me no attention at all; he kept walking up and down and looking at his watch and sucking through his teeth at every one of the increasingly loud explosions. I was translating Virgil, the bit where Neptune calms the waves: "*Solemque reducit . . .*", scanning the verses as I went: "*silent, arrectisque auribus adstant*" – or something like that. Klement was listening to me rather fitfully, and when I came to the bit about the god parting the solid bank of cloud and restoring sunlight to the heavens he looked at me and gave a nervous laugh. It was April 1944; three days later they closed the university. That was horrible, because now I couldn't go back to the hostel: everyone had been told to vacate the building at two hours' notice because the Germans wanted to take it over as a military hospital. I was allowed to stay on until I finished doing *Iphigenia*.

Orestes' family took me in. Orestes' sister Piroska Kapros was in the same year as me, though we weren't in any way friends. Her mother, however, jumped at the idea; she thought being in the play would keep her son safe; they might call him up if he was no longer in it. Béata Géc was the original Iphigenia, and when her family fled to the West, Kata Tóth took the role; she was doing well until her father took them all off to their farm to escape the bombing, so they tried the middle Kóvács girl, but she had a bit of a lisp, and Dózsa, the professor of Hungarian, clapped his hands to his ears at the first audition; she took offence and withdrew; by then everyone else had taken fright and either left the country or moved to the countryside or to their farms, and Dózsa gave the part to me.

Géza Kapros grabbed the role of Orestes with both hands, as did the people offered Thoas and Pylades, because Klement had said that no-one would be called up into the army while the play was still going on. Mrs Kapros put me in Piroska's bedroom and it wasn't a bad arrangement, only I hated their constant fits of panic and the way they kept listening out and trembling with terror in case the postman came, or there was a bombing raid, and what would happen to Piroska if an air attack took place when she happened to be in the house alone? She kept moaning about her fiancé and snivelling all night and switching the light on to read his letters, but otherwise they left me in peace; I ate very well there and learned my lines. I learned them as thoroughly as I would have for an exam I was afraid of failing. Dózsa directed the performance; he had also chosen the play, having been Rector at the time; he had been asked to do it by the mayor and by members of the governing body, they thought it more appropriate and politically tactful for the students to do a play by Goethe rather than a guest variety show for the victims of the bombing. Bolvári told me that everyone on the governing body had smiled when he announced the title, he had no idea why, but I knew better. Dózsa did not like the Germans and he did not like the war. Finally two posters went up on the noticeboard, side by side, one for a charity performance of *Iphigenia at Tauris* given by the students and the other a variety show with guest appearances by artists from Budapest. Pipi's name was at the top of the second, in large letters.

"Those whom the gods condemn to a turbulent existence are given a dear friend, raised on a distant shore or in a neighbouring land, to be near them and support them in their hour of need." Angéla always had someone around to help her. During the war Elza never left her side. Pylades looked really dashing in his little headband, and whenever I was on stage with him I always felt horribly in love with him, but in real life I never gave him a second thought; he was as poor as I was, he had had to do everything for himself and he never asked for help – "a dear friend, raised on a distant shore". But for Angéla the time has now come when neither Auntie Ilu nor Elza can help her anymore. She's an adult now.

It's still thundering, but the rain has stopped.

You mustn't be cross with me. I can't help it, Pipi even less. The sky has now turned green – it's always green after a storm.

"When the refreshed foliage holds up a thousand mirrors . . ."
That wasn't my line, it was spoken by Géza Kapros. When I
first met Pipi I didn't know what he really looked like; I hadn't
spotted him in the audience during the performance, so when
he came up onto the stage during the interval and told me
who he was I was in a real whirl. I thought he was joking; I
had only seen him in films and in the papers, looking very
handsome; in real life he had no more than two hairs on his
head and the skin around his eyes was full of wrinkles. It
was only when Dózsa told me it really was the great Pipi that I
finally believed him; then everything became very confused; the
strap on one of my sandals had broken, I got the jitters because
it belonged to the theatre, and I thought that everyone had
gone mad – people were shouting out and stamping their feet
and the applause just didn't stop. The university gave a banquet
afterwards, paprika chicken, quite marvellous. I'm hungry right
now, horribly hungry; the reason I am crying is because I am so
unbearably hungry. You know how hungry I get. A few months
ago we had a puncture on a road out in the country and we had
nothing with us to eat, so you went into a peasant's house and
bought some cottage cheese and brought it out to me in the car
wrapped in vine leaves. Angéla hates cottage cheese.

Pipi sat next to me at the banquet; at the time I thought he
was completely stupid and I kept shrugging as he rattled away;
I was still in my school uniform, in that hideous white blouse
I'd cut the blue sailor's collar off to create a completely incongruous plunging neckline that showed the hollows around my

neck; Dózsa was sitting on my other side, I was trying to be as nice as possible to him because of my teacher training bursary and I found the attention he was paying to me that evening quite terrifying; Pipi was drinking his coffee without sugar, which amazed me, and I listened to his chatter with only half an ear, I was keeping my eyes on Dózsa and trying to see if I could move the bread a bit nearer, then Pipi started to talk about the fee and I turned my back on Dózsa and gave him my attention again.

Three weeks later we no longer had a home. Mother and I were out in the timber yard when the bombs came, the Gámáns were at the cinema when they heard the sirens going off, everything they had was destroyed with the office and she cursed me for literally taking her in; she took her two girls off to find a cart and they trundled off that same night back to the town. We slept in the school in Homok Street; everything we now owned was wrapped in two bedcovers, including the washing-up bowl that Ambrus had recovered from the reedbed. They gave us plenty to eat; the other people who had lost their homes kept running around shouting because they didn't even have quilts, then the Women's Institute gave us blankets and I slept really well on the straw.

Why did you take me to see where you lived before the war? It had been my favourite part of Budapest until then; ever since that visit I get cramps in the stomach whenever I go there. You showed me where a mine had blown off half the wall and told me you used to live there, what colour the furniture was, how all your houseplants had disappeared and that you found some of your books in someone else's courtyard. Frankly, I have never been able to bear the thought that you had a home in Budapest that I knew nothing of – a place where you lived and breathed and had a servant and a cat and a telephone. In all our years together I have been unfaithful to you only once; it was when you showed me St Anne's Church and told me how nervous you were and how deeply moved you had been at your wedding. I didn't go to the theatre that night, as I told you I did, I went to Pipi's. He thought I had gone crazy. He didn't want me, and he was almost in tears. You know how I hate alcohol; I can't bear to drink it; he drank the whole evening because he was in such despair; the next morning even the pillow stank of brandy. In all my life I have never loved you as much as I loved you that night.

When the Russians broke into the school they were looking for weapons. They went through all our bags and I really wondered what they thought they were looking for – all we had in that way were the skimming ladles we found once at the start of the dyke. Elza told me once that Angéla used to run out into the street screaming and crying in fear for her home, but no-one ever accosted her. "Her nerves were weak," Elza said, "and ever since the war she has been afraid to go alone into the streets after dark." The thought that the Russians had frightened Angéla made me rather like them. They even stood guard outside the hotel where I was living with my mother; when Pipi came to see me after the siege had ended they smiled at me and I smiled back at them; the only thing that got on their nerves was when people shook at the sight of them; they would immediately shout out to reassure them. It was the first time in my life that I had stayed in a hotel.

When you came to look for me in Szolnok I should have told you about everything that had happened, but I just couldn't find the words. We spent our first night together in that hotel on the road to Budapest. We were being taken there on Pipi's truck; my mother was sitting on a sack of potatoes and I was at her feet. Pipi had a large scarf tied round his ears and throat against the cold. It was the end of May, the first time I saw Budapest, and I have loathed it ever since. The theatre was in ruins; the director auditioned us in Pipi's apartment. I did an extract from *Iphigenia*, then a poem by Margit Kaffka, then we did a sight-reading and I chose some of Desdemona's lines. For three months I had been tortured by lessons with all sorts of different drama teachers; in September, when I signed my contract, my mother didn't come to the theatre. I saw Pipi at the front door; he was like Ambrus when I fed the pigs, standing there whistling, and he patted me on the bottom. I stopped in my tracks. I had my contract in my hand. "What do you want for it?" I asked grumpily. He didn't answer, he just carried on whistling. He lived out towards the woods; his place was miraculously untouched and he had plenty of food in there, even American condensed milk. I couldn't remember when I had last tasted milk. "Marcus Vipsanius Agrippa," I thought while he kissed me. "Marcus Vipsanius Agrippa." His head was up there on the shelf above Pipi's bed. It didn't take long. Pipi got up, in a terrible mood. "That was really stupid," he said and lit a cigarette. I did the same. I had never smoked, I was too afraid to start: I was afraid I would never be able to afford it. I was back home by supper time.

I have always wanted to tell you that you gave me back my body. If you had ever asked me how it had been between me and Pipi I would have said at once that there had been nothing like that since; but you didn't ask, and I didn't feel free to raise the subject. The first time you spent the night with me and informed me that I loved Angéla I became wary and miserable, I felt let down and my body rejected you. But in Szolnok, when I was squatting down on my haunches so that you wouldn't see the way my feet had been deformed by Auntie Irma's shoes, the scent of the land and the rain came flooding in through the window and I finally forgot Pipi's brandy-smelling breath and his yellow sofa bed with the bronze bust of Agrippa above it, and the books on his bookshelves all in the same binding and the black vignettes on the covers of Shakespeare's history plays – which I kept my eyes on while he embraced me. But when I was with you in Szolnok I kept my eyes closed so that I wouldn't miss anything, and so that I could follow you blindly by touch alone into a place where I had never been before.

Pipi never loved me the way you imagined, and I never loved him. He never understood something that Ambrus and I did, and after that there was nothing more between us. He taught me everything I know about the stage, and he even politely let me pay for his dinner, but there never was anything especially wonderful about him. It was only much later, when the half-year that we had been together was long over, that we talked about what had passed between us; we were both very glad that it had ended and we could at last behave normally towards each other, like two fellow actors. On that one occasion when I was unfaithful to you with him he was so angry he almost beat me. I had just lain there on the bed looking at the books and at the head of Agrippa, tears trickling down my face. "That was really stupid," he said in the same tone he had used before, and pushed a cigarette into his mouth. "Eszter, why don't you marry Lőrinc?"

9

The rain has now stopped. The air is steamy and mist is rising from the flowerbeds; the mountains behind the house are still covered in cloud, but the sky over my head is clear and bright again. The water will have washed away the mud challah loaf I made; there will be nothing there now to show that it ever existed. It was Béla Kárász who taught me how to make them, but I never learned how to plait them as beautifully as he did. He once brought me a tiny one with a letter baked inside it; he expected me to eat it, of course – he had no idea that in our house every little delicacy like that went straight to my father to break in half and the letter would fall out into his hand; there was a picture of two turtle doves kissing in one of its corners.

There are doves in my garden up on Eagle Hill. They always remind me of Ambrus. I love watching the way they flutter their wings, the assured way they swoop through the air. We once hit a pigeon, do you remember? We found it next to the car spread out in a strangely unnatural way, already dead. I sang a little dirge and you mumbled something, but we both felt very bad about it. Yesterday Elza was wearing a hat with a black pin through it, I couldn't keep my eyes off it; it ended in a dove with its wings spread wide. Elza's face has become a lot thinner and her nose is more pointed than when she was younger; she looks not so much Spanish now as Indian, and at the same time more conventional, more respectable, but her eyes are more restless than other people's, it's as if she's never quite sure that people aren't looking askance at her; she was arm in arm with Auntie Ilu and I spent some time watching the way they moved together and supported each other; next to Auntie Ilu's soft, yeasty-looking body Elza looked hard and bright, they were like a knife and a sponge laid side by side; Angéla was with them, it was as if she had two mothers, only she never once looked at either of them. Hovering between the two of them, or above them, invisible but almost palpable, Uncle Domi was their one great reality; I had to smile when that idea struck me, because he's been dead for so many years now.

It was you who told me he had died; you told me briefly and tactfully, in the midst of Auntie Ilu's shrieking, while Elza stood dry-eyed by the telephone trying to call the doctor. Today everything is sweetness and light between them: with the passing of the years Elza has come to be seen as a sort of second wife. That's only natural: Auntie Ilu has forgiven whatever there was to forgive, Elza has called no-one to account for her wasted years and everyone loves everyone else the way we are told to in the catechism; they put their hands together as in prayer and remember him; nothing but love and kind thoughts follow him into his tomb. On All Souls' Day they kneel side by side to sniffle and whimper over his bones, and every day of the year they give their memories a good shaking and airing and try to outdo each other over which of them has the more. Ugh! But they are absolutely at one in never taking their eyes off Angéla, they are like two anxious maters dolorosas. I have never been able to decide which of them I loathe the more. I think it must be Elza, because she has become so meek and virtuous in her old age.

The only thing missing is a picture of Emil, the same enlarged one of him surrounded by rosaries that they put on the flag in the university chapel – Emil the martyr, the guarantor of his family's livelihood, the domestic saint they were so secretly ashamed of while he lived, become the boy who redeemed himself and his name by the manner of his death, whose tiniest bones have been pressed into service.

And I have realised why Auntie Ilu's bedroom is so full of photos of him: baby Emil lying naked on his belly on a rubber blanket, Emil playing with a hoop, Emil in traditional all-white Hungarian costume, Emil with a feather in his school cap . . . ; once in 1945, when I was dashing off to a rehearsal, she was the first person of my acquaintance that I met; she stopped me, gabbled something about Angéla and her son-in-law, and something about Emil, and that he had died, their apartment had been plundered during the siege, Uncle Domi was ill, and what sort of thieving world had their unhappy son wanted for them? But as the years went by his image grew and grew, and now he is both a martyr and a true believer. I wondered what they would be cooking for Angéla's dinner that night.

How strange it is that Gizi spent her whole time on her knees facing us but not looking at anyone and not minding that it's what the Protestants do; and how interesting that I too was on my knees the first time I saw you.

"Noble sir, I am but a poor village maid, while you have been heaped with every blessing the Almighty can send; might you deign to touch my hand and be blessed for that, My Lord?" While I was down on my knees I became aware of a knot in the floorboard; I wasn't wearing trousers at the time but I was kneeling as if I was, the line was the cue for Pipi, who was playing Bluebeard, but he didn't pick it up, he was standing looking the other way, into the auditorium, and he could see what I couldn't, because I had my back to it. "Would you grant me your blessing, My Lord?" I asked him again, but he just ran off the stage and Pécsi, Ványa's predecessor, yelled something at me, I stood up and turned round, and there you were standing in the doorway with everyone hanging about your neck, hugging and kissing you. I was really annoyed. I sat down beside Pécsi, waiting impatiently to get on with the rehearsal – I really don't enjoy being interrupted like that – and then they led me over to you. I had real difficulty in all the hubbub working out that it was you, the translator of Shakespeare, the English specialist in the team. Eventually the rehearsal started again; you took a seat and kept making remarks from time to time, which again irritated me: I didn't see why I should have to put up with that.

I knew who you were of course; ever since 'forty-five people had been grieving over you because you were a prisoner of war; the theatre had made great efforts to get you out because without you nothing could happen: you had translated the new *Romeo and Juliet* and all the Shaws, and I knew that you also worked in the English Department at the university. Someone had said that you were married and your wife had missed you so much that she had hardly ever gone out into the street; that evening, back in my room, I mimicked you and the way you had stood there like a Christmas tree, with the whole company hanging like Christmas presents from your branches and a little smile on your lips, gazing at the backdrop, the one with the medieval map of Paris on it – it had already been lowered for the first performance. I copied the way you stood there look- ing over everyone's head, not in a coldly distant sort of way, you just weren't interested in anything that wasn't to do with the theatre. I practised it in the mirror for so long I couldn't look any other way myself. I once gave you a demonstration of what you are like when you really turn your attention to something.

*

The going is easier now, the rain fell plentifully on the already soggy marshland. I left Gizike's shoes under the marble cover at the top of the staircase, a little surprise for anyone who comes along. The water butt is half-full of slimy green water; the fresh rain churned up the slippery muck at the bottom. I've just this moment peered at my face in it, I had remembered the way you studied me, so attentively, as I knelt on the stage to deliver Joan's speech to Pipi, looking much as I always did only a bit paler than usual, with some red greasepaint around my mouth – I must have smudged it when I was standing in the chapel sobbing into my hands. Anyway, I pulled my mouth in, tucked my hair behind my ears so that it lay as flat as yours does, and peered into the water barrel, copying the way you used to look – but not for long, the likeness was so good I couldn't bear it anymore; I might have been your younger brother, so very like you and at the same time so unlike, just an image on the surface of the water, caught inside the rim of the barrel, a colourless face in a circular frame.

I'm whistling because I really don't want to cry. "The spring wind brings the rain, my flower, my flower." Juli brought you flowers, blue immortelles, the ones that last so long; I didn't bring you anything, I just stood there clutching my door key in my hand. Juli noticed and looked away pointedly. You can always tell what she's thinking – when she thinks about something and turns it over in her mind, she puts her index finger to her lips at the corner of her mouth; if she despises someone, she raises her eyes and stares at them scornfully – that was the look she gave me yesterday. If I do something to annoy her while she's dressing me she tightens the belt round my waist till I almost turn blue. I adored the black uniform I was wearing when I was burned in *Joan:* "I, Joan, a miserable sinner, confess that I am guilty." The new Personnel Manager will be expecting to see me; this is about the time I am supposed to be in the theatre. Will he be just like the others? When they first pestered me for a CV I wrote down everything that had happened to me – my father, mother, grandmother, the way they abandoned us . . . even Ambrus – but somehow it was also about Aunt Irma and her shoes, not in so many words of course but there to be read between the lines. When the last one called me in he underscored a passage with his finger: there was no point, he said, in trying to hide anything, everything would come out in the end and it would only make difficulties for me. But he wished me no harm, he assured me, all I had to do was to write down the truth, what really happened; I had proved myself sufficiently at Margaret Island in 'forty-five. I had shown there how much I had changed, but I really must write the truth, blah, blah, blah.

He didn't look very much like Father Dobay – he was tall and grey-haired, in comparison, like a modern forty-year-old St Imre, good-looking, cultured and severe – but he did bring him to mind, and I immediately knew what he wanted. When I left his room half an hour later he was radiant; it's ridiculously easy to make those people happy. He was responsible for my first major prize, and when I was given it he shook my hand and growled at me benevolently. If he wouldn't accept the truth or bear to hear it said, then I could always tell him lies – thank God there wasn't a stone left of the house I created for him, and my father and mother were in their graves, so there was nothing to contradict my story. "What a long way she has come!" the last Party boss declared admiringly. But of course! A long way indeed. It makes them all so happy to hear about how I grew up in the lap of luxury, how carefully I was raised, how my governesses took such good care of me, especially the last of them, called Elza, and how ignorant I was, having only ever lived on the sunny side of life shut away from the real world. The story grew with every telling; in the last one I concocted I had a horse all of my own, I used to ride him on the family estate at St Marton out on the Puszta, wearing a soft, broad-brimmed hat and carrying a white whip. Once they had seen me with that wheelbarrow I could have been anyone I pleased.

On New Year's Eve we had dinner in the Margaret Island holiday resort owned by the theatre. At midnight we went out onto the terrace to look at the snow and the hoar frost on the trees and I started to laugh, but it wasn't at what Hella had just said, I was looking back through the glass door watching the opera people dancing and all looking so beautiful and self-assured, and I remembered what they looked like in their finery after the place was bombed during the siege and the trade union officials ordered us to clean up the rubble after the next union meeting; all that was left of the building was the cellar; the ground and first floors had fallen into it. When Hella caught sight of it she was left speechless, and the singers complained that it would damage their voices – all that digging and hauling bricks about – and Pipi wailed that he had rheumatism so he for one couldn't push a wheelbarrow, then they started to finger the shovels gingerly and hobble about on supposedly stiff legs and they started coughing. I sat on a small pile of rubble for a few minutes laughing at them and watching the actors moaning and groaning, then I shot up to the top of the heap and started throwing down bricks and bits of metal – I'm not as strong now as I was in 'forty-five, and I still had full movement in my wrists then, from chopping firewood and mixing bran; a couple of the choir members followed me nervously, then the men became ashamed of themselves and started scratching about in the fallen rubble, though none of them actually knew how to use a pick. Pipi kept whining and whimpering and quoting *Lear*.

Kertész, the Party secretary, worked alongside me. I was aware of him throwing me occasional glances, but we didn't speak. I was quick, adept and perfectly natural; I didn't stand about dreaming and emoting, like Dorottya Kanizsai, I was actually enjoying the activity after the endless hours of memorising scripts and rehearsals. It was only years later that Kertész told Pipi that it said in my record that I had "completely extricated myself from my class background, and had managed to tear myself out of my old environment". He and I had been mixing concrete on that same terrace where you and I had stood that New Year's Eve; it was even written up in the local newspaper. I never met a Party official who had any imagination. Unlike Father Dobay, the school chaplain.

At first I tried to tell him the truth, but he wasn't up to it either; when I started to whisper through the grille for the third time that I didn't think I had committed any sins in the last week he flew into a rage and hauled me off to the staffroom; he told them I was obdurate and stubborn and did not love Christ. I then realised what I really should have said – that I had stolen that egg, or the string of garlic, that I had been eavesdropping in Ambrus' loft and every time I was left alone in Kárász néni's kitchen I licked the half-whipped cream; but the egg wasn't for me, I needed it for my father, and the peasant woman still had fifty of them left, and when I stole that string of garlic in the market I hadn't deliberately set out to steal, I just felt the need to do something exciting, something that would make them chase after me because I was so happy that Angéla had at last got into trouble, and the cream was sweet and soft and she still had a whole bowl full of it, vanilla-flavoured, and at home everything like that went straight to my father. I told the Reverend Father a string of lies simply out of pride, because I was ashamed to tell him the truth, and I worshipped my father and didn't want people to say bad things about him, and of course I cursed and swore, but everyone who has to do real work does exactly the same: I've cut my hand often enough with an axe and I know how hard it is to lift the tub over the fence for the pigs. I could have told him anything, although I didn't think I had done anything wrong: but I deliberately didn't tell him I had taught wrong things to Gizike so that she would fail. If she passed I wouldn't be giving her any more lessons, and I couldn't help people without charging because I needed the money to live on, and because others depended on me.

He pestered me for weeks about my "spiritual life", until I

got thoroughly bored and gave in. He was so pleased when I cracked; he felt that he was leading me down the True Path. The sins I confessed to poured forth like water. I made my parents' lives a misery, I stuffed myself with food and drink; I had a new sin for him every week, sobbing and choking before the grille, watching all the time to see the pleasure it gave him. Of all my teachers he was the only one who stuck by me; when I left the school he blessed me and gave me a St Antony carved in ivory. I sold it straight away to Baum bácsi, the jeweller.

I didn't sell the St Antony medallion you gave me, I threw it into the Danube. You were standing with your back to me and you thought I had thrown a handful of pebbles because I kept throwing them and I still had several more in the palm of my hand. That evening I was very happy, do you remember? Every so often you put your fork down to look at me; you had no idea what was going on in my head. I could have danced and sung at the thought that that medallion was at the bottom of the river, but when you undressed and pulled everything out of your pockets and weren't able to flash its silver sheen in my eyes, you didn't get the same bitter taste in your mouth that I had, the feeling of having been poisoned. Once it had gone missing and you had looked for it everywhere and not found it, and then seen me sitting with my legs hanging over the side of the bed, swinging them to and fro and whistling a little tune, you should have realised that something was wrong, that there was a reason why I couldn't bear to wear your little keepsake and didn't want to. But you found a little hole in your pocket and blamed it on that. You never suspected me for a moment – and that is why all this has happened.

If you had had just a moment's suspicion, if it had occurred to you just once to look at me, even for a second, really look at me, with the same kind of interest you showed when you looked at my body, which you knew even better than I did, perhaps you might have noticed how much distress you had unwittingly caused me, and you might have realised that I was trying to tell you about the diffused but unremitting pain that you gave me with your endless reminiscences, your stories about your past, the names of all those foreign dishes, and when you pointed out which storey of all the buildings it was that you had lived on when you were first married, and the awe and respect you felt for your new friend who had been already married for two years and seemed to you as old and wise as Methuselah. Whenever you went on like that I would jump up and tear handfuls of leaves from the branches of a tree and clown around and encourage you to carry on and tell me everything – and after that I would never set foot in that street again. Pipi took the brunt of my outbursts of rage. I tied ribbons in his hair as if he were a sick baby and rocked him back and forth, and when he got a headache I plied him with aspirin and made him walk with me arm in arm for hours around the city centre, because I was hoping that after your evening seminar you would come out of the university and "happen" to see us wandering around as if we couldn't bear to be apart, and all the time Pipi was sobbing and cursing and begging me to let him be – he was freezing cold, he would have no voice the next day, so why in the name of Christ did we have to drag ourselves up and down the streets like prisoners in an exercise yard? Why didn't I just let him go home? The fact is, I love you. More than I loved my mother. More even than I loved my father.

An old fellow has just come alongside me; he's got a lunch box in one hand and a watering can in the other. Why a watering can when there is water all over the path already? He hasn't acknowledged me, but I am sure he knows who I am. I ought to rush over to him, pluck the lunch box from his hand and tell him he has no need to be here, the birds are singing again, so why don't we both just clear out? I'm sure if he knew what I was thinking the poor old fellow would run a mile, taking his watering can with him.

I think the second time I really looked at you carefully was three days before the premiere of *Joan*. We had just left the theatre, you were going back to the university and I was on my way to Zugló, to the school where I was going to adjudicate a verse-speaking competition; we were standing at the bus stop and you told me you would be bringing your wife to see the play. That evening, when I mimicked the expression you had had, what I saw in my own face made me realise that you had been watching me intently, almost furtively, your gaze was so tense and searching it was as if you were calculating something. I have often copied the way you looked at me that evening, especially your forehead: your mouth and eyes give nothing away but your brow furrows up anxiously. Pipi had often said that you came to the theatre so often because of me but I always dismissed the idea; my mother had recently died, I was tired and depressed, and I spent a lot of time wandering aimlessly round my apartment, which I hated – it was right in the city centre, walls everywhere, a mean little balcony and a tiny square of sky; I was earning a great deal of money by then but I just stashed it away in a little iron safe, the way Juszti always did. They said of me in the local paper that I dressed unostentatiously and observed the simple ways and serious-mindedness of a true Socialist actress; it never occurred to them that I was just mean. You know how much I begrudge every penny I spend. On one occasion, just to annoy me, you smeared cake cream all over the bathroom floor. I yelled with rage and scraped it up with a knife while you split your sides laughing at the idea that I was actually prepared to eat it.

*

The way I did Joan was very different from the way I have played every role since. I used to think of myself that once on stage I became the person I was acting – Ophelia or Desdemona, or Tünde in the Vörösmarty. But in *Joan* I always knew that I was simply being myself, and in the premiere I acted that way for the first and last time in my life. Pipi used to keep an eye on the audience to see if anyone of importance was out there; I never bothered to look, I had neither the interest nor the time for it, I was too busy going mad or being strangled or having to run. Once I was in role I really couldn't open a door that was supposed to be stuck, when they stabbed me I was absolutely terrified, and when someone rushed at me the blood drained from my hands and I felt sick with fear. For me, every stone in the set was a real one, and the moment the interval began I knew exactly who I was, that the stone walls were nothing more than canvas nailed to a wooden frame, and I smiled and bowed and it all seemed to me really rather comical – the beaming faces and the clapping hands and the shouts of applause, and I had to force myself not to burst out laughing. I wasn't interested in what happened afterwards, it was the acting I loved.

At the end of the first act I stood in front of the curtain looking out to my right, because Pipi had said that you were in the first box on that side, with your wife, and I wanted to see your face and gather from it what you thought of the play now. When I finally picked you out amid the uproar you were standing there with your hands behind your back, the way you always do, the only person in the theatre who wasn't clapping, and there was a woman standing beside you beating her hands together in their dainty little gloves; she was wearing a hat, a comical little hat with something shiny on top that glittered in the light of the chandelier as she nodded and smiled at me; but you just stood there, and I forgot to make my bow. The audience went wild, but I kept looking at you, taking in the fact that the woman beside you nodding and clapping her tiny little hands was Angéla.

10

The old fellow has put down his watering can, opened his lunch box, and is now sitting on a bench with it perched on his knee; he's eating something bright red and he keeps wiping his eyes; his meal must be cold, it isn't exactly steaming. Paprika potatoes – eaten cold they must taste like soap. After I left the hospital on Tuesday they served me something similar-looking in the Swan, I have no idea what it was, but I ate it all the same, all I remember of it is the colour, bright red. It was Gizi's day off, Tera was standing in for her, she leaned over into the cubicle with her ugly blond face and asked, "Would you prefer to wait?" Force of habit had led me to the last place we sat, the cubicle at the end; it was six-thirty, their slack period, I was the only person there, I muttered something barely comprehensible, but Tera doesn't care what people say, as soon as she saw it was me she brought a black coffee, put the menu and a bottle of sparkling water – the usual Parádi – down on the table, and two glasses. I read the names of the dishes on the menu and drank the coffee; the table had just been scrubbed, it smelled of soap and caustic soda; the last time we were there I arrived really late because of my rehearsal, you had waited for so long and were so bored you drew a picture of yourself on the table, standing on one leg, with a long beard you had grown while you waited for me. It took me a while to pluck up the courage to look in that particular corner, then I remembered that the top had been cleaned that day so it couldn't possibly still be there; when I did finally look there was nothing left of it, only the little points of grain raised by the fierce scrubbing. Tera looked in on me again, like a patient cow, opened the bottle of spring water and filled the two glasses.

"He's late today," she said. I gave her a cold stare to shut her up, but you know how stupid she is, she just stood there staring at me with a big smile on her face. She commented on how red my face was – I certainly felt hot – and she stood up on tiptoe and started the ventilator. I asked for something to eat but I have no idea what it was; she brought it, looking very offended, and shrugged as she set it down before me; she hates anything out of the usual and she'd never seen me eating on my own before. I ate two mouthfuls, put my fork down and started on the water, taking first from one of the glasses and then from the other; she was still hovering around the table, I could see from her face that she was flustered but also very happy that she was on duty that day instead of Gizike – the next morning she would be spreading the news around that I waited for you in vain, I had had to eat on my own and I had paid for myself.

"Would you like to leave a message for him?" she asked as I was leaving; I exploded with laughter even though the tears were streaming from my eyes. She couldn't understand why, but because from the very first I had always behaved differently from what she expected, she probably just thought that I had responded to her question in my usual sulky way. But what she had said was so ridiculous, so wildly hilarious, that I had to prop myself up against the wall while I finished laughing; when I looked back I saw that her face was still clouded in confusion. I had imagined you arriving at the door, stepping inside and peering around, asking for the menu and starting to draw on the table because I had gone and I clearly wasn't coming back; meanwhile Tera had noticed the blood on your shirt, crossed herself, worked herself up into a tizz, sicked herself and rushed out with her skirts flying up around her fat bottom. The message I asked her to give you was that I was going home and that I wouldn't be coming back the next day, neither for lunch nor dinner; she pinned her ears back and kept opening and closing her mouth, because it was such an appalling thing to say and she couldn't imagine what the consequences would be when she told you – with none of the usual winking at you with her fat eyelids and nodding to where I would be sitting waiting for you. The place smelled of roast meat and beer and salad dressing; they had only bottled beer on Tuesday evenings because the barrels ran dry; when I got to the door I didn't turn round, and I didn't look back once I was in the street, I kept my eyes on the tower and the sky. Dusk was falling.

When I got home the house was in complete darkness. I thought that Juli wasn't in, but she was, she was sitting in the kitchen waiting for me with a prayer book in her hand; when I turned the lights on she clapped her hand to her eyes, stood up, came up really close to me and studied my face intently. I was wearing my green dress, the "indecent" one, the one that when I take the bolero off you can see my naked back. She hated that dress; she never washed it when I asked her to – if I wanted it cleaned I had to do it myself. She grabbed hold of it for a second, as if she wanted to haul me out of its depths, I took a step back and we stood there looking at one another. Her round peasant face was the colour of clay but completely expressionless, as was mine.

The fireplace was cold, there were no cooking utensils to be seen and there was nothing to eat; I opened the fridge, but there was nothing there either; the only remark I heard from her that day was that there was no food: we were going to fast. I went and lay down, she came in right behind me, kicked her slippers off, climbed up onto the sofa and took my candle-holders down from the top shelf; in one of them she had put a coloured candle, the half-blue spiral type that we always lit on your name day, in the other one there was a white kitchen candle that she had already lit; she put them down on the windowsill and went out. The phone rang in the other room; she picked the receiver up and promptly put it down again; I could hear the click as she pulled the cord out and it went dead. The shadows were soft and homely in the candlelight; I took the pillow out from under the bedcover and pulled it over my eyes. Through it and my closed eyelids I could just about make out the candle flame, and two images instantly came to me.

In the first I was leading the usual funerary candlelit procession, with Pipi and Hella following me and Péter Pap and Suci bringing up the rear; we were like a bunch of overgrown primary school children, each with a candle in our hand, and Ványa calling out: "Concentrate, would you please concentrate! Take it naturally, don't try to shade it, one-two, one-two, slowly but naturally . . ." and we went, like horses being taken to water, only this was round and round, holding the candles, with Pipi whispering wicked things in my ear from time to time.

In the other image I saw Angéla; she opened the door of their apartment to me, there were candles on the radiator in the living room and smaller ones flickering everywhere – it was like a muted *Te Deum* or a great family celebration; red button candles blazed in the lobby, and you laughed and put your arm around her shoulder for a moment, like a father proudly showing off his daughter, and she danced around me, danced and clapped her hands; the table was heaped with flowers, and something swooped down through the shimmering gloom and settled on her shoulder, a blue parrot, and I noticed its cage, it had sneaked out of the open door, it was the same lyre-shaped cage with the golden grid and the green bird in it that she had been holding in that memorable dawn.

"My dear Eszter," she said, "dear, dear Eszter." She was love incarnate, a little flame of light; she took my hand and pulled me after her, and I went obediently, laughing a bright, slightly hysterical kind of laugh, as if we were real childhood friends and everything in that room delighted me – her portraits on the wall, the balcony, the flowers, the door handle, everything; her little fingers were like flames, mine were ice-cold, when she touched me she must have felt the scar on my palm from that wound when I caught my hand on the axe. She left the lights off while she brought the turkey in, she had roasted it to a bright red, with pink potatoes rolling on a platter, and the silver carving knife shone in your hand. When I saw the meal I uttered a delighted "Wonderful, I'm starving!" and you gave me a look – you had spent so much time with us you instantly recognised the actressy tones – but then you smiled and you too believed in me, you always do when I'm being sweet, and I rolled up my sleeves so that I could do full justice to the meal; I stuffed myself and took a potato and drew moustaches on my face and Angéla's; you weren't to know that when I stood up, made my bow in thanks for the dinner and then held up the two candles, I was secretly longing to hurl one of them at your desk and your books and papers and the other at Angéla, to light everything up properly.

After dinner she made black coffee in the kitchen, singing as she did, then she suddenly cried out that she had remembered that when we did *János Vitéz* she had never seen me as Iluska because she had been ill that night, so I dashed into the kitchen. I gathered up all the tea towels on the drying rack, threw two of them over my shoulder and hooked one onto my dress to serve as an apron – and instantly became a peasant maiden. You became very serious, as you always do when I am acting, and everyone else did as well; I knelt before the watery-blue Persian carpet and sang as I washed and wrung out the fourth of the tea towels; Angéla clasped her hands together and looked on in wonder, laughing until the tears ran down her face at this person who was no longer me but a little girl, kneeling in front of her Persian carpet doing the laundry; the transformation was so perfect that she danced and clapped and flung herself at you and kissed you in delight, and you laughed too – at the little girl doing the laundry in your living room, the sweet and solemn little orphan girl who was now lamenting in her childish soprano that she had no father or mother to care for her, but all the time I was singing I was thinking about the semolina and the fawn, and the herd of cattle at the inn, and Auntie Irma's shoes and everything – and again my father sprang into my mind: he was standing before me; he had a ribbon sewn round the edge of his jacket because it was so badly frayed, and my mother was at his side, looked at him anxiously and asking him something, looking very worried, but he just smiled; when I saw that smile I took myself off to the woodshed and leaned my head on the board where I chopped the firewood because the ribbon was horrible, really horrible, only once I had sewn it on I couldn't work out why it had to be so cheap and awful; and I heard my father praising me for my beautiful sewing. "Where's my little girl?" he asked, and they decided that I must have gone off to see Ambrus or

Kárász néni, but by then I was sitting on the floor using my calloused index finger to draw circles in the sawdust.

I finished my little number and stood up; I was still in my Iluska costume but once again myself. I laughed and noticed that the two of you were also laughing; Angéla had enjoyed herself so much she had to blow her nose. Seeing her laugh brought back the sight of her with the parrot on her shoulder squawking away and the turquoise feathers caught up in the black coils of her hair and the way she spoke to it filled me with rage: she was going to pay for her entertainment! I threw off the tea towels and stood facing the two of you in the full light. I stood as tall as I could, with a slight stoop, put my left hand into my pocket and pushed out my chin: I was no longer a woman, but a man. She immediately stopped laughing and stared at me. She could see the black suit I was wearing, the pearl-grey cravat, and the white scarf I had just that moment wrapped round my neck as I stepped out of the children's room; she put her hand in front of her eyes and the tears poured out through her fingers. "How are you, Angi?" someone else's voice asked through my mouth – a deep, rather pleasant voice with a slight musical lilt. You gave her a handkerchief but she was beyond comfort: the delightful evening was over. She wept and wept, she was weeping for Domi bácsi, the festive candles were all in vain, in vain the aroma of roast turkey and coffee: Domi bácsi had appeared amid the flames – and yet he wasn't there at all because I was there in his place, once again my real self, and she wept on your shoulder, "Oh, Papa, Papa!"

When the time came for me to leave I realised that she now loved me more than ever: one look from me and her father had been back in the room again. She kept squeezing my hand, rubbed her tear-sodden face against mine and murmured how much she longed to be with me; her beautiful lips and eyes were wet with tears. "What a delightful evening," I said, and thanked her for the dinner.

11

The old fellow is now washing up. He went over to the water barrel and rinsed out his lunch box; I'm pretending that I'm not watching him, I don't want to embarrass him.

Now he's leaving, with the watering can and the lunch box banging together as he goes. Poor old chap, there must be something wrong with the sole of his shoe because he's limping at every step. I think I was never happier than when you took me to buy shoes.

It isn't true that I didn't notice you from the very start. I am constantly observing things, places, objects, people – I do it all the time without realising. Hella is the same, and so is Pipi. I know your face and every inch of your body so well that I could model you in the sand beneath my feet. When you leave me in the street and set off home I always turn round and watch you go, following the rhythm of your footsteps. Once, in our early days together, you came into my dressing room; there was a small spot on your necktie and it bothered you so much you covered it with your hand; another time you had banged your head in a taxi and there was a large bruise on your fore-head. In the theatre I always kept my eye on the door to see when you arrived. Hella, who is the biggest gossip in the world, told everyone, including the firemen, that I was in love with you even before I was, and that I was still waiting for you to say the word. I would sit beside you like a good, wise sister and ask you all about Angéla, but I was trying to work out whether you knew why you came there so often to see me or whether I would have to give you a little help to realise why you did. One half of my heart leaped up at the thought that you were deceiving her by coming to the theatre, the other half hated you because you slept in the same bed as she did, drank from the same glass and bathed in the same bathtub. I hated you because in your moments of intimacy you would have had special names for each other that no-one else knew, and that one day, in a moment of forgetfulness, our two bodies, hers and mine, would blur in your physical memory and you would use that special name for me – but I also longed for that moment, because I would then know for certain that I had taken you from her.

We spoke about her a lot and it really irritated me. It took all my strength to stop you noticing how much I hated talking about her. It was all very confusing in those days because I really did want to know about her, about how easily she caught a cold, and how she had to look after her ears so carefully, and how hard she was working at the Women's Association and yet she still had to prepare your meals and she was often in so much of a hurry that she ruined them and cried and the tears fell in the soup and she would hunker down, the dear little thing, in her flame-red kimono, and she looked at you so with such a sad expression on her face that your heart longed to help her in her heart's desire. How brave of you! How loyal! To smooth the way forward for those delicate shoulders, so very unused to real work and now labouring under the burden of Emil's legacy! Angéla the convener of seminars, the constant presence at the orphanage, forever improving herself, her eyes glued to the copy of Karl Marx in German that Emil left behind and buying all the latest books on Party ideology. When people were turned away from the butcher's because there was no meat to be had she opened her eyes wide in astonishment and the tears flowed down her cheeks, and when she got home she took an economics book off the shelf to find out why there was nothing for sale. A very large book, to be sure.

Yes, we laughed at her, but you were always just a little moved by all this, and so was I. I made my eyes fill with tears and declared how she had been just the same as a child, so self-sacrificing, and I knew that it was true – that she would always take on other people's problems, and shoulder all sorts of impossible burdens – and again the rage rose up in me, because she always had the time and the means to do that sort of thing, she had no other business than to be the benefactor of mankind. How good she was, you once said, to dash about hither and thither to get you an early release from the prisoner-of-war camp, and lug your manuscripts in an impossible wooden box from one cellar to the next, and fish out your desk lamp and your mother's childhood photograph from the rubble when your apartment was hit by that bomb.

And now she lives for her brother's memory and wants to carry on his work. Your tone was deadly serious, and appreciative and full of feeling. "Dear, dear Angéla," I whispered, but I was choking with rage. Emil, the tall, slender Emil, what a substantial figure he has become, so much more impressive than his father, for all his service as a judge and his daughter's lacquered fingernails and the three-stranded gold necklace around Auntie Ilu's neck – Angéla holding that bird in her hand once again, dandling her latest toy, smiling her wonderful smile at the sky. "Give me your hand, Angi," murmurs the immortal Emil. "Come, I shall lead you on." She follows him, and instantly her old existence is rolling away under her foot like a ball, and the Movement gives strength to her poor weak back; once she poured out cups of tea at lavish parties for her father's colleagues in the judiciary, now it is milk into the mugs of the children of the liberation heroes. She has become "the younger sister of Emil Graff". No-one thinks of her now as the daughter of the late Justice Graff.

One afternoon in 1948 I was leaving the theatre rather late when I realised that I had left my new script in the dressing room. I was on my own; Pipi, Hella and Suci were still at a Party members' meeting. I ran up to the second floor, grabbed the script, gathered up the empty jars on the table and threw them into my bag to take to the recycling centre. On my way back down I heard the sounds of a discussion filtering through the door of No. 12: "Because the Future that we all want to build for ourselves . . ." It was a voice I didn't recognise, a man's voice, so I stopped. "The Future . . ." That was something I had no desire to build. I had enough of the past about me already for the thought to do anything but horrify me. "The Future." The door opened and out came Ványa, but the conversation carried on behind him. His stare froze, I raised my bag and felt myself blush. "This meeting," he said, "is for Party members only. Are you waiting for someone?" The jars in my bag clinked loudly as I fled down the staircase.

Dear little Angéla – she sat with us in the theatre, she accompanied us to restaurants; by then you were going everywhere with us, with me and the other actors too; we all took coffee together, and if you and I happened to sit next to each other we always talked about Angéla. I told you about the bedroom she slept in as a child, and her books – and all the while I was watching the way you looked at me. I was waiting for you to put an end to this stupid chatter and say what I really wanted you to. I had begun to hate you – as if you had dragged me along with you into something shabby and tasteless. What I wanted to happen between us seemed to me perfectly natural and necessary; all that sitting around rabbiting on about Angéla sometimes took all the strength I could summon to bear it.

I had to wait so long for you to speak out at last, and to kiss me. We were in your room at the university, we tore the manuscript of the end of the first act of *King Lear* out of your typewriter and Pipi dashed off to the theatre with it. I stayed behind, though it was now evening; Angéla's picture was there on the table opposite me – the only thing that made the sight of it bearable was the thought of the pain it would cause her now if she had seen you holding out your arms to me. You closed your eyes and gave yourself up to the kiss; I just watched you. Your face was full of sorrow, the arch of your eyelids showed only sadness, no passion. Your suffering made me choke with revulsion; your conscience was tormenting you and afterwards you would go home and be even nicer to her than usual to make up for what had happened between the two of us.

That night in Szolnok you were really worried because you couldn't work out what was the matter with me; I had started to cry because you had told me that it was such bliss to hold me in your arms for the first time that it hurt, that the feeling was so overwhelming that it caused you pain and suffering. "I had so desperately wanted to know that you loved me," you said, and my eyes filled with tears; I lay beside you in the bed, limp and relaxed in your arms, but it was all pretence, inside I was cold and rigid: I was thinking what you must be like when you embraced Angéla, and I hated you.

But I never hated Elza, and I never felt more sympathy for her than the day she suddenly appeared on my doorstep. It was a Sunday morning, Juli was away at her church, and I opened the door myself. I knew at once what had brought her. I helped her take off her coat and gloves; I was filled with a wild exhilaration as I let her in. She was about to sit in the chair you always sat in, but she just perched on the side of the armchair, as if she wanted to maximise the discomfort she was feeling. She went on and on; I could see she was thoroughly embarrassed and I took pleasure in observing it.

You remember the first time you left the theatre with me; when we got to the Korvin department store in Rákóczi Street Angéla suddenly emerged, walking ahead of us, her burgundy red dress glowing in the summer light. You slowed down and waited for me to follow suit, but I simply walked faster; you thought I hadn't noticed who was just ahead of us and you caught hold of my wrist. I pulled it away. At that moment I loathed you as much as ever; it was just like before, the same old conflict and suffering. I turned round and started to run. Behind the theatre the Megyer bus was about to leave, so I jumped onto it. Did you never realise that I actually wanted us to catch up with her, the two of us together? I wanted to see her face turn white against the burgundy dress as she stared at me in confusion.

I made Elza a cup of tea – I had remembered that she preferred it to coffee. I lit a cigarette and listened to her moaning, in fact I felt rather sorry for her: Auntie Ilu was so very tactless, she really should have come herself; she, Elza, knew that I knew all about her, so it must have been especially difficult for her to bring the subject up.

"You're a clever girl, Eszter," she said to her teacup. "All I want is to spare you something that sooner or later . . . Only you can talk to Lőrinc; Ilu can't and I certainly couldn't. It would be terrible if Angéla noticed. The poor dear still doesn't know anything."

She put down her cup and gazed at me. I put mine down as well and smiled.

"Someone will have to tell her," I replied.

She clasped her hands together and stared at me. She was speechless. She was the one person who might even for a moment have seen through into the hatred that lay inside me; only she could have realised that I was just waiting for the time when someone told Angéla about you and me; and she was the only person who understood that if she really wanted to help her she would have to say nothing.

12

Well, she certainly knows now.

She didn't find out the way I had always wanted her to, or when, but at least she does know.

When I was coming out of your hospital room on Tuesday I almost bumped into her; she was standing behind the frosted glass door, close enough for it to blur her image and conceal any suspicion that she was listening. It was already quite dark in the corridor and the wall lamps, shaped like red crosses, were already on; when I pushed the door open the light from your bedside lamp flooded the entrance and she clapped her hands in front of her eyes at the sudden blaze. I don't know what her face looked like because it was covered by her palms. Elza and Ilu were standing together next to the laundry basket embracing each other and crying, and Péter's cage was on top of it; the bird was swinging back and forth and banging its bell every so often with its beak; Angéla's handbag had been left in the doorway – I almost stumbled on it when I went out.

There were now more people in the corridor than when I

arrived; a nurse came bustling in and busied herself by re-arranging the flowers on the stand, then a doctor went and stood beside her and the two of them started whispering and nodding from time to time; the professor was standing with Gyurica at the top of the stairwell, and when the door handle squeaked everyone turned to look at me. Auntie Ilu immediately looked away and started to sob even louder. Elza tried to stand up but Auntie Ilu stopped her; Angéla didn't move. I didn't speak, not even to greet them, I desperately wanted to sit down but I didn't, I left the room immediately, but I looked back when I got to the staircase; Angéla was just going in, followed by the professor, all I could see was her back, and Weltner putting his arm around her waist to help her through the door; when Gyurica stopped me at the lift, the doctor and the nurse stared at me as if I were some strange monster, and the two old women went on whimpering. Gyurica stammered that he had his car and would take me home, but I told him I couldn't go home, I had things to do, so he let me be and I went down on my own; the lift was noisy and stank, surgical spirit, carbolic acid and chlorine; on the second floor a girl was washing the stairs and singing a song about a round bun, very softly, so as not to disturb the patients.

When I got to the garden I just had to sit down; I went to the fountain, to the red-stained benches beside it, but they were all full of convalescing patients in hospital gowns chatting and smoking; I went up to the fountain and collapsed on the rim; the fine spray fell on my neck and I plunged my hand in up to the wrist, then someone told me not to disturb the fish so I pulled it out and placed it in my lap; everyone was laughing and happy, the sun was still shining, I looked up at your window, it seemed so strange – it was still daylight and yet the lights were on inside; no-one seeing it from outside would guess how gloomy every room and corridor was because the trees were even taller than the building and cut out the light; there were fruit flies swarming around the fountain, a young man blew his smoke at them, I couldn't smoke myself, I had nothing with me, not even my ID card, only a few crumpled ten-forint notes, change from the fifty I had paid for the taxi; the driver brought my handbag to the house later that evening.

I had never got to know this particular district. To me it's like a country town; I went past courtyards surrounded by wooden fences and single-storey houses with embroidered cushions on the windowsills and cats dozing behind the panes; the multi-storey hospital seemed to belong somewhere else, floating above the low houses, and the square belonged nowhere at all; the noise from the local bus terminal, the clattering trams and hooting buses were all too much for me, so I kept walking around the winding, unfamiliar streets; I never looked back, I kept my eyes on the Buda hills, the twilight air was bright and clear and I could make out the individual houses; one particular fleck of white stood out among the green and gold; it was mine, and I thought of Juli and walked even more slowly; there was a refuse lorry ahead of me and clouds of dust flew up every time they opened the lid.

The smell of fresh bread came wafting out of the door of a bakery; not since I was a child had I seen such crisply edged bread rolls and square brioches as the ones painted on the metal sign; I found a photographer's shop on the corner and stood for ages under the arched doorway staring at the pictures on display behind the reinforced glass; we had had similar pictures back at home, in Csoma bácsi's studio – the same naked babies and smirking soldiers; I hung about so long that the owner appeared at the top of the steps and I stopped staring and moved away; a child ran up to me with a milk can in his hand and some drops spilled onto my shoes; when I got to the ring road I had a sudden urge to look back, then I turned my head away – I only realised that there were tears in my eyes when some people stopped to stare at me; a woman took me by the arm and said something to me but I pulled my hand away; by the time I got to the Swan my eyes were completely dry. Angéla would have found my photograph in your briefcase by then.

I had long wanted to ask you to keep a different photo of me in your wallet, but the one you took of me at the lake three years ago, all so innocent, in stark black and white, was still there. You were so happy the day you developed it! It caught the whole of that summer in its little square frame – a bit of sky, a corner of the lake, a stray dog and me squatting down next to his square-shaped head with my basket full of apples on the ground in front of me, peering out between two strands of hair hanging down in front of me and smiling.

When you took it Angéla was still in bed asleep. You and I are both early risers; it was barely seven when you sent the maid to call me; you had arrived the night before, Pipi and I had reserved a room for the two of you, and we had all dined together at the Water Fairy. I sat between you and Pipi, facing Angéla, and I was watching to see if she noticed that your tone of voice had changed because you were so happy to be sitting beside me again. Dogs were prowling around between the tables begging for bones and fish heads, and Angéla was enjoying her sour yellow wine. You asked her to dance because she had remarked that it was years since she had last done so and she felt a sudden urge to now; Pipi groaned and complained about his stomach and put some bicarbonate of soda in his coffee, and I sat and watched the two of you spinning round and round on the concrete floor to the slow music, and sipped my coffee, never taking my eyes off you. Pipi went on moaning and complaining that he wouldn't be well enough to go to Badacsony the next day; Angéla's lilac cape was on the chair, you had brought it for her, she hates wearing it, Elza always had to take it to school after her and now it was your turn because she caught colds so easily and the evenings beside the lake would be chilly. I knew that you had been working hard for six unbroken weeks to raise the money for this summer holiday, and that you were never in a state to work on the days when you hadn't been able to be with me.

I asked Pipi to call for the bill: we would play a trick on you and steal away; he was very happy, it meant he could go and lie down, so we paid and left; when the dancing ended and you noticed that we weren't there we were already out in the park. Angéla told me on the beach the next day how worried you were not to have found us there.

When we got back to our rooms I put Pipi to bed, with a warm cover over his stomach because there was no hot water bottle, and went out again, down to the pier. The air was still, I could see the lights on the far side of the lake coming from the restaurant where I had left the two of you, and I could hear the music; someone was rowing across the lake and I could just catch the sound of the oars; the night was warm, and the sky was ablaze with stars. From then on I found it increasingly difficult to endure your company. If I could avoid it I never went to the phone when you rang, I never sat at the same table as you, I never let you kiss me, but I kept smiling and telling you I loved you, that every day I didn't see you was a meaningless one and I couldn't act if I couldn't see you; I knew that Elza was getting on Angéla's nerves and that Auntie Ilu had no idea what to do about her and that you were the only person Angéla would listen to, the only person who could get her to wear a scarf and not forget to eat something before she rushed off to care for the children at the orphanage. Which was named after Emil.

When you sent Manci for me the next morning it was so early I was still in the bathroom. I raced out to meet you happily with my locks flying round my head like an unruly little girl and begged forgiveness for walking out on you the night before. I went off with you for a stroll, through the next little village beside the lake, I had my little basket with me and we bought some apples from the vicar; I danced down the road half a step ahead of you, singing all the way, I made goat noises at a goat, shook my fist at cars and feigned terror when they hooted at me: I was all smiles, and at the same time I kept thinking of the room where Angéla was still asleep, the best room in that refurbished peasant's house with the Gobelin tapestry on the wall showing a Rococo Our Lady beside Jesus kneeling in the Garden of Gethsemane and gazing down from the picture at the two beds pulled side by side the night before to make an improvised marital one – after lowering the blind in the window so that the morning light wouldn't wake her too early.

It wouldn't have been quite so hard if your attachment to her had lessened even slightly, if I had noticed that since you had been with me you had behaved any differently towards her, but you took her with you wherever you went, you nearly killed yourself with translation work to pay for her clothes, you pandered to her every wish, you paid Auntie Ilu's phone bills and had an electric boiler installed for Elza because when Domi bácsi retired his pension and the compensation they received for Emil's death weren't enough for them to get halfway through the month . . . No, you were still just what you had always been, only you now happened to love me. So I kissed you according to the script I had written beforehand; I fell on my knees, made my waist and body completely relaxed and held your arm to regain my balance; it was the only way I could contain the hatred I felt towards you. You had become a burden to me, but one I couldn't get rid of. As we tripped along the path beside the lake I would rather have been anywhere than with you; the others were getting ready for Badacsony, I was desperately missing Pipi and Hella and everyone, I would even have put up with chatting to Ványa rather than stay where I was with you. "Wait a second, I'll take a picture of you," you said. We had got to the end of the path, where the poplars formed a double circle around a little clearing. A dog was running ahead of us, you lured him over to us and I squatted down beside him; all I wanted was to be back at home reading a book, or lying sunbathing with my head in Pipi's lap, or swimming out to the buoy with the straps of my swimming costume loosened – anything rather than be there with you, standing opposite me with your hand on the camera, with my hair falling over my face and the dog sniffing at me. "Smile, please," you said, and I smiled into the camera.

13

"Here lies Gyúla Sokoray, awaiting the resurrection promised by Jesus. Laid to rest by his inconsolable widow Klára Benedek Gyúla Sokoray."

I had nothing carved on my father's grave below his name, not even the date; I only put his name there because something was required. I know that once people are dead they mean nothing to anyone else.

My greatest joy as a child was when we went to the cemetery in early November to light candles on the graves; I was already looking out for them by the time we were up on the bridge, it was still quite a distance – our cemetery was on the other side of the railway line, beyond the raised embankment – but you could see the angel above the family crypt from all that way. When we arrived my mother always crossed herself and knelt for a moment at the entrance; we went to Grandfather Encsy's grave but we never dared go into the little chapel next to it – it was on a slight mound just above the crypt – because on All

Souls' Day the whole family would be there, it was where the Martons worshipped, and my mother didn't want to show herself because of my father. As we came nearer after crossing the bridge there was a clear view of the tombs; it looked like a carnival, with cheerful candles fluttering in the damp November gloom; it was the sort of place where they burn candles as thick as your arm, there was one near my grandfather's tomb of some army general, with a blazing red St Andrew's cross in the centre and glass candlesticks. I stole one once, the day after the festival, and kept it in the woodshed under a pile of sawdust. My mother always led me by the hand while my father ambled along behind us, but that was only in the early days, later he wasn't allowed to go out in damp weather and my mother wouldn't leave him on his own for even an hour. Our candles were as thin as my little finger. I set mine down on grandfather's grave, lit it and went from tomb to tomb marvelling at the different ways people were commemorated.

I went there once with Gizike and Angéla and the rest of the school; it was in the spring; our form tutor's husband was being buried; we sang beside the grave and didn't have to go back for lessons for the rest of the day. We walked there three abreast and Gizike and Angéla were talking about what sort of dress they would wear as brides. The cemetery wasn't as beautiful in the spring light as it is in November, when the sky hangs low over the ground – in spring the branches are so heavy with the damp you expect them to break and the graves lose their meaning and look incongruous in the strong sunlight. "I shall be married when I'm eighteen," Angéla announced, and Gizike repeated, in a meek little voice, "Me too, me too!" I kicked a clod of earth away. Angéla was now describing her veil and what the church would look like. We duly sang the funeral hymn, and on the way back they were still talking about their weddings; Gizike, sounding more confident now, was going through the reception menu, a long list of dishes, all tasting very different, and the drinks to go with them. Angéla listened distractedly, then they both started to question me. I just growled that I was never going to get married – it rather shocked them. The birds were chattering away above our heads, the form teacher wept, everything was merry and bright, spring-like and radiant; Angéla's face had turned red from the April sun; I thought, "Who on earth would marry me?" And in any case, I couldn't get married because I didn't have a white dress.

Last night, looking up at the picture of Juszti above Gizike's bed, I remembered how passionately I had once wanted you to die. She had just finished changing the compress on my foot and hadn't got back into bed; she was still sitting on the side next to me and looking at me very solemnly, almost expectantly, the way she did when she was a child and didn't understand something and was waiting for an explanation. I lowered my gaze; it wasn't the light that was worrying me, it was the look on her face; people only ever look at me like that when I am on stage, wearing wings and a wig, or when I happen to be playing a boy – otherwise you were the only person who ever looked at me that way, with an expression that seemed to ask if there was another face beneath my mask, the one you would really like to see. In the beginning, whenever we were together, that was the way you looked at me, and if Angéla was also with us, you looked at her that way too.

Angéla almost never asked for anything in restaurants. She ate very little and drank only the driest white wine; you would study the menu until you found something you thought she would like, and then she would eat it very slowly, almost reluctantly, giving you a grateful smile every so often, like a child. Once we dined together up in the Buda hills; Pipi was late, then he phoned to say he wasn't coming – he was chasing a girl at the time, a really young one. It was a wonderful evening, cold and hard, with light glittering on the mountains. Angéla had her coat on but was still feeling the chill; you were afraid she might catch a cold and suggested we go home; I didn't want to leave so I told you to go and leave me there; I watched you go all the way to the bus stop and get on, and I followed the bus down the winding road until it had dwindled to the size of a star. I read *Macbeth*, smoked a cigarette and enjoyed the chilly evening – my bare legs and arms were as cold and hard as stone – then I saw you coming back, making your way between the tables, your coat over your shoulder and your hand in your pocket, looking around for my table; I put the cigarette and the book down; you were surplus to requirements, I didn't want you, I was tired of you, I had been utterly bored watching you feeding Angéla, then taking her arm and guiding her over the crossroads, I had had it up to the neck with the two of you and it meant nothing to me that you loved me and had come back when you had to give two lectures the next morning at the university and you had told me while we were eating that you would have to work the whole night to finish the day's quota of translation.

As you got nearer I imagined what it would be like if you suddenly dropped dead; you would collapse in your stride, the waiters would rush over to you, people would bend over you, someone, me of course, would have to call Angéla, they would take your body away and I would carry on reading *Macbeth*; she would cry her heart out, the whole problem would have been resolved and I wouldn't have to be bothered with you anymore. People watched you as you came, it really made me smile, you were obviously far better known than I was, more people knew your face than knew mine, and you greeted people to right and left all the way, and then suddenly there you were standing beside me. You sat down in the chair you had recently vacated, told me you had put Angéla to bed, then reached out your hand to mine just as naturally as you always did wherever we were.

I tore my hand away, then immediately smiled at you and quoted *Macbeth*: "How now, my lord, / Why do you keep alone . . .?" Once again you couldn't tell whether I was just playing the fool or if I really was displeased to see you come back.

We sat there until dawn, talking about your mother and the dishes your father had liked and your little sister who died; you drank white wine, I drank soda water, and we smoked. I was only half listening to what you were saying, I had *Macbeth* open in front of me and was memorising the text; at one point I actually laughed out loud, I was thinking that here you were, nattering away, and you had no idea that you had dropped dead some time before, that I had killed you and you were now lying somewhere, down in the waiter's room or a junk room, Angéla had no idea that she was now a widow and that from now on no-one would be there to order her pancakes and caviar to tempt her to eat; watching you go down the hill in the taxi I was thinking that she would sleep on and you would have to work the whole of the next day to catch up. I was still living in the city centre at the time, you were kissing me as I stood waiting for the gate to open, "I shouldn't have kept you up so late," you said; you were now worried that I might be tired the next day, but going up in the lift I felt anything but tired and sleepy, I was so happy to be on my own again, to be able to make myself coffee and carry on studying *Macbeth*. I looked down from the window and saw you glance up at the light from it, and when you got to the corner you turned back to see if I was waving to you. It would have been Angéla who told you to go back up the hill and sit out the night with me, because you had spent the whole day sitting in your office, you needed a bit of fresh air, and it wasn't very nice to leave me there on my own. I didn't wave back, I just pulled down the blind.

*

"Here lies Gyúla Sokoray, awaiting the resurrection promised by Jesus . . ." I have never for a moment believed that I will see my father or mother again. Now that I think about it, it never occurred to me that Jesus' promise could possibly apply to me; growing up in the Barrage I often used to think that none of us would rise again, it was all so far away, life and death equally; I would go and eavesdrop outside the door of the other room and it would occur to me that one day even they would have to die. I would burst into tears and stumble back to bed. It was so painful to think that we had no place of our own in the church, as Juditka and my grandmother's family did, and we could only afford to put two fillér in the collection at Mass, so how could we ever rise again? Suddenly the light from a candle flickered on the bedroom wall, Ambrus was pottering around, he would surely be saved, I thought, he had pigs and a large pan for boiling plums and a pile of bran in his storeroom. The greatest hope I had then was that at least my father might be saved; he was gentle, he talked to the flowers, he never hurt anyone, while I cursed and swore, stole and told lies, and my mother had a lot of hatred pent up inside her, so we wouldn't be going anywhere; and then I thought that perhaps my father would be able to get my mother in with him and I would be the only one left behind, because nobody loved me; it seemed the most natural thing in the world that no-one should, it never surprised me and I was never offended by the thought; instead I was rather amazed when anyone was drawn to me, people like Gizike or Pipi, but then Gizike had grown up with me and Pipi was a fellow actor. Here in the theatre we have a sort of secret bond – we love and hate one another just a little, it goes with the profession; the feelings are never straightforward but they are very strong and they bond us together; you and I are bound in much the same way. At first I revelled in the idea, but later it began to annoy me, because she was somehow always with you; you plied her with food and made her drink, you wrapped her up warm, you took her away on holiday, you offered her your handkerchief when she forgot her own and you visited the children in the orphanage and had them sit in your lap to make her happy. The fact that I was the one who really dictated your day meant nothing: she was always around somewhere. You had to phone the doctor and order the ice for the fridge, she had to have special sardines from Scandinavia because she was sure to eat those, and between all the work you had to do you ran from her to me and from me back to her.

If you had spoken earlier all this might have turned out differently. You were late at the cafe, you said, because you had had to take Angéla for an X-ray. That was it, I had had enough, I could no longer put up with this triangle between you, me and her; I don't remember what I said, only the look on your face and the way you kept smoothing your hair down on your head; I remember your tone of voice when you did finally speak, and the way my hand felt when I banged my fist down on the table, and the bright light that shone on my red glove. "Have you gone mad?" you asked; my legs went weak under me and I had to prop myself up on the table; the glass was full of mineral water and your face was reflected in miniature, all round and twisted. "You're mad!" you said again, and I felt my heart start to race. "Have you never realised, Eszter, that it is you that I love, not Angéla?"

14

It was Gizike who brought those flowers, I saw her put them down; she must have bought them from one of the sellers in the market and not in a shop, because they are tied together with string. Delphiniums and antirrhinums – I'm so tired I can't think of their common names. Józsi must have had to sleep with his brothers that night; it's almost three years now since I last met Gizike, and she has never once allowed me to see him; if she could have, she would have kept away from me completely and we would never have met again, though I did see that photo of me nailed to the wall above the washstand, a really poor one from a newspaper taken five years earlier. The first time she and I came face to face in the Swan she tried to treat me like a total stranger.

I had gone there with Hella and Kertész for dinner; our eyes met briefly as she came over to me with the menu, I could see that she had recognised me, just as I had her, but it was obvious that she didn't want either of us to show that we knew each other. I studied her as she stood at our table with her thin childlike neck turning red from the rush of blood. It was my first time at the Swan; whenever I could I ate in the theatre refectory, if I ever did go anywhere it was with either Pipi or you; Pipi took me to the restaurant opposite the theatre, you took me up to Buda or to Margaret Island.

I was afraid you would come looking for me; you knew every nook and cranny of the theatre, but if I hid in the trade union club I knew you would never look for me there. I got into a discussion with Kertész, about Morozov's interpretation of Shakespeare, and I kept pressing him with questions, I knew that you would have to go back to the university at six to examine someone and I had to spin things out until then. Hella opened the door, saw the two of us deep in discussion and came in and settled down with us. Kertész was warming to his theme, waving his arms about and explaining everything; I watched Hella sitting there, all studious attention and anxiousness to keep up with me, and I wondered what she would think if I told her what I was up to – she hadn't realised that I wasn't following what Kertész was saying, I was only there because I didn't want to bump into you.

When he had finished his disquisition Kertész invited the two of us to have dinner with him. I liked the Swan because it was small and friendly, and the white bird on the sign tasteless in a countrified rather than a big-city way. Gizike brought three glasses of beer and put the menu in my hand. I ordered a frankfurter and horseradish and avoided looking at her, so I sensed rather than actually saw a small smile on her face; at the Three Hussars her father used to bring me a whole grated horseradish – I adored the taste; it brought tears to my eyes and I had to gasp for air, but I ate it all the same. When I had finished the meal I left the two of them there, I felt a strange urge to sneak out into the corridor where the waiters brought the food from the kitchen, and at just that moment Gizike came out of the kitchen carrying a large dish, enough for two people; she saw me standing there, stopped and put it down onto the serving table.

We just stared at each other without speaking; two waiters dashed past us, averting their eyes, astonished to see me with my arms around her neck and sobbing, and she was crying too, not as angrily as I was but still despite herself, with her eyes firmly closed and lots of embarrassed whimpers; Tera – I didn't know her as such then – suddenly appeared, with her soft body and her stupid look, she clasped her hands together and stared at the two of us. I don't know what Gizike was thinking – perhaps about Juszti, or the well where we had washed her prayer book; I wasn't thinking of either of my parents, I was thinking about you, and that I never wanted to see you again.

*

Yesterday the telephone operator was standing outside the theatre; I asked him not to put any more calls through to my room; it would be easy to avoid a private conversation with you during rehearsals because I was never alone then, and I went into work so early the cleaners hadn't finished, and I stayed there so long that you weren't able to wait for me. That was when I became a patron of the kitchen factory and bought my house – the hardest thing I had ever done. I had never put money into savings, I didn't trust the banks and all I had was my monthly salary and anything else I could get my hands on; I counted it out and tucked it away in a box – the Kossuth Prize money, the other awards, the fees for my films and radio broadcasts, it all added up to a mountain of hard cash; I lived on my salary, which was now very large, and still kept the greater part of it; I had so much I could have covered the entire floor of my apartment with one-hundred notes. When I bought the house, the solicitor watched in amazement as I counted out the full purchase price in cash, in hundred-forint notes.

I moved in before my furniture had arrived; Juli had agreed to be with me for only a fortnight, and she wasn't sure she would be able to do the shopping, but I just shrugged – it said in her papers that she had been born in a village up in the mountains so I didn't think Eagle Hill would be too much of a problem for her, but she also wanted to have her devotional objects out on display, that was the reason why she had to leave Hella. That first evening, as we were about to lie down beside each other on our mattresses, she took out her Virgin Mary, her Saint Antony and Christ with his bleeding heart, set them up on one of the trunks, knelt before them and started to pray by the light of a gas lamp, throwing hostile and challenging looks at me as she did. I propped myself up on an elbow and stared at her and her sacred objects and thought what a stupid person Hella must be – stupid and cowardly. I yawned and turned the other way; she carried on mumbling for a few more minutes, then lay down beside me and I caught a whiff of her – she smelled of starch and potatoes – before she undid her hair for the night; it was tied in a bun the size of a walnut and she had a long pigtail – it was more like a cat's tail. Before we went to sleep I told her, "I am not at home to anyone, ever." She looked long and hard at me and mumbled something; at dawn she prodded me awake and announced that she had to go to Mass but she had prepared my breakfast – on a spirit stove, because there was no electricity and it was all we had – and when Pipi struggled up the hill at midday, moaning and cursing, to visit me in my new house – and she had known him for ages – she turned him away without even putting out a chair for him to sit on in the garden and get his breath back; she just shut the door in his face and parroted her message that I wasn't at home to anyone, ever.

I was sitting on the kitchen floor cleaning my shoes, listening to the exchange and giggling, then I suddenly threw the brush down and rushed out onto the path after him; I hauled him back to the house and nearly suffocated him with kisses. Juli looked me up and down, stomped off back to her room and refused to come out the whole time he was there. By the evening all the furniture had arrived and the power was on; she laid the table and put her kitchen book down in front of me, she had written the shopping list in it. "Write down who it is that I mustn't let in," she added. We had had spinach and fried eggs for supper, and there it was: "One kilo of spinach and four eggs." I wrote your name and Angéla's next to it.

The next morning I looked out of the window towards the city and there you were, sitting beside the fence, with your back to my window, your hat perched on the top of your head and your briefcase lying on the grass, reading. Juli was doing the washing-up and neither of us spoke; I never did ask you how long you had been there, and Juli never told me. I didn't want any breakfast, I took my shoes off and went out the back of the house via the kitchen path to the side fence, taking the kitchen stool with me, and climbed over; the grass was long and soft and you didn't hear me coming; on my way down the slope with the shoes in my hand something cut my foot, and that made me even angrier than before – if I hadn't been at the bottom of the slope by then I would have gone back and told you to clear off and leave me in peace, now and for ever. Instead I needed to sit down and examine my foot, it was still early and the ground was cold from the dew; the car drivers stared at me as they went past, the milk float slowed down and the milkman called out something to me, but I just shook my head; I leaned over and rested my head on my knees, I was tired and miserable, and I was working out how long it would take me to get to the theatre by bus.

That afternoon we had a Peace Meeting; I sat next to the technicians, as close to the door as I could, my foot was now throbbing and every step counted; the Party secretary was talking, we were sending a telegram somewhere and we all had to sign. While I was signing my thoughts turned to the war again, and the fact that I now had a home of my own. The person I had once been came from the sort of town where people thought in terms of rented houses with small gardens and would not have considered a house their own unless it was listed under their name in the Land Registry. During the meeting I also thought about the reedbed, and Palla bácsi wiping away his tears, and our little home and the gaping hole where it had once stood, and the way I had laughed when I saw it – there was no point in crying, all you could do was laugh; that was when I told myself never to fall in love with a house again, people build them only to set fire to them and bomb them . . . "And now I do have one," I thought, as I sat there in the meeting, with the opera group playing Schiller's "Joy, fire from the heavens, daughter of Elysium".

I kept my eyes down, staring into my lap and not looking around; I knew you were somewhere near; you had waited on the doorstep for some time before Juli went out and told you that I had either gone out or hadn't slept there that night – I was very happy to hear her say that. She added that you had gone back to the theatre, but the tingling on my back told me you were somewhere close by, and it struck me that I had bought the house simply so that I could be with you without our being disturbed. I could have screamed with rage, I no longer wanted to see you, I wanted nothing from you anymore – and it made me wild to think I had spent good money on such a stupid idea. Money? All my money. Pipi, poor dear, recited a dreadful poem about Peace, and I kept saying to myself, "My house, my home!" The decor was so ugly that neither of us dared look at it, even less so the workmen who had put it up. It's hard enough decorating in a theatre, where everything is made out of papier mâché and everyone knows what flimsy materials the decorator has to work with.

When Father was dying my mother stayed up all that night, kneeling beside the bed and breathing on his hands and lips, like an animal. I did the cooking, I knew I wouldn't have time for it the next day.

Towards dawn he became calmer, and she came up to me and whispered in my ear that he was a little easier now. Something inside me told me to let her leave it at that. She hadn't slept for days, and I thought she might sleep for an hour or two if I could persuade her, and I needed time to myself anyway, to gather the courage to face what lay ahead of us if he wasn't going to be with us the next day. I didn't try to reassure her, it was now too late and I didn't have the courage to steal even a few minutes from her by lying; I pushed her back towards his bed, I could feel the frail bones through her shawl, and I told her to go back to him because he was going to die at any moment.

When we left the theatre you were waiting for me at the door. I couldn't escape because of my foot, but I didn't want to anyway, so I let you follow me, we went out onto the ring road, not saying a word; the sun was scorching hot, the street was airless and there were people everywhere. I avoided your gaze for a while, then I raised my head, looked into your eyes and we stopped; there was a smell of petrol and the blaring of motor car horns. It was then that I finally admitted to myself that I was in love with you.

15

When I ran out of the cafe after you had told me that you loved me and not Angéla I didn't go very far, I took cover in a doorway, it was a building that I knew, the one with the furrier's workshop – he worked for the theatre. I watched you come out some time later; you stood at the traffic lights looking to left and right wondering whether I had gone home or back to the theatre, then you set off for the theatre and I carried on to the Danube. I stood looking at the water thinking how I could never get used to the idea that it ran under iron bridges and between stone riverbanks with soaring hills on the far side; the hills themselves never ceased to surprise me, they seemed not quite natural, just as you thought the Great Plain wasn't; the wind was blowing and that made me happy, it was something familiar, back home it came from the other side of the Tisza; there were barges hunkered down in the water.

I felt that you had duped me, the two of you. My loathing of Angéla couldn't have been any greater by then, but the hatred I felt for you was mixed with a sense of shock, the feeling of professional envy a clown gets when he suddenly realises that his partner is just as good a trickster as he is, that he hasn't been spinning that ball on his nose because he likes doing it or has a natural talent for it, it's a trick he has learned in a school for performers. In all the confusion one thing was clear to me. I had no wish to carry on. I have more money than Angéla does, I am well known, one day my statue will stand in the theatre foyer and books will be written about me; she is transient, ephemeral, a chain around your neck that you drag around with you, and she will feature in the literature, if you are ever mentioned, only in a biographical note. So you don't love her? You are just being kind to her, the way Domi bácsi was, and Emil, and everyone else who ever knew her? So what does it mean to the two of you that you got involved with me and that you love me? What more can I take away from her than I already have? Your love that, as you had just told me, you hadn't felt for her in ages? Your body that hers hasn't responded to for ages, ever since she became a reincarnation of Emil and turned her gaze away from everything transient, from actual people, to contemplate eternity? What could I possibly take from her when you are so very good to her and will continue to be because it is in your nature and simply because she is so very good to everyone else – mad dogs would lie down trustingly at her feet and fishes would sing to her – and the less she means to you the more you think about her and the more you do for her? The fact is, she doesn't belong in this world – Angéla in a red kimono, Angéla with a coffee grinder or a roast turkey in her hand, Angéla in a hat with spangles in it, or a nylon nightdress, it's all an illusion; all the time she's making very sure that she won't ever suffer because her Marxism has made her deny the terrifying "merciful" God who is the only one from whom she can hope that she will one day meet again the person for whose sake she is doing all this; that's the truth about your dogmatic-materialist Angéla, she has turned against God because of Emil; she took that St Antony medallion from around her neck to give you as a memento of something that doesn't exist anymore, something that is over and done with and can never be brought back, like childhood; she tortures her head with books on political economics, but she has for so long now been a sort of weird nun who has nothing to do with actual people and wider humanity, so what can I possibly take from her? You? You have never been hers; she belonged to you only so long as her horror of the war and fear for her life were stronger than the pull of Emil, and the moment he died she lost all her emotional certainty about what your love meant to her. So what are we to do now – about you, and her, and myself?

I stood under the arched doorway reading the names of the residents and looking at the posters on the wall; there was one from last year asking everyone to sign up to the compulsory monthly deduction for World Peace.

I went home and began learning my next role. Pipi came up the hill but I didn't let him in. I made supper, there's no kitchen in the house, only a little cooking area, the smell of the onions frying stung my nose and brought tears to my eyes; I ate right there, standing up, straight out of the pan to save washing up, then went back into the sitting room, opened my boxes and counted up all my money; I washed my hair and darned my socks; the phone rang three times, but I didn't pick it up, I had no wish to speak to you ever again.

When my father died I had to force Mother to hand over his clothes, all the patched and mended shirts and worn-out slippers, to sell at the second-hand market. She sobbed and tried to hide them from me and I had to tear them out of her hand when she clung on to them; the only things I didn't sell were his gardening clothes, the ones that Béla had worn for those three weeks; I had looked for them but couldn't find them, it was only much later that they turned up in the cellar, my mother had hidden them under the copper sulphate container; with the money I got for them I topped up the barrel of lard and made a huge amount of dried pasta; I also brought home one and a half sacks of potatoes. The first time I cooked them my mother blanched over her plate and rushed out to be sick; later on I spotted his coat, there was no mistaking it. I had patched it with the wrong sort of cloth and the buttons were too bright and didn't match the material; it had survived the siege and the bombing and a young lad had taken it off and put it on the steaming rump of a horse harnessed to a refuse wagon outside a house. I went up to the horse, patted it on the neck; the coat was covered with spots of grease and smelled of sawdust – the rancid odour of poverty. When our house disappeared and we were put up in that school I used to sit and hum little tunes to myself in the toilets – you couldn't hum in the classrooms, everyone there was sobbing and crying and nursing what was left of their belongings. There was nothing of my father's left now. Even his flowerbeds had been dug up.

My mother died here in Budapest, in the Kútvölgyi Street Hospital; the nurse had put everything on her bedside table into her little lacquer bag: an unopened bar of chocolate, a life of Bach, some toiletries and a nightdress, the one she had been wearing when she died. I gave her the bag as a present, she just stared at me as if I was mad; I whistled as I went down the stairs but the tears were running down my cheeks, I was whistling because I knew that it was finally all over and done with: I had only to give the house a good clean and then I would be on my own, completely on my own, and would no longer have to worry about anyone. I got the caretaker to take everything to the welfare shop. Everything – the books, including the sheet music I had bought for her in Budapest, the fur coat, the expensive shoes she had hardly ever worn, her dresses and the money I had got for them, I put it all in the welfare box; the photo of the two of them as a young couple had been destroyed with everything else in the bombing. I have rarely dreamed about my parents since then, I try never even to think of them, and if they ever do enter my thoughts I distract myself by starting to learn my next role.

Sometime after that Pipi took me to a concert so that I could hear his current mistress perform. We sat in the director's box. He was so excited he nearly fell out as he leaned over the balcony to get a better view; reading programmes bores me, I'm only interested in what the performers actually do, but she played several different pieces, all of them rather well, with her strong white arms flashing in the blaze of the chandeliers; I suddenly realised she was playing Chopin's *Scherzo in B Flat Minor* and I closed my eyes to hide the tears; when the interval came Pipi kissed me on both cheeks – he was always so grateful when anyone praised his mistresses. We went down to talk to her, she simpered prettily, looked very pleased with herself and flirted with him, and when he told her that she had made me cry she blushed with pleasure, I smiled and shook hands with her, and he grinned with delight; I looked at him as if he were an idiot: he had never seen my mother at the piano, with her mane of black hair flowing down over her shoulders, playing by the light of two tiny candles – they were cheaper than electricity – while the room smelled of cooking fat. The supper often burned as I stood entranced because she was playing Chopin.

I never wanted to see you or speak to you again, but as I went into the room I was aware of the imprint of your hands – the book you had sent me, the little souvenir pot you put the raspberries in that you bought when we were on holiday by the lake, and the little patchwork dog on the shelf above my bed, the one you were forced to buy to stop him looking so sad in the shop because he was so ugly – and so that I wouldn't be all alone in my house; I stood there looking at the dog and thinking about the coat on the horse's rump, and the scherzo, and you. I have never thrown or given away any of your presents. You duped me and I hated you, but I know I can never forget you.

and anything about the most on the lap as a fountain, and the chosen, and are. I have never thrown or given away any of your presents. I have done in and Claude or José: I love I can beyond and you.

16

The bird is drinking now.

Water has collected in a crack in the concrete next to the cistern. First he drank, then he bathed, and now he is shaking out his wings and his legs are gleaming. I have never hated birds; they used to arrive in a flock and descend on the crumbs when I shook the tablecloth out – they knew when we had lunch and they always know when you are doing the washing-up. In winter the twilight came early and they arrived with it, filling the garden with noise and pecking up the crumbs and chirping away around my feet; the cold raised goosebumps on my skin and it turned red where my rolled-up sleeves exposed my arms; if I left the door open in the spring I could see them hopping about in the lilac tree, and we had swallows under our eaves – people call that a blessing from Heaven, because a house where there are swallows will never catch fire. I thought of the swallows when I was coming into town from the Barrage, the day after the bombing.

The only bird I ever hated was Péter, the one you and Angéla had. You were very fond of him and were very amused by him, as you were with every living creature; he adored you, he would land on your hair and shout at you, and take food from your plate, and when you and Angéla had nothing to say to each other he would fly up onto the table between you, clean up the rest of the meal, tweet at you for a while, cock his head from one side to the other, hop onto her head and then back onto yours; he was so light and fragile and clumsy that you had to be careful not to tread on him; you had to make sure he always had something to eat and drink, and not to leave the windows open; your love for him was obligatory under the law that makes you care for anything weaker than yourself.

Every Sunday Ambrus would make pigeon soup; he would go out to the pigeon house, pull out a couple of birds and wring their necks. "Péter looks like a jewel on you," you said. I was standing on your balcony, it was the last time I went to your house, after the fair at Máriapócs; I opened my hand and he flew up onto my fingers; I immediately thought of Ambrus and those pigeons and my fingers started to tremble.

The bird here has finished his ablutions and flitted up into the willow tree.

I wasn't jealous of you. You probably never understood that. It would have been easier if I had been . . . "Let my coronet be dressed with willow flowers . . ."

Two years ago Hella was a far better Emilia than she is now. We should swap roles, you said, at the end of the first act: I should do the Moor and Pipi Desdemona. I was gluing an eyelash back on that was getting in the way and I glanced at you in the mirror, you were lounging in the doorway, with a cigarette in your mouth; my hand was clumsy, Angéla had come to see me before the play started and I had shaken hands with her and scrubbed it so hard afterwards I had almost taken the skin off.

I was never jealous of her. I knew that you loved me and not her. I just found her repulsive; I shuddered whenever she touched me, and on those rare occasions when she visited me and I had given her something to drink I would smash the cup she had used when she left. Her touch, her breath, the way she walked, the scarf round her neck, instantly brought it all back to me – everything that had happened to me in the past, and everything in yours: she had had a striped ball, you fell in love with her and married her, and I thought of the fawn and the fact that you slept with her, and the thought would make me put down my knife and fork on the dinner table. I thought it would be enough just to get away from you and hide myself in a suburb somewhere where I wouldn't have to see you, and all the time I was aching for you so much I was actually trembling.

Everything to do with you and Angéla – Péter, a packet of cigarettes, Elza – seemed to me unclean, and when I thought about your having any dealings with her I would run madly down the street, as if running could drive a thought out of a person's head. One day Pipi came to the house, he arrived just after you had left; I was down on the carpet attacking a book, the book of fairy tales you had just brought me to read; I had been looking for something by Hans Christian Andersen and you brought me one from your own shelves; on the first page, in large round letters, were the words "Angéla Graff"; there was a large swan on the cover pulling a shell, with a fair-haired boy sitting on it wearing a huge hat. I had knelt down to tear the book to pieces. Pipi went and got the brandy, then sat down beside me on the floor with the bottle between his knees; he didn't speak, he just watched as I swept the pages under the wardrobe, then lay on the carpet with my head on his thigh and he stroked my hair and my brow, the way you do to someone who is ill. By the time Juli came in he had finished the whole bottle, I was still lying on the floor and the tears were running down my face; she switched the lights on, gathered up the glasses and the bottle and started to lay the table for supper. She glanced at me only once, then turned her head away; she had looked at me as if I were the scarlet woman in the Bible.

The gardener is planting now. It's rather late in the year to be moving such a large plant, but it might take all the same, if only because so much rain has fallen, and perhaps it will survive; I can't make out what sort it is, only the colour, a sort of coppery red. When I first brought you back to the house I was afraid of Juli and what she might say when she saw you, and I wasn't sure she would even give you any supper; I didn't dare let you come inside at first, so I wandered about the garden with you, you were looking at my trees and measuring the distance between them – you had said you would bring me a swing. It was already quite dark by the time I got up the courage to go into the kitchen; she wasn't there but one thing stood out, it was the weighing scales that Kárász néni had given me when I went to say goodbye. I don't know why she chose a pair of scales, she took me in her arms and kissed me, and she smelled of sugar. In one of the pans was a note: she would be away for two days, tonight's supper was in the fridge, tomorrow I would have to eat in town; she was going on the farewell pilgrimage to the shrine at Máriapócsi; she had taken care to close all the windows; the kitchen smelled of the wet mop, and gas. I handed you the note, I didn't look at you, I just straightened the tea towels on the rack. You took the key from my hand, went back to the door and shut it. I don't know what you told Angéla when you phoned her, I "accidentally" released a loud blast of water into the bath so that I wouldn't hear a word of it. Sometime before that, about two weeks earlier, before I was hiding away from you, it amused me when I heard you lying to her; I knew that she believed every word you said and it tickled me to know that there I was sitting with you in some restaurant while she thought you were at a meeting or rehearsal at the theatre; now it just irritated me. The truth is, I would have liked to hear you tell her you weren't going home, you were going to spend the night with me. That was the day I started to shudder whenever I heard her name. Lying there on Pipi's bed under the head of Agrippa was very difficult, but it wasn't easy here at my place either, that night when you said you knew that I loved Angéla.

*

Now the gardener is mumbling something. He's right, it's good to talk to flowers; when my father was planting he always stroked the little leaves and said, "Now do be good." He's started to hum, and he's stooping down to create little mounds of wet earth around the bottom of each bush, they look like nests of mashed potato, with new shoots sprouting out of the top. You left at dawn the next morning; I watched you all the way down the path to the main road, and I felt nothing but bitterness. You whistled as you walked and kept turning to wave to me – you knew I was sitting on the windowsill watching you; it was the same tune: "Blow, spring wind, my flower, my flower . . ." Your figure slowly grew smaller, then disappeared from sight at the corner. The clouds drifted away, my face and hands were bright red in the morning light and the dew had settled on the flower boxes in the window. I just stared at them, I had no idea what to say to them, I don't know how to talk to flowers. The gardener isn't stooping now, he's kneeling.

"Stooping" was the word you used that night. Last night, at Gizi's, I realised what you had meant. I had never thought about it. I realised I hadn't been listening to you properly and you had already talked so much; my brain must have been paying attention but my ears and body were just lying in wait, listening for the tremor in your voice that wasn't intended for me. But for some reason the word stayed with me, and last night I realised that you were bristling with accusation and a sense of grievance because I had abandoned you and you were begging me never to do that ever again. You had been stooping all your life, you went on to say – I watched the smoke curling up from your cigarette and wondered if you smoked at home at night when you were with Angéla; you had stooped before your mother, so as not to make her worry about you, and you stooped before Angéla, because you loved her, and before everyone else so that they wouldn't think badly of you and chop your head off because you were taller than they were. You said that no-one had ever liked you for what you really were, you were always playing a role to make people accept you, but with me you stood up straight and didn't feel you had to sing if you wanted to show me your teeth, like the wolf in the story.

I wasn't paying attention, I wasn't interested in what you were saying. I was wondering if when you left me and went home you would give her a hug, and if it was true that there really hadn't been anything between the two of you for so long. As you were going down the hill and I was sitting on the windowsill, a cold hatred ran through me: it had occurred to me that if she trusted you so much that she believed every word you said, then the two of you must be in complete harmony. The morning light was cold and hard; I could no longer see you but I could still hear your voice. "Blow, spring wind, my flower, my flower . . ." I closed the window; I was tired and miserable, and bitterly disappointed.

That morning the phone rang – you were calling from home. We exchanged some neutral words about the rehearsal, I threw in the occasional yes and no. I knew that Angéla would be sitting somewhere close by, with the coffee steaming on the breakfast table. I put the phone down and took out a book. I had no idea what I was reading. "So you did manage to deceive her," I thought, and was not pleased.

*

It's a chicory.

A drop of water is clinging to one of its petals . . . and now it has run down under its own weight and been swallowed up by the soil. *Cichorium endivia.* Gizi must have told you that I like salad. Juszti always made it, Gizike served it to the guests with a large multi-pronged glass spoon, and the two of us finished off what was left in the bowl, trying to outdo each other at eating it like rabbits. I even loved the way it looked – the curl of the green leaves, the crispness of the younger ones. I have never been able to eat it since I found that poem in your briefcase, the one you wrote about Angéla's salads when you were younger.

I always see writers in their settings: Ovid sitting on the sea-shore with foaming black waves at his feet, a black cloud flying overhead and a bird circling. On one occasion Gizi came into the study and suddenly let out a scream: I was lying sprawled out on the floor with my brow bathed in sweat; she wasn't to know that I was having a terrified fit because I was reliving the Battle of Segesvár and horses were running over my body, stamping on me as they went, and I could feel the weight and sharpness of their hooves cutting into my flesh; I was so happy to see her standing there, now I could get up and no longer have to relive the battle of Segesvár, and no longer see those waving fields of corn – I could see my father's law books again, and the blackened mirror, in its mother-of-pearl frame, hanging from a gold thread in the corner of the room; it always made me reimagine the heroes of the poets and other writers, Piroska Rozgonyi and Cordelia and Klärchen, and man's long journey through the dark wood of life.

When Pipi dug out that old poem of yours you simply said, "Oh, that was so long ago, it wasn't the real me." We were sitting in the Swan and Gizi had just brought me a salad she had prepared herself, done the way I remembered them. I instantly recognised the smoothness of the oil and the smell of the vinegar and I couldn't take a second mouthful, I just pushed the plate away. After that you always ate all the salad yourself; you had duly taken note, as you had with the fact that I don't like alcohol and eat bread with everything, like a peasant. You were always delighted when you came across any oddity or peculiar fussiness in me, but they held no interest for me. "It's an allergy," you declared, as I pushed the plate away. The leaves had left a tight knot in my throat, you dipped them in the paprika sauce and spooned up the layer of vinegar and oil dressing beneath them. I just watched. I was thinking of Angéla, and that first meal she cooked for you when you were newly married and you wrote that ode to it, and the first spring you spent together, and I thought of the journal that had published your poems, and that they were always there on her dining table and would still exist when we are both long dead. Their hideous immortality made me choke.

*

Now the gardener is silently mouthing some sort of formula, like a magical incantation, the way old women in the villages do when they are planting, or he is praying and muttering non-stop.

You too talked non-stop; it was as if after the long years of silence you had at last found someone who really took an interest in you. You talked about your godfather and how prickly his beard was and how his huge fur cloak – the one that was so black and shaggy – shed hoarfrost everywhere when he came into the room in winter. I just listened in silence. You talked about your time at university, and the first trips you made abroad, and about Angéla, how you first met her and how her radiance gradually faded during the war and put a distance between you – and how she had distanced herself from real life to devote herself to her dead family and you had grown apart. I watched you and said nothing. I was silent and helpless beside you, like a stray animal who follows you down the street then looks up into your face and whimpers, and you have no idea what he is trying to tell you. My bottomless silence should have told you that there was something truly terrible in my past and that I was begging you not to let me look back – if I did that even for a moment it would drown me again. You didn't understand. "You're jealous," you told me irritably, after you had gone on and on about how you went with her to the children's home because the night was frosty and you didn't want her to be out alone on the slippery streets – and all I could do was shut my mouth and push the plate away. That was always your answer: I was jealous. You would spend half an hour trying to persuade me that I had no reason to be, there had been nothing between you for years now . . . and I listened in silence. I couldn't bring myself to tell you that *anything* you shared with her – the bird Péter or a letter about the rent or the electricity bill – was more than I could bear.

"Think," my eyes were saying to you, "about the ugly fits of rage, the uncontrollable moods that come over me; try, because you love me, to understand that there is something inside me that I cannot talk about; I need you to reconstruct in your mind the house in the Barrage that you never saw and that has vanished for ever, and Kárász néni's kitchen, and Béla's kisses and Ambrus and everything; try to acknowledge the fact that I really hate Angéla, and why I hate her." If I could restrain myself sufficiently I would sit there and hum a little tune while you told me all about your day and I would be telling myself that you are weak and corrupt and I despise myself for loving you and I hate the pair of you – Angéla because she exists and you because you take her by the hand and hold out her coat and say goodnight to her.

*

The gardener is looking this way now – he doesn't know whether to greet me or not – he's fiddling with the loose button on his coat, and now he's turned away and started to hum again. "You are a genuinely great actress," you once told me; you weren't just being nice, you said it in a calmly matter-of-fact way; I was sewing the top button on your jacket at the time. It had just fallen off; while I was stitching away I noticed that someone had reinforced the middle one with a weak, light-coloured thread – clumsily and very badly. Angéla never learned to sew, she always pricked her fingers in the needlework lessons and started crying.

I put the coat down on my lap and just stared at it. I could see her very hand, the thimble sitting clumsily on the end of the index finger, the way her narrow shoulders moved as she wrestled with the hard material – and my stomach heaved. You asked me what the matter was, I said the scissors had cut my finger and I sucked on one that hadn't been hurt, and started to sing and dance and pirouette around the room, and all the while I was thinking that the next day I would refuse to let you in, I would go down to the river somewhere – the company were doing *The Marvellous Brigade* and I wasn't in it; I wanted to be alone, I wanted to freeze in the snow until I shook and trembled and the winter had seeped into my bones. "Where are we eating tomorrow?" you asked, and I said, "At the Swan, for lunch." I didn't see you for three days after I got back from Szentendre, I had left a note for Juli saying that I was going to a rehearsal and phoned her later from the Margaret Bridge to say I would be travelling for a while. The next time we met I could see from your face that you had been searching for me high and low: you could have murdered me. I lay in your arms staring up at the ceiling and at the light moving across it from the cars in the road down below; how could I have possibly explained that I had hidden myself away from you for three days because Angéla had reinforced the thread on the middle button on your jacket?

Old Ince used to sit like this on the ground on the corner of Török Street, under the crucifix next to the well where Gizi and I washed the ivory cover of her prayer book; he always called out, "I kiss your hand, young lady," even when I was only nine; I never acknowledged his greeting though he went on doing it for years; I never gave him anything however soulfully he looked at me, I just walked quickly past him with my head held high – I was proud that he was even poorer than we were; in the winter he had rags tied round his hands and feet, it made him look like a rag doll. Then one winter he died, the City Council arranged his burial; it was a great event, even the three gypsies who performed in Józsi's inn were there, they had known him since the start of time. I went too, with Gizike; on the way there they were saying how proud they were of him because he was so horribly old; he didn't have a single relative – a man from the Council walked behind the hearse instead. I thought it interesting that they were going to all that trouble for him and were so proud of him and yet they had let him freeze to death. After they had covered the grave and taken the magnificent hearse away, everyone went home. Gizi and I were the only ones left; it was very cold but we didn't feel it, I never do and Gizi had her snowshoes and handwarmer; she knelt down on it, said a last prayer, then took a pengő out of her little purse with the clover leaf on it and buried it in the ground. Whenever I think of Gizi smiling, it is always that smile on her youthful face as she knelt there on her handwarmer in the half-light. When Juszti was still alive there was always dripping being melted in the kitchen and they slaughtered a pig almost every day.

An hour later I was back at the grave, I was horribly frightened; the snow was even thicker now and I didn't have snowshoes or a handwarmer, but I knew Gizi would have been home for a while by then, the electric light on the little table would have been switched on and she would be drinking cocoa, with a brioche next to her cup. It took me a while to find the pengő and I had difficulty digging it out of the hard soil under the snow. They were selling roast chestnuts and pumpkin slices in the street, I wandered between the braziers and heated tiles for a while but didn't buy anything; when I got home a piano lesson was going on. We kept our money in a cup on the dresser, I threw the coin in it and shed a quick tear, I didn't have time for anything more. I had to start getting supper ready.

I did love you. I haven't told you very often and I have never known how to show it. But I did love you. That evening when you took me up to the Castle to show me the view and you tossed a coin into that beggar's cap, I laughed at you and said,

"At least he'll have something to get drunk on tonight." Then we got to the corner of the square and stood in the shadow of the Holy Trinity Statue; light was flooding out of the open door of the church and I stopped there for a moment and looked back at the way we had come. You shook your head, but I pulled my arm out of yours and ran back and poured out all the money I had in my purse onto the old fellow's lap. Then I ran up to the Fisherman's Bastion, you could barely keep up with me. "You're crazy," you said as you kissed me, but standing there snuggled against you I thought that you really had no idea how crazy I was: I had never in all my life given money to a beggar, the tears were pouring down my face and got smeared all over yours and you never realised that I was crying because I was afraid. I was afraid of this stranger I had become, this person who gave away money and wished a beggar goodnight.

17

Schoolchildren.

Each child has a ball and a lunch bag and one of them is eating. There are two teachers with them, one of them walking at the front, the other at the back. What are they thinking? The one at the back, the younger one, looks fairly natural, almost like a real person; the one at the front is grey-haired. Now she's stopped and is looking around thoughtfully, and while she does so the boy in the checked shirt picks up a snail and throws it in the water barrel, but neither teacher sees him; they all have netted bags hanging from their shoulders, with bread rolls and rubber balls gleaming inside them.

They stand there in silence, looking at everything but not discussing what they see – the sun, me, the bird, the drying crowns of the trees. The boys start to point things out to one another; they are very taken with the gardener sitting there talking to himself; the grey-haired teacher is explaining something and she keeps glancing in our direction: she finds both of us disturbing, the gardener talking to himself and me sitting on the ground with no shoes on; it bothers her, we don't fit into her idea of what is proper, we don't conform, we are alive.

The younger teacher is now peering into the barrel, the sun is glittering on the surface of the water. "The gratitude of the nation," the older one intones; my bird flies up from the tree; it isn't a sparrow, I now see, it has a yellow breast and green feathers around its neck; it passes over our heads and the children watch it entranced.

What will they write in their essays about the walk? What did Angéla write about me when we had to compose portraits of one another in that Religious Studies lesson? The priest never gave our work back or even mentioned it again. We had to describe each other's appearance; I was rather nervous about it and spent some time thinking about what she would make of me, and more generally what people saw when they looked at me; we didn't sit in our usual places in Religious Studies, the two denominations were separated and those who sat at the back were moved to the front, so I always sat next to her for those lessons, otherwise she would have been in front of me. Every so often we would gaze intently into each other's faces and study them at length, very carefully, as if for the first time, while the priest walked up and down between the rows of benches and leaned over to see what we had written. I loved reading and learning things by heart but I hated writing essays, it was much harder work, I thought it stupid to have to write things down and have to search for the right words when I could just mime them and act them out. I tilted my head to one side, the way Angéla always did when she was concentrating, and the priest burst out laughing and tapped my exercise book to tell me to write something; I looked at her again, she was studying my clothes, and I was filled with such a violent wish that she would die, right there beside me on the bench, that my face turned white. "You are God's favourite children," the priest said when we were confirmed. The little boy has now found another snail and thrown it in the water barrel.

Pipi loved children. If Angéla had told only me about the event and had not met Pipi and Ványa in the theatre later we would never have gone to the orphanage; Pipi would have been game for any fir tree festival in an orphanage, only no-one ever dares ask him, so when she explained her plans for the carnival that afternoon he was delighted, and so was Ványa; by the time I got there everyone was laughing and saying how happy the little orphans were, Ványa made a speech about the social responsibilities of actors and talked about Emil the martyr, and Angéla was all blushes and smiles as she thanked everyone, and I stood there smiling too and saying yes of course, what a brilliant idea it was. Pipi was whistling with joy when he rang me on the internal phone in his changing room to discuss what we should do for the poor little things to make them happy, but I didn't respond, I just banged the phone down. I was standing at my window looking down on the ring road, there was some sort of gathering outside the pharmacy across the way and I was watching it with great interest, then Juli brought me my costume and I happened to look at her as she was helping me put it on. She was smiling. That smile looked so distorted and unfamiliar on her normally sour, expressionless face that I just stared at her from under Puck's slanting eyebrows and glitter-powdered eyelashes. We looked at one another like two wicked elves; she was so pleased that I was going to perform for Angéla that she was laughing at me.

They're moving on now; I scared a lizard out of their way in case they saw it, picked it up and threw it in the barrel like the snails. They are being moved away down a different path to make them turn their backs on us all the quicker, so that they can apply their minds to less transient things. The older teacher is now at the back and the younger one is leading the way; they really ought to be singing "I would love to live in a dark forest" but none of these children would know it, they've been brought up on Bartók and Kodály. The show at the orphanage started with a song by Kodály; the children lined up, then one of them came up to me, mumbled something, took me by the hand and led me off down a corridor; Angéla went with us everywhere, all happiness and anxiety; I walked slowly, keeping pace with the child, the walls were lined on both sides with enlarged amateur photographs, many of them of Emil, then I suddenly came across one of the town where I was born; it must have been taken from somewhere on the roof of the church tower for a view of the main square, because I could see Köves Street, and the villa. In one of the pictures Angéla was standing in the children's room with Emil, he was leaning over the table and I remembered that they were looking at a mathematics book; Emil knew nothing at all about arithmetic, he was only there to add a bit of glamour to the picture. The next one showed him on his own, standing outside the university holding books under his arm and squinting into the sun; at the turn of the corridor there was a photograph of the tannery – it must have been a recent one, there was a large star emblazoned at the top and a flag flying above it, and you could see the corner of an alley and the wall of a house to the side of it. If it had been taken from any further back you would have been able to see the entrance to the Three Hussars – it was always open – and the big main gate, which was opened only for Rózsi and the wagons coming in from the farm.

The children at the orphanage were all in white – even their shoes were white. Auntie Ilu and Elza sat perched beside them like two old ravens; the chair beside Auntie Ilu was empty because you had gone out for a cigarette in the corridor (you got back just as I was about to come on, so you sat in the corner and watched from there); it was the Kirgiz pantomime and I was the bear; the children screamed with delight and one of them ran up onto the stage to give me flowers and sweets; Angéla was so happy she was in tears. There was a portrait of Emil behind me, hanging over my head; it had been painted from a photograph and looked vaguely like both of the two siblings but not much like either of them individually. Emil never looked quite as manly and smiling and cheerful as it suggested.

The next scene I did for you and not for the children. I knew you were worried about the consequences of getting me involved and would be wondering if I would run off into the country again or simply refuse to let you into the house: it couldn't have come at a worse moment – you were up to your eyes in work, preparing for a panel discussion at the National Theatre and translating Kyd's *Spanish Tragedy* for the Katona; the moment I stepped out onto the stage you knew there would be trouble – there always was when I was forced to have contact with Angéla. Only later did I realise that you thought I was angry because I felt sorry for her and was hearkening back to my fond memories of our shared childhood, and Szolnok, and everything that had happened there. You never once took your eyes off me the whole time I was on the stage.

Afterwards they gave us afternoon tea, hot cocoa in mugs, and a film crew came from the news; Angéla hid herself away from them, she kept pushing the orphans in front of her; it was my best-ever television appearance, I sat with one of the children on my lap, holding her in my left arm, like a good mother, and pushing a brioche into her mouth with the right; it was snowing heavily – the road sweepers never got on top of it, they would brush it away and immediately more would fall, I loved the sound of it crunching under my feet. Angéla didn't leave with us, she stayed behind, with Auntie Ilu and Elza. That evening was the last time I saw her looking happy and beautiful. I looked back and saw her standing among the children – they were clinging on to her hands and her skirt; the once timid Angéla looked like a self-confident adult, and in that setting, with its little tables and huge building blocks, everything around and about her looked homely and natural.

We walked about for a while; Pipi was in excellent humour, deliberately sliding about on the icy street; you took me by the arm to stop me falling, but I pulled it away without a word – I was furious that you should presume to tell me what to do: I am not Angéla and I was well acquainted with slippery streets; once, in the Barrage, I was running home in winter and tripped on a stone concealed by the snow; my knees were covered in blood, but I didn't show them to anyone – it was bad enough having spilled almost all the milk in my bottle. The windows in the orphanage were brightly lit, the sign at the gate had been decorated with a winding ribbon, and white paper roses and a blue lantern, and the words "Emil Graff Children's Home". Pipi was ready to go home but I didn't let him, I told him he was having dinner with me; the three of us took our leave and we left you at the bus stop. I didn't take him home, I got off two stops later, he stayed on the bus and I went back to the theatre. I went into the members' box and scribbled your name on the back of an invitation to the orphanage event. The first act was already in progress; in the interval Hella sent a message asking me for my notes: she felt that the opening scenes hadn't gone as well as they should have and she wanted to improve on them.

I arrived home thinking that Juli would greet me with the information that you had tried to phone me, but she said nothing, and supper was served in silence – jellied pork; I couldn't face the meat but I ate the jelly; the snow was drifting down and she went out into the garden every hour to sweep the steps; Angéla had given me a mug for taking part in her event – I threw it in the stove and left it to burn in the flames. I rang Pipi, he wasn't at home; the phone rang later and I raced to it; it was Ványa, to say he approved of what I had done.

The gardener has gathered up his things and left; he was planting cosmos, I now see. Hella brought me some yesterday; first she paraded them around for everyone to see, and only then did she put them down; Juli will have told you that I didn't throw away the bunch you gave me: she knew they were in my wardrobe in a box on the top shelf.

My mother kept her bridal bouquet in a box with the name of the hatmaker printed in gold letters on the lid; once when I was little I took the box out – it had a strap so you could carry it on your arm; I carefully lifted the shrivelled brown wreath out, packed it with cherries, and walked up and down the garden with it, singing. My father always said, "Spring is coming, bringing us flowers!" and I always saw immediately what he meant – the image perfectly matched the reality: I could see March striding along with a sack on its back, full of flowers and branches of fruit trees. It was the very end of June, so I picked a bunch of crimson cherries, and there was an old straw hat in the house, so I cut the rim off and placed it round my head, filled the box with cherries and marched about the garden singing; I was the personification of summer and I knew it.

In the afternoons the smell of Ambrus' pigs vied with the

perfume of the stocks in our garden; the mixture of the two was heady but not unpleasant, there was the whole of summer in it – the overwhelming clouds of stock scent and the pungent smell of the animals. I was barefoot, I had just watered the ground and it was soft and warm.

*

Your bouquet was still in the cellophane box you had brought it in; every time Juli did a major clean she put it out of the way on top of a piece of furniture so that the petals wouldn't be shaken off. The snow was falling heavily now, you couldn't see more than two steps in front of you in the street, you had lost your gloves again and your hands were red and swollen from the wind; I just looked at you, I was suspicious and hostile – what were you hoping to achieve with this box of yours? You never brought me things like that, you used to buy your flowers in the street and you often forgot to give them to me – you left them in your pocket and by the time you found them they were ready for the bin. You were whistling a little tune when you arrived; you asked for a cup of tea and walked up and down the room and talked, while I listened warily. We had parted earlier that evening without a word to each other; Pipi was sliding about on the ice and I was silent, watching him in admiration; I made a snowball and threw it at him and simply ignored you. When you stepped in the door you brought the whole business of the orphanage and Angéla in with you, and before you had even opened your mouth something rose up inside me – I knew that whatever you were going to say no good would come of it, so I just watched you: would it be yet more about your translation of *The Spanish Tragedy* – or something else for a change, about us, for example? The quarrel was waiting in my throat. The day before when I pranced about on the stage in front of you I was a bear, I was eating honey and I had been as sweet as honey myself, so of course you thought I wanted you to come, I would have been waiting for you all day. I looked at your flowers – they were long-stemmed roses – and I calculated how much they must have cost you. They are always so expensive in February.

Juli brought the tea in, took a good look at the flowers – a very good look – put her tray down, went up to you and put her hand on your arm. I just stared at the pair of you. Had she taken leave of her senses? What on earth did she want from you? "Don't!" she said. You laughed at her and shook your head; to our surprise she burst into tears and ran out of the room. "She disapproves," you said. "Do you hear, Eszter, she disapproves of us." You tried to embrace me but I tore myself out of your arms. I was exasperated; I hadn't understood a word of what had just gone on, and I was furious.

I was so upset I spilled the tea while I was pouring it into your cup; I was expecting the usual lengthy explanation – I wasn't to get upset by the fact that you were going to leave Angéla, she had everything she needed, it would be just as if she had someone to care for her; she wasn't a woman she was a child, she thought of herself as a good member of the Party, and the last two statements summed up all that there was to her; I was watching you closely, I was waiting for you to say something that would make me even angrier and more bitter than I already was. I watched you devour the toast that Juli had toasted for you because you are always so hungry, and you were as happy as if we had parted the night before on the very best of terms; suddenly I was just as hungry as you were, I took a bite out of your toast and the tea tasted good again. I had put the head and paws of the bear on the windowsill ready to take to the theatre when I went back in the afternoon and the moment I saw them all my anger evaporated; I put the cup down, sat on the floor beside you and rested my head on your knees. My hair was in plaits and you undid them. The whole scene wheeled around me in a wide circle, the way it does when you are on a swing, and the wind blew the flakes round and round in spirals. By the morning the Danube had disappeared – it was often like that in winter, up on the hill; it was as if you were the only person in the world, there was no city, no form of human habitation, only the mountain and the sky, the elements, the wind and the snow.

I had already put the flowers into water, they even had a perfume, then I stared at you in astonishment because I had just noticed that you were quietly amused by something and that the flowers seemed to have some connection with it, you weren't taking any of this seriously – you had brought me roses in a cellophane box and at the same time you were laughing at me for putting them in a vase and even sniffing the scent, it was some sort of game, only I didn't know what you were up to, just that it was something to do with the flowers. Juli did, both of you knew, and neither of you was going to tell me.

I was almost always given flowers at Christmas, some exotic species that my father had grown in secret and presented me with only at Christmas – flowers covered with little spots or looking like fish; I thought them so wonderful I hardly dared water them. While my mother was decorating the tree he and I were shut in the kitchen and sang carols and songs from old operettas; in the other room she would be rummaging among the decorations – they were actually older than I was. We baked potatoes for supper and the snow swirled around outside; "An angel from heaven," I began, and you laughed so much I broke off and stood there confused and embarrassed: you had laughed and then immediately stopped, as if you had suddenly realised how far back the song went for me and you thought that I was now thinking how much I had loved my father's winter flowers, they were like little siblings to me, something fresh and new and completely different, born from the blood of my mother and father. I had always wanted brothers and sisters, so that I wouldn't have to do everything myself.

"So what's your answer?" you asked, keeping your eyes fixed on me. You went over to the window and gazed out; the snow continued to fall. What question was I supposed to answer? You hadn't asked me one. You picked up the paws and tried them on your hands, but they didn't fit you, so you put the bear's head over your own. At any other time I would have laughed myself silly, but I was beyond laughing now; I stood at the table redoing my plaits, with your flowers beside me. What was the question that I was supposed to answer? The room had become a stage, the scene outside the window was now a backdrop, the bunch of provocative red flowers a theatre prop – they were the same sort that Ványa used to order from the props department every time we celebrated an anniversary in a play.

"So what's your answer then?" you said again, and at last you turned to face me. You have said that my face was never as expressionless as it was at that moment, just a pair of eyes, a nose and a mouth, pale skin and the hair half done up in plaits. I knew how to make myself weep and blush and get my face to blaze with anger, I could do anything I wanted with it, but at that moment I didn't want it to do anything. You were still wearing the bear's head, I just stared at you and neither of us spoke. Finally I realised what you had asked me. For the second time you were asking me to marry you.

18

Yesterday the sculptors were standing outside talking about the statue they are going to put up and discussing who should be in overall charge. At one point Pipi turned round and gestured to them to stop, he was afraid that their chatter might annoy me, but I shook my head to say let them be – what should they talk about if not their work? Ramocsay was with them, we had been to see his ceramics at the exhibition. "Are you on your own?" he asked you, when he found the two of us looking in the glass cabinet. He didn't know who I was and I stepped back so that we wouldn't have to be introduced. There was a jug in the cabinet and while you were talking to him I studied it carefully – I can still see every little curve on it; I kept repeating the phrase "On your own?" to myself, with my ears pricked in an attempt to hear what you were saying in reply; you were speaking very softly, much more so than usual, so that I wouldn't be upset by what you said in case I happened to remember your telling me that in the early years of your marriage you had gone to a lot of these exhibitions with Angéla.

Between the display windows there were narrow little passages. I left the museum through the side door but I didn't go to Pipi's that afternoon – if he didn't open his door to you it wasn't because he was with me but because he was with Marica, he thought that we didn't yet know about her. I waited for a moment for you to turn round and look for me, and if anyone asked you if you were there "on your own" you would tell them you weren't, you were there *with me*, you had come *with me*. Ramocsay knew Angéla, he had made a Tanagra-style statuette of her, and I was expecting him to be taken aback and stammer out something. But you just said, "She isn't very well at the moment . . . She never goes anywhere these days . . . She is too busy with the orphanage."

I didn't go to Pipi's, I only wanted you to think that I had. I was with Ványa. I went straight to his apartment. He opened the door, stuttered out something and let me in; his mother looked at us from the kitchen, her face was red from the cooking and full of disapproval; his wife was due back later so I waited for her; by the time she arrived Ványa was a nervous wreck. I turned my head away and tidied my hair while she calmly put her prayer book away – the church bells rang at noon and I was wondering how many trams the poor creature would have had to take to get round all those far-apart shrines to pray for forgiveness for her husband's many sins; and I thought of you too, and what you were doing then and if you would be out looking for me, and I kept deliberately stumbling over the line, "Good my lord, / How does your honour for this many a day?" Ványa groaned and scratched his neck as he tried to explain where I was going wrong in the text; the wife stood watching us with her hands clasped together. She was very young, barely twenty, she just stared at us, clearly both very angry and wondering what on earth had possessed us that I should be working with her husband on a sunny Sunday morning. When we came to the line "Go thy ways to a nunnery. Where is your father?" the text suddenly came alive for me: my own father lay in the Marton tomb, I couldn't enter a convent myself because they had all been shut down, but on one or two days of almost every month an itinerant nun would spend the night in my house wearing everyday dress; Juli thought I was so stupid I wouldn't notice them, but there was a strong smell of cooking – some kind of meat broth; I did my best to speak the lines as badly as I could so that he would have plenty to correct. The old lady rattled the saucepans in the kitchen and he asked me to stay for lunch; they served an excellent meal, but I had no appetite for it.

*

"Only his wife can go in," the professor said, and again I thought about Ramocsay's remark and stopped where I was, at the top of the stairs; I couldn't move my feet, they were paralysed with hatred, I couldn't take another step. I had already spotted Angéla in the distance, she had arrived just before my taxi got there, she had come in Gyurica's car and she was having trouble persuading them to let her in because she was stammering so much – she always has difficulty expressing herself when she is frightened, and the doorman had stopped her straight away because she was carrying so many parcels and it wasn't visiting time; if she hadn't been with Gyurica they probably wouldn't have let her in. In her bag there was some apricot preserve for the patient, some flowers and one other small parcel, and Péter's cage hung from her right hand, swaying back and forth. I stopped a little way behind her, I was wearing only the slip of a dress I had on when I raced out of the house for a taxi, and I watched as Gyurica finished his explanations and I noticed how the doorman's manner softened when Angéla looked at him. She's come straight from home, I thought, she's packed everything one does in these situations, something she's cooked for him, his pyjamas, his slippers, his toothbrush – everything – and now she's going to put Péter's cage on the windowsill, reorganise the room and ask for a screen to hide the spittoon. By now Gyurica had seen me but she hadn't, her eyes were so full of tears; the doorman tried to say something to me but I stopped him with a look, he took a step back and opened the door. It was then that I realised that I had left my handbag in the taxi and had no identity documents with me.

There were two parallel concrete paths leading to your room; Angéla and Gyurica had taken one and I the other, we came face to face only at the covered entrance. When she saw me she tried to smile at me, it seemed only natural to her that I should be present at such an important time and she obviously wasn't wondering who had told me that you had been hit by a car; it was obvious from her face that she thought you had simply grazed an elbow or broken an ankle, and I thought of Pipi, he had seen you fall, he was standing at a window in the corridor at the time and he watched the ambulance arrive – he was still sobbing into the phone when he rang me. Gyurica was waiting for the lift because Angéla had a weak heart, but I ran up the stairs and we turned into the corridor at the same moment. It was only when she was standing at the door and saw Elza and her mother with the professor that she grasped what had really happened. My face is much more frightening than it looks when I'm wearing make-up.

The moment Pipi rang I knew what had happened, I didn't have to be told, there are things you just know. Pipi doesn't really cry if he can help it – he has a very dry skin and it isn't good for it – but it was only when I stood in that corridor that I realised that I hadn't taken it all in; only that morning we had been together in my garden, measuring the site for the new pond, and when you left at midday I didn't even watch you go because I knew we were having dinner that evening – you had something to see to, and we would meet at the Swan after you had taken Angéla to the dentist. Juli was the only one who said goodbye to you – she always gazed after you until you were out of sight; she was humming a tune, some old hymn to the Virgin as she cleared the table. I finished off your coffee and chuckled at the thought that she was in love with you, it was so comical; I wondered if she had ever realised it herself.

It was only when I saw first the professor, and then Elza and Auntie Ilu collapsed against each other on the bench, that I finally believed what I had been told; sitting there next to the laundry basket they made a proper *tableau vivant*; the red light above one of the doors into the corridor was on, like the ones you see in cancer hospitals when they switch on the radiation and put a NO ENTRY sign on the doorhandle. I recognised Weltner, he had won the Kossuth Prize the year after I did and I had seen his picture on the news; I knew he didn't know who I was, he probably didn't even know my name; he hated the theatre and the cinema and only went to concerts. I have no idea what I was feeling just then, probably nothing, I was still taking my surroundings in, trying to make sense of them, and I only summoned up the strength to feel anything when I heard him say that only the wife was to go in and Auntie Ilu and Elza started to whine and beg to be let in too – but Weltner stood his ground and blocked their way as if he hadn't even heard them, and Angéla put the bird cage down on top of the laundry basket.

"Are you on your own?" Ramocsay had asked. I took a step back, and you turned and looked at me, hoping that I hadn't heard what he had said; while you were answering him I kept my eyes on that vase, there was a blue bird perched on it, ruffling its feathers; this Weltner had a mouth like a beak, and again I felt that deep hatred for you. "Well, die then," I thought, "die and get it over with, die your miserable death, and may you suffer till your very last breath. Clear out of my sight, let the earth cover you, and if there really is a resurrection I never want to see you again!" Angéla looked very frightened, the tears were running down her face, Weltner was so impatient he almost struck her – why was she standing there wasting his time, staggering around and being patted by those two old crows? Péter banged on his bell – there was apricot conserve in Angéla's bag; I was still standing at the door next to Gyurica; on the way in the taxi my hands had been freezing cold even though it was the height of summer, now they were thoroughly moist. "The wife only," Weltner repeated. Well, let her go in then, worthy little Angéla, Mother of Mankind with her forty-eight children – let her go in then and be there to receive your last breath! At least Ramocsay will be glad that you won't be alone, may God punish him, and may he punish you too, may you die in agony, choking in torment, to choke and suffer the torments and thrash your arms about the way my father did; for that one reason alone I hope there is a Purgatory for you to spend time in until you burn in Hell – but of course you don't believe in Purgatory, or in your religion either, let alone mine.

Weltner and the figures in the tableau, even the flowers and the faded lace fern, all seemed to be waiting for something. I was waiting too, waiting for you to get on and die and for there to be an end to it all. Who was it who sent you to be fitted out with a smart new coat? Who filled out the request for that prescription when you fell ill, and took you to the shirt shop when your cuffs were frayed? Who listened to the story of your day and slept with you, and who did you tell you wished you had never been born? And who did you talk to about every single line you had ever written?

"Are you the one called Eszter?"

Weltner had put the question to Angéla. I pushed past the two of them and went in quickly through the door.

19

Something down there is shining. A ten-fillér coin. It must have been trodden into the ground and then washed clean by the rain; it has been flattened out and the inscription is barely visible – some child must have put it on a tramline. When I was little, children used to drill holes in coins like this and hang them on a cord round their necks; I always put mine aside to spend at the bakery: Csák bácsi had very poor eyesight. Angéla never learned how to handle money; even today she doesn't know the difference between the pengő and the forint.

Snow was falling outside the window; I was watching the flakes swirling around and not looking at you standing there with the bear's head on, and I was thinking that it had been just too hot in the orphanage the day before. You now felt able to leave Angéla, you said; you had needed all that time to be sure that she would still have a circle of friends around her, and the orphanage would be there for her as a kind of sustaining illusion, if you were to leave her permanently; those forty-eight children, the whole set-up and the work she so much loved would keep her together somehow, because she couldn't survive on her own, and if she didn't have someone to watch over her and love her and take care of her she would fall to pieces. I took the bear's head back and put it on mine with my pigtails sticking out, I sat down on the carpet and gazed back at you; the snow was swirling around behind your head and I was sitting at your feet, in my trousers, with a red ribbon in my hair, and I had no face, it was a bear that stared back at you, a stupid, faithful bear; my eyes blazed through the chink in the mask but they told you nothing. They were looking at you the way a wild animal would.

"Angéla may know her ideology," I heard you say, inside the bear's head, "but she doesn't even know how to fill in an identity declaration." Every quarter you were the one who had to draw up a work schedule because she simply couldn't plan, and she couldn't do percentages and when the accounts came in at the end of the year you would have to carry on doing all that, both for the time being and ever afterwards, even long after we were married.

You were laughing and smoking a cigarette while you said this, you were talking about her as if she were a charming, incompetent baby; I kept nodding and growling, then I pulled the bear's paws back onto my fists; I was thinking that while I was down there bowing before you, supposedly clutching my paws to my heart in gratitude that you should ask me to be your wife, all I wanted was for her to fall into little pieces and disintegrate completely; I wanted her to have to find out how to fill in an identity declaration and make up the end of year accounts, and bring in the coal herself, and know what it is like to be hungry and to have to flee for your life – all those things the rest of us have had to deal with. I just wanted her to evaporate, and never to see her again.

You would of course have to call on her from time to time, you went on, to make sure she had brought the firewood in – she was quite capable of forgetting to do so; she might order enough fuel for the orphanage but without you there wouldn't be a shovelful of coal in the house when the winter came.

I tore off the mask so that you could see my face, and your expression changed instantly. "No," I said, and I began to gather up the things on the table. "Thank you very much but no, I prefer you as a lover."

You didn't kiss me again that evening, and you left shortly afterwards, much earlier than usual; I assumed that you had to do the accounts for the orphanage fair and write Angéla's report for her; she has never, in all her life, managed to fill in an official document.

Juli was still out in the garden, sweeping; I went out to join her, I tied her scarf round my waist, took the broom from her hand and started to sweep – I was sweeping away the tracks you had left along with the snow. Juli stood on the kitchen steps and watched the way I was handling the broom and singing as the snow fell all round me; she had seen from your face what I had said to you. She gaped at me for a short while, then went back into the kitchen, no longer able to stand the sight of me. I was thinking how utterly immoral you were, with your kindness and good-heartedness; as you made your way down the hill you were no doubt thinking how immoral I was too.

*

Some scraps of food are still there on the side of the water barrel, lumps of that disgusting red potato mixture. Back home in my childhood people put that sort of thing on the step outside people's gates – you were never to touch them because people thought your fingernails would fall out, and you had to have a Mass said all the way through because it was a sign that an enemy had been to your door and left it there as a mark of the Evil Eye. One day Kárász néni found some next to the iron boot scraper and she cried the whole day and kept going to the sty to see whether her pigs were still alive and well, that was in winter too, and they were about to be slaughtered and she was worried about them; Béla was ill at the time but all she could think about was the pigs. I was the one who cleared the mess up, she was too scared to; I didn't dare touch it with my hands, I swept it onto a shovel with a broken broom and threw it on the fire. When Angéla put her bag down on the doorstep the apricot conserve was peeping out of the top of it and I nearly cried out, "The Evil Eye." The corridor had the damp smell of communal bathrooms, like the ones they used to have in the university hostel, and suddenly it was as if it had all happened before, as if I had seen it all before, not as a single image but in fragments – all it needed was the damp towel around Auntie Ilu's silly head, Elza looking younger and dark-haired as she sat there in the shadow of the laundry basket, Angéla with a bird beside her and the two of us standing in the doorway together like two devoted sisters. Gyurica was behind us, and the professor in front. NO ENTRY it said on the sign. As I went in through the door the red light above it was switched off and it went out.

"Tomorrow is St Valentine's Day / All in the morning betime, / And I a maid at your window . . ."

A doctor was sitting beside your bed and there was a smell of camphor in the room. It stayed with me all that Monday after I left you and went home, and it was still there when I went to the Swan. When I undressed I accidentally caught sight of myself in the bathroom mirror and stood there amazed by the thought that you had actually loved me.

I was thinking too that perhaps I should have told you to leave Angéla to her fate, and also that I should have shown you the town where I was born, and Köves Street, and the Barrage, and told you how I got to know Auntie Ilu and her family, and that when I was a little girl I had to cut the fronts of my shoes off so that I could walk in them, and that we were known as "the mad lawyer's people", and how Károly beat me in Ambrus' workshop because he thought I might betray him for putting into words everything I felt in my heart but had never been able to express; or that I had always paid my own way, and how Ványa had told me, "This is not an open meeting, it's for members of the Party," and I had to run out, with the jars clinking in my bag, even though someone in the room had just wished me and everyone else a Happy Future. And I should also have told you that the Personnel Manager had dismissed my CV, the only true one I ever wrote, with a wave of the hand, but no-one ever mentioned that Angéla had three servants or Auntie Ilu had bracelets all the way up to her elbows. It wasn't me who won the Kossuth Prize, it was my talent and a purely fictitious person, the daughter of a lawyer who had overcome her class limitations and learned to love the common people. But who had I ever belonged to, and where else, if not the common people – you excepted – and to Ambrus' pigs and Auntie Ilu's shoes and the racket from that piano, and the free suppers at the Three Hussars – my whole world of hopeless longing, and my desperate sense of oppression?

If, just once, someone, anyone, had been able to accept me as I really am, without reservations, not censoring out Auntie Irma and my memories of the Barrage, the whole truth. But not even you managed that. You can accept the truth only when it comes to Angéla. It seems to me no-one has ever, ever, genuinely tried to help me.

And I thought of the smoke that evening, when we were standing on Castle Hill looking down Lovas Street and at the city and the mountains beyond – there was a stream of smoke rising from the chimney of someone's house and you said you would give it to me as a present; as the smoke billowed up and drifted away I thought, "No-one has ever given me a column of smoke before," and I couldn't keep my eyes off it. "I don't have a real home, Eszter," you said reproachfully, "how long do you want me to wait?" and I started to quote from *Hamlet*: "Imperious Caesar, dead and turned to clay, / Might stop a hole to keep the wind away." I hugged you and squeezed you and all the while I was thinking that I had no home either, I had nothing, nothing, only that smoke, and I kissed you again and again and I wept.

How difficult the early mornings have been this week! I really should have told you everything. There was a time when I even thought of murdering Angéla; I would take her down to the Danube and throw her in – she never learned to swim – or I would lure her up to the top of a building under construction – I would tell her she had to see it because it was going to be named after Emil – and then somehow contrive to push her off the top, and she would no longer be in the same world that I was and I wouldn't have to keep feeling that you were thinking and worrying about her and none of that would matter anymore.

Then I had to laugh, because I thought about the articles you had written in the journals that would live on for ever in the libraries, and that your name would be carved on her gravestone, only by then it wouldn't matter anymore. I cannot live with her alive, but I would have to as long as I lived with you.

For three years I have watched you and studied the way you forced yourself to live an inhuman life, and you taught yourself to stay silent – you, who so love to talk. I heard all about your time in the army and at the university where you studied, you even once told me about your first love, and I noticed the way you watched my face in case I was upset by it. I nearly laughed out loud, it was so funny – you were all of seventeen and you were telling her to swear by the Holy Sacrament that she would never again allow her husband to touch her again. You talked about your work at the university, and what went on at the Writers' Union and what your mother cooked for you on your birthday, and how every year she waited for the precise hour of your birth to begin. The only thing you never actually mentioned was Angéla, and all those years since you had first met her – as if there had never been the war and you had missed out on the meaningful time of your life, when you got married and found your true style at last and really became a man. About all that you said nothing. Since that evening we spent at the orphanage you have never spoken to me about Angéla, nor did you ask me why I was sitting there in silence without asking a single question or telling you why – and when Ramocsay remarked that you were there on your own you just whispered your answer so that I wouldn't be upset by hearing you say her name; and yet week after week you kept asking me the same question and I always said no and laughed and shrugged, I told you no every time and watched your face as I did.

Then I thought no, what a shame it would be to kill Angéla. People never vanish completely from this world, they live on as long as there is someone who remembers them, and I looked at the streets and restaurants where you had taken me, and at the books on my bookshelf you had given me, and I thought that she would still be around somewhere, even if you never mentioned her name again – Angéla as a little girl swinging her legs from a branch, or walking up the aisle with you if we happened to be passing St Anne's church, or crying because she had cut her finger or wanted a book to read, and how whenever we were in that bookshop and choosing what to buy I would have no idea if you were choosing books of the kind that she liked; and when you pointed out a house to me, yet another example of your "fine Hungarian Biedermeier", I would never know if you had previously pointed the same building out to her.

If you had ever come to me and told me that you had left her for ever, and said that you would never go back to see her, that you were no longer interested in what was happening in her life and what she was doing, and you were no longer going to give her money because she already had enough to live on so you didn't feel sorry for her and didn't feel responsible for her in any way – the way everyone who knew her did – then I would have been prepared to marry you, but even then I would have woken you up in the middle of the night and shaken you and demanded to know what you were dreaming about, because I know that we never forget anything, and that old

Ince and Ambrus and his pigs and Angéla are still around somewhere and the memory of them grows and spreads down the years, like a cancer. You always said that you had no proper home and that I never gave you one, I only gave you a few hours of the day; but I didn't have a home either, I had only a house, where I could be with you undisturbed for a little while, but you always left afterwards, you didn't really live there, and Juli didn't either in any real sense, she just sheltered there and was always on her guard. She handed in her notice on Tuesday morning and I was delighted. It is the only good thing that ever happened in all my dealings with her.

While we were all rushing through the hospital garden I noticed a chain glittering on Angéla's dress, and when I came out of your room afterwards the light picked out a pendant shaped like a snowdrop, attached to a long golden thread and hanging down almost to her waist; it would have hung at a more natural height on an ampler bosom, so it must have once belonged to someone much stouter than she was, and I remembered the picture you had given me of yourself as a child – it was the only thing in the house Juli made it a point of honour to dust every day; it showed you as a baby in your mother's arms, you were reaching out to the camera and behind your little blond head there was an antique pendant on your mother's ample breast. When I came out of the room it wasn't Angéla I was laughing at, it was at something I couldn't put into words; I was laughing because I couldn't help myself, because I had once asked you what had become of that piece of jewellery and you told me it had been lost and promptly changed the subject; so when I saw it hanging from Angéla's neck at that moment and in that place I couldn't help laughing. I wasn't laughing at her but at what you must have thought of me then, if you had taught yourself to lie to me like that. And I was also laughing at the monster I really am.

*

I'm gathering up these wreaths and throwing them in the bin, then I'll take my time setting out. I forgot to close the shutters before I left and the kitchen will be boiling hot; I drew the curtain in your room on my way out, there was nothing in there that needed to be covered. The doctor stared at me almost in fear when I picked up your wallet and emptied the contents into my lap; I had always wanted to see what you had in there but I never dared look in case there was some memento of Angéla; there was a picture of Péter in it, standing on your typewriter preening his feathers, and the one of me with the dog at Balaton, and the ribbon I had used to tie my hair up that night in Szolnok. By the time I got into the room I thought you must be dead; the doctor mumbled something and let go of your wrist; if I had been on stage I would have known what to do but just then I could think of nothing – I didn't kneel beside you and I didn't touch you, I just gazed at you. You had died so horribly quickly; your mangled watch was on the table next to you, the one I had frantically put back at lunch while you were washing your hands to make sure you would be late at the dentist where you had to take Angéla because she was afraid she might have to have a tooth out. Pipi told me you had glanced at your watch when you were dashing past the Corvina shops.

20

It must be past two now, the streets are starting to fill up; I forgot to wind my watch yesterday so I'm only guessing – somehow nothing feels real any longer, time either flies or it stops altogether; on Monday, when I left the hospital and went to the Swan, I thought I must have spent a few hours there, but when I got home I saw on Juli's alarm clock that it wasn't yet eight. I went to Pipi's that night because there was no more laundry left to wash.

I hadn't intended to do it that Monday; I lay down and tried to sleep, but then Juli disconnected the phone and lit the candles – they were blazing away on the windowsill – and she had opened all the internal doors and gone into the living room to pray, kneeling on the blue Persian carpet, your carpet, in front of the flowers; she stayed there the whole evening, praying, starting again as soon as she finished. "Release him from the bonds of sin . . . May the angels lead him to the peace of eternal bliss." It was the only liturgy anyone said for you, Angéla didn't dare send for a priest and there was no church burial. Juli had taken the picture of you as a child from my bedside table and set it down in front of her; when she started on the prayer for the fourth time I went into the kitchen and locked the door behind me; I bundled up the dirty linen from the laundry cupboard, I was going to put it in the washing machine but I changed my mind and hauled Juli's washtub up from the scullery; she always bathed in it because she didn't like using the bath after me; it was horrendously heavy, it nearly broke my back dragging it up the stairs; the water I used was so hot it nearly cooked my hands, and I had to scrub the sheets with all my might – they hadn't been left to soak and it wasn't easy to wash them. I also washed Juli's things – I found them in a separate bundle at the bottom of the laundry cupboard; by the time I finished dawn was breaking; I took the clothes out into the yard, the stars were still there but fading; on one side of the hill it was still night and on the other the dawn was breaking, and the washing hung on the line in the laundry area of the garden between the blackness and the flashing red of the dawn. Juli had fallen asleep on the carpet so I took the quilt from my bed and covered her with it; there was slimy water all over the kitchen floor, so I washed the stone tiles, then I sat on the front step and watched the light growing ever stronger; by the time she woke I had already copied out my Russian lesson into my notebook on the kitchen table and done all the exercises and learned the vocabulary; that afternoon I had won the prize in the end of year exam, a book by Stanislavsky in Russian; once again Pipi hadn't a clue, he hadn't even done the exercises in his workbook.

I hadn't really wanted to go to Pipi's; he looked so forlorn when he opened the door, he had been expecting Marica and the sheets were already pulled back on his bed; he didn't have the heart to send me away, so he rang her and told her not to come after all – she was furious and very suspicious but he swore blind into the phone that there was no other woman with him; I was already in his bed and he was still protesting his innocence; he was now shouting at her and I could hear from her replies that she was shouting too. I felt thoroughly ashamed of myself, I felt I really should have gone home, but I was so tired I could barely move my limbs; neither of us spoke, I kept drinking water and Pipi drank brandy and we both smoked; he joined me in the bed at around midnight, tossed about for a bit and fell asleep; I moved as far away from him as I could, as close as I could to the wall.

When night fell Juli would have lit the candles again and opened her prayer book, but it was quiet and dark at Pipi's; the window in his bedroom was in the same position as in the study in the Barrage, not facing the bed as in my house or behind its head, as at Angéla's, but exactly in the middle next to it; the curtain moved gently in the breeze and Pipi snored. The late-night traffic down in Üllöi Street was only slightly less than in the afternoon; I lay there thinking how close I was to you at that moment, and that you were going to be buried.

At one point Pipi stopped snoring and opened his eyes; the glow from the street lights lit up the room as usual, I looked at him, we could see each other's faces clearly; he stared at me blankly for a while, then burst into tears, I started crying too, he drew me towards him and we buried our faces in each other's; he got up and went into the bathroom, took out the face cream, rubbed it into the skin around his eyes and then around mine, then sat on the side of the bed, looked at me for a short while, and suddenly knelt beside it and rested his head in my hands; I knew he was crying again because I could feel his tears trickling down my hand. "You don't want me to marry you, do you?" he asked through his sobs. I just gaped at him, as the tears ran down his cream-covered cheeks. "Don't ask me to do that, Eszti!" I held him tight and kissed him and reassured him and comforted him like a child, and soon he was sleeping peacefully again. I looked first at him and then at myself; you know his apartment, how the mirror is placed so that you can see it from the bed. The trams were now rattling along Üllői Street.

I went home later that morning, Juli didn't even acknowledge my greeting, she just looked at me and turned her head away. I have never in my life felt the need to explain myself or my actions, but I just stood there in front of her feeling that at any moment I would scream or throw myself down on the ground outside if I couldn't make her understand why I had spent the night at Pipi's. She went into her room and shut the door firmly behind her; finally I found something to eat on the stove, but in just one of the saucepans, a single helping of peas – she had cooked only for herself and not for me; I waited a while for her to come out but nothing moved, it was so quiet behind her door you would have thought she was dead, so I took a wooden spoon and scraped the entire meal, all her lunch, into the bin, turned the pan upside down and left it on the stone floor.

Everyone had watched Juli as she knelt there praying and reading from her prayer book at the top of her voice; she was the centre of attention; they also kept glancing at Angéla and me; Angéla only started to sob aloud when your coffin was lowered into the grave; until then she had just wept silently, the way she used to as a child until it turned into loud, plaintive sobs if no-one was able to console her. I looked only at you. Yesterday, when I saw you in the coffin, I almost screamed with relief. Pipi had warned me that your face looked terrible, but I didn't find it so; it was you that I saw, in your dark grey suit, with the striped tie I had bought you, and it was your face, your hair – you felt close to me again, I kept wanting to take you in my arms and caress you and kiss you: your dead body seemed more natural to me than that you should not exist at all.

That was on Thursday, by then I hadn't seen you since the Monday. When I stepped inside the mortuary and caught sight of your face I stood rooted to the spot, it had all come flooding back to me, I felt connected again, it was as if just seeing you had brought all the different strands of my life together – I felt hungry again, I longed for the taste of good food and, sleepy as I was, I wanted to drink coffee and run and swim, and do everything I loved. Pipi took me by the arm and studied my face – he was hoping to learn how someone reacted in the presence of a coffin. I just smiled, Angéla was in tears, I leaned against the wall for support; I was reliving the experience of seeing her face when you were still alive. Then Gizike arrived, set down her bunch of flowers and a wreath in the shape of a cross and knelt beside Juli; it made me think of the Swan and the dishes she had brought us, and of her long, fine fingers as she picked out the palest croissant for you and poured the first glass of wine.

Last night she told me you were only sleeping. I was eating a *lángos* and looking out of the window; whenever I had bad dreams, about the Barrage, and my father, and that Károly is beating me, you know that I never cried or shouted out in my dreams, instead my limbs would go rigid and cold, I became so frightened I couldn't speak – when I had those dreams I always lost the use of my voice; if you were sleeping with me you would wake in fright and immediately realise what was about to happen, even before I had started to shiver and my back became rigid; you would pull me against you and shake me awake and everything would melt away and disappear – Ambrus, the war, the Barrage, whatever it was that had come back to upset me – and I would instantly relax and fall asleep in your arms; so when Gizike said that you were just sleeping, the mouthful I was chewing turned to rubber in my throat and I could hardly swallow it.

At the hospital I had a pretzel. It was Wednesday, visiting day. I had called on Hella at midday and had some of her soup; we were rehearsing *A Midsummer Night's Dream* – it's on next week in the theatre on Margaret Island. I was finished by half past four, I looked into shop windows for a while, then thought I would call in at the hospital as it was a Wednesday and it would soon be five; I jumped on a bus and went there. At the entrance to the hospital they were selling ice cream and black market lemons; I bought a comb, the whole place was buzzing, I had no idea where you might be, I just wandered around between the buildings, then stood for ages round the back – I somehow had the feeling that they had taken you somewhere in there; I tried to see in through the windows but the first floor is very high up and they were frosted anyway, but I stared up at yours, the one where I had opened the curtain on Monday, then went and sat down beside the fountain; there were children playing all round me, a man came past selling balloons and another selling pretzels; I bought one, people were talking about how their operations had gone, and a little boy with his leg in plaster dropped his ball in the fountain. The light was on behind your window – it seemed so strange, because I knew that someone else must be in that room now and here I was down in the garden – and at the same time it suddenly seemed that I were up there too, as if there were somehow two versions of me, one looking down at the other version of myself, one looking up and able to see the drawers of your bedside cabinet and the brilliant shine on the polished knob.

At seven they rang the bell. The traders were the first to leave, then the crowd slowly drifted away and the garden emptied; I had dinner near the hospital, the place was filthy and the beer warm; I bought a newspaper and scribbled all over the front page and blanked out the title and the date with my fountain pen: *Evening News*, 1954. A dog came up to my table begging for scraps, it took the bone from my hand, very cautiously, started to gnaw it, then put it down because there was more leftover food under the table, trodden-on lettuce leaves. When they buried you they kept piling more and more soil over you and I glanced briefly at Gizi, praying softly there, and I thought how sure she was that you and she would meet again one day – her face was filled with both grief and certainty. I was wondering if I would be able to dig you up with my bare hands. At Megyer I found a shell at the edge of the water and used it to scratch marks in the sand.

I had never gone that way before on the train, we always went to the holiday centre by bus or by car. When I left the restaurant I mooned about in the square for a while, thinking about Pipi and Juli, then I went to the corner of Gyöngy Street; from there I could see Eagle Hill, where my house is, just under the peak, but it was in darkness, only the street lights were on; the block of hospital buildings was also in darkness, there were cars racing round the square and again I felt that strange sense of heightened alertness that had been with me since Monday as soon as night fell. I went to the Margaret Bridge and got on the local HÉV train; there were very few people on board and they were all asleep – my neighbour's head was slumped over his wooden box of tools and he slept beside me all the way to Aquincum.

I got off at Megyer and they told me at the station how to get down to the river. I set off between ploughed fields; the path ahead of me was shaded by acacias and poplars and there was the scent of carnations somewhere nearby, a sharp, almost suffocating scent, as if I were walking in a cloud; the panes of the glasshouses in the horticultural co-operative glittered in the light, a train blew its whistle and there was a sudden thudding of hoofs; two girls were chatting at the gate of the co-operative and a radio was blaring out from the workers' holiday houses beside the shore. Once I got to the crossroads I knew my way; I came to the holiday centre and scuttled past at speed so that no-one would recognise me, but I spotted Diósy in the garden, lying in a deckchair smoking a pipe, and little Jolán was making the swing squeak extra loudly.

I went down to the riverbank. The river there seemed more familiar than it was in the town. If I didn't look to the right, towards the factories and the chimneys in the distance, I might have thought I was back at home. A breeze was fanning my face, coming from the trees huddling on the island opposite. I sat on a stone and stared at the water. It was Wednesday evening, when the new guests arrived and the old ones left, and music was coming out of all the workers' holiday resorts.

After the final exam on Tuesday Ványa told us that we were going to West Germany in the autumn to do Schiller's *Love and Intrigue*. I realised I would probably be Lady Mitford. I would be the only one who wouldn't be leaving a family member behind as security – even Pipi had his mother, she lived somewhere in the country – and it occurred to me that it was a chance to escape. I walked out of my hotel room thinking that I would get used to it. I would put an apron on and a cap and go out through the kitchen one way or another – and Ványa could shout and scream in rage and weep and go back to the theatre without me.

I came across half of a shell, picked it up and started to poke around in the sand. The evening boat was coming in and the waves lapped almost all the way up to my feet. I made a little pile of sand – that was the Barrage, this was the bend in the river, that pebble was Ambrus' house. "Daddy saw Reiner in Josefstadt Square!" Angéla told me when she was a child. "She's a great actress." The water sloshed around it, I bent down and put my hand in it. It was still warm.

I used the shell to dig up some pebbles from the sand, piled the sand up to represent Eagle Hill and patted the sides firm; a car stopped behind me, a man and a woman got out and went off to the municipal holiday resort; I thought how I had never seen the sea, and never seen any of the great cities of the world, but I had been to the Mátra Mountains once, and laboured up the steep paths intoxicated with the thought that I was all of a thousand metres high. Then I decided I didn't want to upset Ványa, and what would I do abroad anyway? What would be the point? And I realised that none of the great cities or the mountains interested me now, not even the sea.

I've put my shoes back on now because the going is rougher underfoot again. I took the wreaths and threw them in the waste bin; the gardener in the furthest plot stopped working and looked at me suspiciously, but he didn't say anything. Juli used to stare at me just like that, suspicious and distrustful. There's nothing else here now, only the earth between those four little stakes and the board with your name and age on and the number of years you lived: thirty-eight. The earth there was damp and crumbly: I pushed my fingers into it; it was so soft and moist I could have dug up the earth above you with my bare hands. Juli's train must have set off by now; if I went home now the house would be deserted.

The gardener is looking towards the main road; he can't see anything but he can hear a military band somewhere; I can hear it too; they must be parading down Kerepesi Street.

The band music went on for such a long time in Megyer that it was only after midnight that the shoreline became quiet again; by then the lights in all the windows were out and the couples who had been strolling up and down behind me had disappeared from the paths. I was cold, I had no more cigarettes, my foot was swollen and numb from sitting on that rock. I went back to the holiday centre. It was so late there was no-one sitting outside and the front gate was locked, so I went round to the back gate, reached in and pulled the latch up and went and leaned against the wall of the boathouse; it was still warm from the heat of the sun falling on it all day. There was nothing but sky and more sky, stars and the moonlight, the chirruping of the cicadas and the frogs singing in the field behind the holiday centre where the stream runs across it; the line of hills and the trees on the island seemed to hold up the sky above my head, the moonlight glittered on the roof of the bus shelter, the main road was dark and deserted and the shadow of an acacia with a broken branch slanted across the ground. I stood there, with my back against the wall, gazing at the road, the sky and the trees. I think I was waiting for you.

I didn't say it aloud, I didn't really think it either, I just stood there looking towards the town and remembering the time when Angéla's burgundy-red dress suddenly appeared ahead of us as we were walking past the back of the theatre and you tried to slow me down but I tore away from you, and then went back round the theatre and jumped on the holiday bus to Megyer; the Party secretary told me I was a good member of the co-operative and at dinner I sat with the drama students and the extras and we sang and played tombola till midnight; then we all went to bed, they put me in the girls' room. Hella was the only actress who was well known there, and she lent me a nightdress.

I couldn't get to sleep so I went into the garden. I was filled with a sudden feeling of bitterness – it hit me like a wave, I lashed out against it, I felt I was drowning in it, then I spotted the headlights of a car, it was coming closer all the time, it stopped at the beach and you got out; you tried to get in through the main gate, then went round to the little one at the back; as you put your hand through to draw the latch you saw me leaning against the wall, I was still in Hella's long frilly nightgown. "Are you coming like that?" you asked, and I went back in and put my dress on. I fell asleep in the taxi as soon as I felt your body close to me.

I know I shall never see you again. I knew that yesterday afternoon, and all the time I was standing beside the boathouse wall the tears were running down my face and I mocked myself, I told myself that I was no different from Gizi or Juli and that to have heard your footsteps approaching was perfectly natural. From time to time there came the blast of a whistle, from the boat or the brick factory at the foot of the hill; smoke was billowing up, they must have been working through the night and it rose a rich pink against the black background of the sky.

After a while I went and knocked on the caretaker's door; he gave me a blanket and set up a folding bed for me in the dining room. At breakfast there was milk, a little butter and apple jam.

I am going away now, and leaving you here. If my foot wasn't so painful I would walk, though I would never make it up the hill. Today I shall be myself again, I wouldn't be able to do the laundry again – Juli has ordered a carrier and sent the washtub to her new address. Gizi said you were just sleeping, and I would see you again one day, I nodded and thought, yes, I would call on you, Angéla will spend today in bed and Elza won't have time to plant flowers over you, so I thought that I ought to go and dig up your body, so that when they next came they would find the grave empty, like Christ's tomb, and I would take you up to Eagle Hill and gaze at you and watch the mould cover you over until there was nothing left of you. Last night, at Gizi's, the first light came very late, the morning was cloudy and the sun came out only later.

Last year, when we were together in Megyer, you always ran

to the jetty ahead of me, while I hung behind, dipping my toe in the water and pulling faces, dipping my feet into the Danube and stamping and rubbing suntan lotion on my shoulders after you had been in the water for ages, swimming towards the island, and then suddenly I no longer knew where I was, I began to panic, I was no longer sure of who I was; I could still see you but you were getting further and further away, it looked as if the island was moving further and further away and the amount of water behind you was getting wider and wider, and I started to shout out to you to wait for me, I was coming now, and I jumped into the water, I surfaced and was with you again, gasping for breath and flapping my arms and clinging on to your shoulder with my hair dripping behind me . . .

I shall go out through the side gate, the way I came in. If there were an afterlife, you would have come looking for me at the boathouse, or at Gizi's, or in my kitchen. *Székely Bertalan*: the drops of water will still be shining on the bronze curls of his beard. *Here lies Adam Clark.* The rain has washed this little seedling away. From here at the gate I can see the clock on the tower of the co-operative hospital; it's a quarter to four, but I can't look back and see you from here. The flower seller is having her afternoon tea, there are slices of green paprika on her bread; the gate is open just as I left it; a child is racing down the street on a scooter, ringing his bell.

Wait for me, I'm coming.